Minnesota Memoirs

Stories by

Duff Brenna

Minnesota Memoirs

Stories by

Duff Brenna

SERVING HOUSE BOOKS

Minnesota Memoirs

ISBN: 978-0-9838289-5-2

Cover photo: Lois Shaw

Author photo: R. A. Rycraft

Serving House Books logo by Barry Lereng Wilmont

Published by Serving House Books
Copenhagen, Denmark and Florham Park, NJ

www.servinghousebooks.com

First Serving House Books Edition 2012

For Edwin R. Brenna, Medicine Lake, MN

Acknowledgements

Most of these stories, in various incarnations, were previously published; acknowledgement is due to the following magazines and anthologies: *The Literary Review, Cream City Review, The Madison Review, Milwaukee Magazine, StoryQuarterly, Web Del Sol, The Nebraska Review, New Letters, MacGuffin, Ducts, Pif, The Girl with Red Hair, Contemporary World Literature, Quarterly West.*

The author is indebted to the Centennial Committee of the Golden Valley Historical Society, Golden Valley, Minnesota, for their publication of *Golden Valley, 1886 – 1986.*

The author wishes to express his heartfelt gratitude to Walter Cummins, Thomas E. Kennedy and Susan Tekulve for their kindness and patience and all the hard work they've done to make this collection as clean and accurate as possible. Special thanks as always to R.A. Rycraft.

Books by Duff Brenna

Fiction

Minnesota Memoirs
The Law of Falling Bodies
The Willow Man
The Altar of the Body
Too Cool
The Holy Book of the Beard
The Book of Mamie

Nonfiction

Winter Tales: Men Write about Aging (co-editor: Thomas E. Kennedy)
Murdering the Mom: A Memoir

Contents

Who knows the interpretation of a thing?
Ecclesiastes 8.1

The Grindstone Martyr

Based on a true story

After his wife died in the spring of 1851, Fergus Foggy moved his rotary grindstone, his distillery, his two boys, Ignatius and Seth (ages nine and eleven), from Chicopee Falls, Massachusetts, to the Minnesota Territory. They traveled via ox-cart.

At the edge of a meadow six miles west of the Mississippi River and north of Bassett Creek, surrounded by pine and sugar maple, white oak and poplar, Fergus and his sons built a one-room cabin.

They had heard lurid tales of bloodthirsty savages who lived in the woods near Medicine Lake, and so when a few Indians showed up one day, Fergus grabbed his rifle and stood in the doorway. He was trembling. Ignatius hid in the belly of the stone fireplace, while Seth grabbed the ancient flintlock and stood beside his father. The hammer on the flintlock was broken, but the Indians didn't know that. There were five of them staring curiously at Fergus and Seth.

In the gruffest voice he could muster, Fergus said. "We'll go down fightin!"

"Down fightin!" squeaked Seth.

"Fightin," echoed Ignatius within his stone nest.

The Indians looked at each other with puzzled expressions. Seconds later, they shrugged and went away. In less than a minute they had vanished into the forest.

After such a terrible scare, Seth was posted on the roof with his flintlock, while Fergus and Ignatius worked to finish the cabin. They gave it the final touches, constructing shutters for the two windows and putting up pole beds laced with rope. Fergus had brought mattress casings and these they stuffed with dried grasses. He made lamps from strips of cotton cloth placed in pie tins filled with rendered deer tallow. He set the lamps on the mantel where they would throw the most light. Using an auger he bored holes in the mantel and in the holes he hammered pine pegs. On those pegs he hung the cooking utensils he had taught himself to use after his wife died. He and his son made chairs from tree stumps. They made table legs from slender poplar branches. They split and planed pine to fashion a tabletop and a workbench. They made open cabinets and shelves for tools. Everything was notched, nailed, roped, pegged, bracketed, angled, strutted, beamed, braced, buttressed—bolstered so soundly that both cabin and furniture alike announced the Foggys had come to stay.

When the interior of the home was finished Fergus constructed a smokehouse directly behind the cabin and dug a cave in the side of the hill to serve as a cooler. Next to the cave Fergus set up his still. Day after day the Indians would watch from a distance. Seth would aim the flintlock at them and make shooting noises. Their curiosity satisfied, the Indians would eventually drift away. After awhile, Fergus understood they meant no harm. He had Seth come down from the roof and get back to work.

Fergus distilled a mixture of corn and potatoes he called splow. He sold it to farmers homesteading the neighboring lands. The farmers would bring tools for him to sharpen on his revolving grindstone—mattocks, axes, shovels, augers, chisels, knives—and while he was turning the stone and honing edges, the farmers would sit outside with a jug. They would drink, smoke, relax, until it was time to take their tools and go home.

In summer, when spring's muddy trails had dried, Fergus would make the three-day trip to St. Anthony Falls, his ox pulling the chirping wagon. The grindstone in its cradle ready for action. Lining the dirt roads were cabins and shacks of all sorts, with here and there the first of the framed, clapboard houses that would come to dominate the town in a few more years. Fergus and his boys would spend as much as two weeks going from street to street, calling out—"Sharpen your tools! Bring your knives, scissors, scythes, razors, axes, hatchets . . . sharpen your tools!"

When they could, Fergus and his sons supplemented their main diet of cornmeal mush and potatoes with wild game—rabbit, squirrel, grouse, pheasant, quail, turkey, deer. Occasionally a moose. They would fish Medicine Lake and when their luck was good they would load the crossbeams of the smokehouse with walleye and pike and perch and bass. They would put dried apples in slung baskets, along with potatoes and

14

corn, which Fergus bartered from the farmers who bought his splow. When the weather turned cold, he and his boys tapped the sugar maples for syrup to pour on fried cornmeal. From December to March they threw meat on the roof to keep it frozen. In summer they salted the meat and kept it in barrels in the earthen cooler.

As the years passed, Fergus thought of himself as blessed by God. He was infinitely grateful for what the good Lord and Minnesota had given him, a hundred and sixty acres of lush meadow and woods that he could eventually pass on to his sons and grandsons. "God's Blessed Boonies" he called his tract. Generous neighbors brought him tools to sharpen and kept regularly buying his splow. The Indians were friendly and seemed to have the attitude that there was plenty of land for all. Fergus learned to greet them in their own language. He didn't know what more a man could ask for. Maybe a woman to warm his bed, but he didn't really miss not having one. In fact the only real drawbacks as far as Fergus could tell were the mosquitoes and ticks and the muggy weather in summer, the brutal winters (January and February mostly), which were colder than the winters in Chicopee Falls. But, as he told his boys, a man could tame the snow and cold by being prepared, by being the ant and not the grasshopper.

"I came, I saw, I conquered!" Fergus might shout on occasion. Adding, "I earned the right to this land!" He thrived on the idea that he was a pioneer. He had opened the way for his children and for other hardworking homesteaders. And perhaps above all, his piece of earth had given meaning to his life and a purpose that he hadn't had before.

In his cups some nights he would feel the spirit of his wife and the spirit of his hundred sixty acres entwining. He would see into the future and he would say, "Boys, her spirit guided us here to find our piece of earth, this virgin soil to make it our own God-given, and that's what we done, we homesteaded her. Made your ma proud. We said we'd do her and we done her. We got our acres and thrivin business. Ain't nothin gonna drive us off here. Ain't nothin gonna make us leave here ever. A hundred years from now, there will be Foggys all over Minnesota Territories, all of them tracing their blood back to us. Think of that, boys. We're the fountainhead, we're Adam in the Garden. This is Eden."

The boys would nod and say yes Papa and wait for the splow to put their father to sleep. Contentedly yawning, peacefully proud, he would finally close his eyes. When he'd wake in the morning, raw-mouthed and coughing, feeling death's toad in his belly, he would swear by the angels never to get so putrid again.

One winter morning Fergus—sober—looked out the window and saw deer tracks in the otherwise spotless snow. A two-day storm had blown itself out and the sun was shining. The world before Fergus was dazzling. It looked as if God had sown it with diamonds. He swiped charcoal beneath his eyelids to dampen the shine and set out to follow the tracks of the deer. He wore buffalo boots tied with rawhide up to his knees. He wore a black bear coat, a wolverine hood and rabbit mittens, all of which he had bought for seven number 4 traps from a Sioux Indian who lived at the winter encampment on Medicine Lake. But even wearing his most formidable winter gear Fergus got very cold that day. His toes were numb and so was his nose. Frost and icicles clung to his mustache and beard.

After hours of tracking, climbing over fallen trees, over frozen ponds and creeks, trudging in circles, backtracking, it was getting late and he decided to give up and go back to the cabin before he got frostbitten or worse. The sun was already southwest and falling fast. He didn't want to be out after dark. As Fergus started for home, he stepped into a clearing and saw the deer he had been tracking. It was a doe. Her head was down, her dainty hoof pawing the snow, digging for the yellow grasses underneath. Fergus raised his muzzle-loader and fired. The deer's head lifted. She stood still for a moment as if deep in thought. Fergus thought he had missed and he knew he wouldn't have time to reload before the doe would be gone. She pivoted in slow motion, staggered, took a few steps toward the gaunt trees opposite Fergus. Her knees buckled.

Fergus whispered, "Thank you, Lord."

He waded through the snow and got to work dressing her out. His knife moved swiftly and it wasn't long before the deer was gutted and ready to go. But as Fergus was about to shoulder the carcass, he saw an Indian standing in the forest staring at him, bow and arrow in hand. Fergus's rifle was leaning on a log. There was no time to grab it. It wasn't loaded anyway. He stood tall and made the sign of peace. The Indian signed back. He and Fergus stood on each side of the deer. The Indian indicated that he had been stalking the animal.

Fergus wondered if the Indian wanted to fight him, winner take all. He remembered Solomon and the quarreling women and the baby ordered split in two. Fergus made a gesture of cutting the deer in half. The Indian nodded agreement. Fergus pulled out his knife again and soon the deer was separated into equal parts.

The Indian marveled at how easily Fergus's knife had divided the animal. Fergus handed him the knife and he tested it on one of the haunches, severing it at the knee. He held the shank up and jabbered in Sioux, some of which Fergus understood. The Indian wanted to know how a blade could be so sharp. Fergus tried to explain about the grindstone, but the Indian remained puzzled. Picking up his half of the deer, Fergus beckoned for the Indian to follow.

They went to the cabin, where Fergus showed the Indian how the thick stone wheel went round and round on its axis making the edge of the blade thinner and thinner, until the edge seemed almost transparent and could cut hide as if it were hardly any thicker than paper. "This stone is what they call a thousand grit size," Fergus explained, while running his palm over the wheel's edge. "A thousand grit is very fine. You want a stone that's fine and not coarse, of course." The Indian got so excited that he grabbed the knife, ran out the door, leaving his share of the doe behind on the floor.

Fergus's sons wanted to know if he was going to let the Indian steal the knife. Fergus pointed to the two halves of the deer and said it was a fair trade. He got another knife and cut off some steaks and tossed the rest of the meat on the roof to freeze.

The next day the Sioux chief came from the camp on Medicine Lake to see what was being called "a magic wheel." Fergus took a hatchet from his supply box and sharpened it. The chief inspected the blade, calling it *shunkahah wanagi*, wolf spirit. Fergus gave the hatchet to the chief. "Wolf spirit is yours," he said. "*Shunkahah wanagi.*" The chief indicated that Fergus was now a brother because he had given away a prized possession. The two men clasped forearms. Fergus felt secure. He believed the Indians were all his friends and he would never have to fear them ever again.

By 1856 there were enough farmers in the area to give a blacksmith hope of making a living. A blacksmith named Dick Story bought an acre lot from Fergus and set up shop nearby. Story had a Swedish wife and two healthy blond girls. Fergus told him about the Indian awe over the magic wheel and the two men decided to make knives and hatchets for the Indians and trade them for furs and sell the furs at the trading post in St. Anthony Falls.

The blacksmith made beautiful horn-handled knives with blades thirteen inches long. These knives eventually became known throughout the territories as Story Knives. They were compared favorably with the Bowie Knives that Jim Bowie had made famous not long before Story was born. Story made hatchets with oak handles. He forged double-bladed axes lethal from either side. Fergus sharpened them on his magic wheel until their edges were so finely-honed they were almost translucent.

The Indians brought buffalo and bear hide and beaver and muskrat and fox and anything else they could think of to trade. The two men built a store and stocked it with Indian goods and with staples they purchased in St. Anthony Falls. Story's wife and daughters ran the store, while he continued to work in the smithy. Fergus continued to sharpen blades and brew splow. In a few years, dozens of Sioux and Chippewa from St. Cloud to New Ulm to Mankato and beyond owned a Story Knife or tomahawk sharpened by Fergus. The two families prospered.

In 1859 a sawyer named Bob Becker bought the lot next to Story and moved in with his family and set up a sawmill. In a few weeks Fergus had a frame house with glass windows and a sitting porch in front and a long bench where he could relax at the end of the day and watch the sun go down over the meadow. He gave the old cabin a rough pine floor and kept it as his workshop.

His sons were growing tall and strong. They spent many days with the Sioux, learning their language and lore and ways of surviving in the wilderness. They could speak the Sioux language as easily as they could talk English with Fergus. They told their father that the Sioux warriors would rather die than lose their honor. Their love of honor brought them closer to Fergus's heart. Many a soldier in the Foggy past had died for honor on the field of battle, none a coward, including Fergus's own grandfather, a Scottish mercenary who fought for the French and fell at the Battle of Borodino in 1812. Fergus had a letter of commendation signed by Napoleon and a bronze medal with French writing on it, which he kept on the fireplace mantel in a cherry wood box. He taught his sons that they must never do anything to dishonor the family motto: *Deliverance or Death*.

"Live like your Sioux brothers and your great grandfather," he told them, "for you descend from royal Scots, honor-bound to the core of your pride and your courageous Foggy heart."

He told them of a duel over some property Fergus's father (drunk and belligerent) had gambled away and how he had insulted the winner (a long-time friend), forced him to fight (pistols by torchlight) and killed him. When he sobered up and realized the horrible thing he had done, he mourned for his friend and the honor lost. Months went by and he couldn't get over it. He slipped into a black depression. And finally hung himself. He left a note saying his suicide was atonement for what he had done to a dear friend and a good man who had never harmed him. His last hopes were that God would forgive him and that he had wiped the stain of dishonor from the Foggy name. Fergus ended the story with, "Deliverance or death, you see? Do nothing to dishonor yourself, for when you dishonor yourself, you dishonor the family. You dishonor your ancestors. You dishonor the generations of Foggys yet to come."

Ignatius and Seth took up land not far from Fergus in what would one day be called Golden Valley. When Seth was twenty and Ignatius eighteen, they had a double wedding, both marrying the sisters from the Story family. The young men had learned farming, but still made money by trading furs to their father and father-in-law. Now and then they visited their father and drank splow and talked of their glory. "Ma's spirit guided us here to find our piece of earth, this virgin soil to make it our own God-given land and that's what we done, we homesteaded her. We're the Foggys! We make Ma proud! We said we'd do her and we done her. We got acres and a thrivin business. Ain't nothin gonna drive us off here. Ain't nothin gonna make us ever leave. A hundred years from now, there will still be Foggys on this here piece of ground."

Year after year more settlers moved in and farmed and built homes and set up shops. A pastor named Paul Turner built a church and called it THE NON-DENOMINATIONAL UNION CHURCH. Everyone, including the Indians he converted, was welcomed at the Sunday services. The pastor preached a simple gospel based on tolerance and love. His favorite verses from the Bible were Mark 12:31, *Thou shalt love thy neighbor as thy self;* and Matthew 7:1, *Judge not that ye be not judged.*

By the fateful year of 1862, the North and South had gone to war and several adventurous boys had already gone east to join the Union. For Fergus and most of his neighbors the great slaughter seemed as remote and alien as Europe or Africa. The talk at the general store was not about war, but about whether or not they were a village or maybe even a town and shouldn't they have a name? They all agreed that they should have a name, but they couldn't agree on what it should be. Golden Rod was one favorite, but Meadowland was also a possibility, and so was Long Valley and some wanted to call the place White Oak or Lily of the Valley.

Fergus was only forty-one in 1862, but his hair and beard were gray and he had lost most of his teeth. He had stomach troubles and drinking splow nearly always made him ill, so he sold his still to a German named Moser, who set up a saloon and distillery in St. Paul. Moser ultimately became the largest maker of whiskey throughout Minnesota.

Besides stomach ailments, Fergus had arthritis in his hands. To cure his arthritis he ate lots of "man root," which was the name for the ginseng root that grew abundantly in the forests and could be harvested easily with a hoe if one didn't mind the insects or working in the humid heat. Fergus would eat the ginseng or make ginseng tea and drink it three times a day. He also hired some youngsters who lived at the settlement to go out and fill sacks with the root, which Fergus would dry and then resell to ginseng buyers for ten cents a pound. The buyers would sell the ginseng to exporters in Saint Paul for a dollar a pound. The exporters would ship the tons of ginseng to China and make a hundred and forty percent profit. "There is no excuse for failing in this country," Fergus told his sons. "Why, this country practically gives itself away."

On the 10th of August 1862, Fergus rose with the sun and found a line of Indians waiting in front of his shop to have their knives and tomahawks sharpened. Most of the Indians were unfamiliar to Fergus. He saw by their markings that they were Dakota. He stood at his grindstone that day listening to the sizzle of the metal on stone as he wetted edge after edge and drank cup upon cup of tea. The more tea he drank and the harder he worked the more his arthritis eased. "Old as I am, look how I can hone these things thin as spirits," he said to no one in particular. He was proud to recognize how many of the knives and hatchets he and Dick Story had made. Animal furs and offerings of food and head-rings made of bear claws piled up on the floor. Fergus worked very hard and by the end of the day all of the Indians were able to walk away flicking their thumbs over razor-sharp blades.

After supper that evening, Fergus sat on the porch and smoked his pipe and watched the sun settle into a nest of flaming clouds. The wind moaned through the pines and Fergus thought of the Banshee who would one day come for him. In the distance he could hear the gurgling of Bassett Creek. In the great meadow in front of him grew wild roses and lily-of-the valley and the ubiquitous golden rod and daffodils. It was poetry for the eyes. Despite the pain from his arthritis, it was a fine life Fergus reminded himself. Everything was calm, steady, predictable. There were many days when his arthritis responded to the man root and he felt more like a younger, stronger version of himself. There were times when he was lonely for his boys, but they weren't prohibitively far away and he could pay them a visit if he really needed to. He didn't miss his wife at all anymore and in fact there were days when he could scarcely remember what she looked like, though he had loved and appreciated her and would always cherish her memory, especially for the fine sons she had given him. He was grateful to God for all the good fortune and he told himself that in some ways he had found paradise without having to die. He finished his pipe and carefully cleared the ash, keeping the unburned tobacco in the bottom of the bowl.

He sat listening to cicadas chirring in the trees and thought about how mysterious cicadas were, how they came abruptly alive in summer. And then, a few weeks later, they all died. Birds ate them. The Indians ate them. Critters of all kinds ate them. The husks of those not eaten would be found scattered under the trees. Stepping on them was like stepping on tiny dried leaves.

"They come and they go just like us," he told himself. "Only lots quicker."

He stared at his gnarled hands and decided it was time to make out his will. He got his quill and ink bottle and a piece of parchment and started writing. At the top of the list was the meadow in front of him. He wanted to pass it on to his sons, but also to make sure it was never sold for farmland or for "… any purpus of dividing unto streets and houses or any bisness venture that would spoil the view." He carefully reread his stipulations, then signed the will and added a postscript saying, "Sons you will thank me one day for not aloting our meadow for develope but to always keep this spiritual kindlyness for all to see and enjoy."

He placed the will inside the cherry wood box.

The Indians continued to show up each day to have their knives and hatchets sharpened. This went on for five days, a steady stream of Indians waiting patiently for Fergus to hone each hair-splitting edge. He wondered at their number and decided they were probably off to a big buffalo hunt somewhere out west.

A few days after the Indians stopped coming, Fergus learned what they had done with the knives and hatchets he had sharpened. They had gone to Acton and Sauk Valley and New Ulm and all the way to the Iowa border massacring whatever settlers they found. Over a four-day period, forty-seven men, twenty-two women and eleven children were known to be dead. Four women and three children were taken captive. They were never recovered.

When Fergus asked Dick Story and Bob Becker why the Indians had gone on the warpath, he was told the Dakotas wanted their land back, simple as that.

Fergus's sons and their wives moved back to the settlement. Seth had gotten very excited about the prospect of chasing evil doers out of the territory and he joined the Home Guard, which numbered 30 men. They organized and drilled in a lot next to the main road. After a few days of drilling, Seth started complaining about how boring it was marching up and down. Where the hell were the evil doers? He'd come to chase them out of the territory, not collide and tangle legs with a bunch of fools that didn't know their right foot from their left.

When the news came that Indians had been seen in the woods

north of Medicine Lake, the men hurriedly gathered together and marched off to track them down. Seth was far ahead of the group, practically running to the encounter. In his hands was the ancient flintlock, little more useful than as an heirloom, something to hang on a wall and talk about how in its glory days decades ago it was hell on rabbits. The day that Seth rushed into battle, the old gun wasn't capable of bringing hell on anything, unless it was used as a club. Which may have been what Seth had in mind. In any case, the hammer was still broken. Seth claimed he didn't care. "If I meet up with those savages, they'll never know the difference," he said.

Unfortunately, he did meet the savages and when he pointed the rifle at one of them, it didn't matter how fierce the old flintlock appeared. Instead of dropping dead from fright or running for his life, the Indian brushed the barrel aside and fractured Seth's skull with a tomahawk. The other twenty-nine men were several yards away watching all this. They hastily fired their guns and drove the Indians back. The barrage made a lot of noise but killed no one else. Two minutes later it was over and everyone had had enough. The Indians vanished into the forest, while the Home Guard went south at a jog.

Two days after the battle, their ranks swollen to fifty-four, the Home Guard returned for Seth's body but couldn't find it. Those who had been there said it was the right spot. But no Seth could be found. Had the Indians taken him? Were they cannibals? They had looked a starved bunch; they might have eaten Seth.

It was decided that the Dakotas had probably divided Seth up and taken his portions to their camp and roasted them. Either that or he was wandering around the woods with a cracked skull. Whatever had happened there was nothing to be done. The men straggled back to town and told Seth's wife they couldn't find him.

"He might have been toted off by a bear or maybe some wolves," her father told her.

When Ignatius told Fergus what Seth had done, Fergus had a dizzy spell and had to sit down. "That damn fool!" he said. "That flintlock's no good. What the hell's he thinkin?"

"He just got excited and took off," said Ignatius. "I couldn't stop him. You know how he is."

"Always the fool," said Fergus wringing his hands.

He got his Bible and opened it and blindly stabbed a page. This is what he read: *I have sent among you the pestilence after the manner of Egypt: your young men have I slain with the sword and have taken away your horses; and I have made the stink of your camps to come up unto your nostrils.*

Fergus put the book down and wept and said, "My boy's dead."

They gave a memorial service for Seth and called him a hero and said that men like Seth Foggy were making Minnesota safe for women and children.

The Eighth Minnesota volunteer army was formed and many Indians were slaughtered and the ones who weren't left the territory, some of them escaping north into Canada.

When the Dakota war was over, and everything was peaceful again, Ignatius and his wife and the other farmers went back to their farms and the merchants went back to their shops. Seth's wife moved in with her parents.

For a while it seemed that Fergus was going to be all right. He was obviously dazed and distraught over the death of his son, but he worked on stoically, sharpening tools and selling man root. A few months passed. Then a year. It was summer 1863 when Fergus built a new still and started making splow again. Despite all his stomach ailments he drank almost as much as he sold.

One evening Dick Story was enjoying a jug with Fergus, and Story started pumping his old friend as to why he was drinking so much. His son Seth wouldn't want a drunk for a father. And there was Ignatius to think about and the news from Mary was surely a blessing, wasn't it? "You're gonna be a grandpa, old boy. Now ain't that something to celebrate? If it's a boy, they're gonna name him Seth. How about that?"

Fergus nodded. Took a long drink. Wiped tears from his eyes and said that he was not drinking because of his son's death. He could handle that. Seth had died with honor on the battlefield. He had taken his death like a man. No, Fergus wasn't drinking to forget Seth. He was drinking because he was responsible for the massacres of August 17, 1862. In his dreams he kept seeing the Indians handing him blades to be sharpened and laying down the furs of dead animals and other possessions for payment.

Thirty pieces of silver kept echoing in Fergus's head. He said that Minnesota history would always associate him with the eighty deaths of innocent men, women and children.

"What nonsense," Story told him. "It's not your fault. How could you know? None of us knew."

But Fergus wouldn't be convinced. "My grandfather fell at Borodino in 1812 and I, his namesake, end up sharpening knives for murderers to use on the innocents at New Ulm. What a legacy!"

"Well, if he puts it that way," some of his neighbors said.

Pastor Paul Turner said, "Pray to God for Fergus. God will forgive him."

And others said, "Oh come on, Fergus, you didn't do a damn thing wrong!"

Over the course of days, then weeks, Fergus went from an impotent anger to a brooding sadness to a deep despair. He couldn't rid his dreams of the screams, the terror, the knives and hatchets coming down on the heads of children watching the blood of their parents and then their own blood drain away. He would walk around mumbling, "Tell me what it means. How? Why? What did I do that You've forsook me? How could this happen to me living in God's Blessed Boonies?"

He would tell those he met on the street that he was an instrument of death, a maker of horror, an infamous Joseph Guillotine. The poor, helpless ones, the women and children, their throats cut with Story knives sharpened on the magic wheel, the blades made to shine like polished silver. "Sick Minnesota. Why did I come here?" he asked. "False paradise. Satan's house."

Eventually he refused to work at his grindstone. It stayed in a corner collecting cobwebs. He sat on his porch and watched the meadow turning yellow beneath a cooling sun. He brooded on death.

Winter came. No one saw him ice-fishing on the frozen lake. When spring arrived, industrious boys brought him ginseng root, but he wouldn't buy it. Wouldn't say a word. Just waved them away.

One day when Ignatius and Mary came to visit Fergus they found him uncommunicative. His eyes were haunted by grief. "But it's not your fault," Ignatius told him. "There's no way you could have known what was gonna happen, Papa. Anyone would have done what you done. Don't take on so, you have a business to run. There was no way to tell by their faces what them savages was up to."

"No man is an island," replied Fergus cryptically.

They scratched their heads and looked at each other and shrugged.

While they pleaded with him to be reasonable, Fergus sat sad-eyed and bow-backed. Unforgiven.

Mary fixed him venison stew and ginseng tea and pestered him to eat and drink. Ignatius found a jug of splow in the cooler and poured Fergus a cup and made him drink it. And then another cup. And then a third. As he drank, his color got better, his eyes got brighter. "He looks alive again," they told each other. "He'll be better now."

The next morning they came again and saw Fergus in his shop, standing over his grindstone, sharpening a bone-handled Story knife. Ignatius and Mary felt satisfied that they had done a good job. They went back to their farm. Later that afternoon, they got a message to come to the shop. It was an emergency. When they got to the shop, they saw a lot of people standing outside. No one said a word. The young couple went in and found Fergus dead on the floor. His throat was cut. On top of the wheel he had left a note that said: DELIVERANCE OR DEATH.

Ignatius found the will in the cherry wood box and buried his father in the meadow a few yards from his shop as he had wanted. When everyone had gathered around the grave, Pastor Turner read a statement, which said in part that Fergus Foggy was a better man than his last act might let people believe. Despite a mind-crippling affliction, here was a man who had somehow remained true to his principles.

"No one who has not walked in his shoes should judge this man," the pastor continued. "His contribution to the massacre of 1862 and the death of his beloved son had plagued his conscience and made him unable to live with what happened. He was shattered by grief and not in his rightful mind when he killed himself. We cannot hold him responsible. He is innocent and God always forgives the innocent ones."

There were murmurs of agreement with what the pastor had said. A few weeks later the town voted to name itself Foggy Meadow in honor of Fergus. The new name was burned into a board and set up on the road that entered the town from the south.

It wasn't long after the death of Fergus that Dick Story and a tradesman named John Pearson bought the shop from Ignatius and turned it into a souvenir store featuring the bone-handled Story Knife that Fergus had used on himself. The area of bloodstained floor where he had bled to death was given a glass cover and surrounded by a railing. His sizable grindstone was set on a pedestal in the center of the room. Dick Story made a trip to St. Paul and bought a block of sandstone. He took it to his smithy and chipped pieces from it, which he carved into thin rounds the size of a silver dollar. Each round he roughened with a file. What he created were miniature replicas of the grindstone itself. Each replica was carved with the epigraph: FERGUS FOGGY GRINDSTONE MARTYR. The disks were drilled with a tiny hole where a loop of babiche was run through, so that each piece could be worn as a medallion.

Penny-a-piece watercolors of Fergus that Mary painted were framed and sold as well. Fergus was silver-haired and bearded, tears running from his eyes and his finger pointing at his broken heart. Miniature replicas of the grinding wheel nestled in its cradle were etched into pinewood plaques, along with the motto DELIVERANCE OR DEATH. His buffalo boots could be seen in a case, along with his black bear coat and wolverine hood and rabbit gloves. Hanging over the case was his muzzle-loader and powder horn. Mary Foggy wrote a ballad and made numerous copies in a scrolling hand. The ballad claimed among other things that--

> *Fergus Foggy was an Injun fighter,*
> *A buffalo hunter as well,*
> *A great explorer of the northern lands*
> *A man who knew no fear—*
> *Fergus—Fergus Foggy—died in the New Ulm Year.*

Nearly a hundred years later "The Ballad of Fergus Foggy" would become the inspiration for "The Ballad of Davy Crockett" and outsell every other song of 1954.

Those who survived the 1862 massacre made pilgrimages to what became known as the Foggy Meadow Museum. They bought the necklaces and horn-handled knives and replicas of the magic wheel. Mesmerized, they studied the fading bloodstain beneath the glass on the floor. Some of them read aloud the Bible verse Pastor Turner had hung on the wall. John 25:

> *I say unto you, the hour is coming when the dead*
> *Will hear the voice of the Son of God*
> *And those who hear will live.*

Eagerly the pilgrims purchased "The Ballad of Fergus Foggy," and they sang it so often near and far that it became the number one hit of its time, known by just about everyone from Foggy Meadow to Milwaukee, Wisconsin, and Chicago, Illinois.

Within a year of his suicide, the story of Fergus Foggy had somehow changed. It was now said that Fergus had martyred himself rather than hone the weapons of the murderous Indians. They had tried to force him to use his magic wheel, but he had refused to the bitter end. When the killers wouldn't leave him in peace and threatened to kill him, he had cried out—"Deliverance or death!" and stabbed himself in the neck. Such was the final version handed down mouth to ear and printed on flyers and written about in newspapers and illustrated in a comic book called *SAVAGE TALES FROM THE FRONTIER.*

For a generation things concerning Fergus Foggy were for sale. Then the interest in him died away as new settlers moved in and raised children who had their own heroes and gave less and less attention to the Grindstone Martyr. The name of Foggy Meadow was changed to Golden Valley in 1886. By the turn of the century it was a thriving timber, farm implements and granary storage town of three thousand souls. And then came Crystal and Robbinsdale and Plymouth and New Hope so on and so forth.

It wasn't long before the cemetery sprawled out beyond Fergus's lone grave. Listed on a monument beneath his name were three other martyrs— three Minnesota soldiers who had fallen in the Civil War. There was also a monument erected for children *DIE KINDER RIEHE*—The

Children's Row—who died in the diphtheria epidemic of 1873. And, of course, there were numerous other men, women, children whose tombstones marked their names and dates. Several veterans of World War I and World War II were eventually given places as well. And keeping to the theme of tolerance and love that was the bedrock of Pastor Paul Turner's UNION message, Lutherans and Presbyterians were buried next to each other; known atheists were buried beside Catholics; a pair of Muslims (man and wife) given place beside a Baptist family of four. And so it went, and so it is to this day. This eclectic plan was made official in the by-laws written down by the Mutual Cemetery Association, founded in 1869, which stipulated that no one, no matter what race, culture or religion, would ever be excluded from burial in the meadow. The cemetery plots (all of them facing the rising sun) grew to cover sixty acres within a hundred years of Fergus's death. The plots were kept neatly trimmed by an appointed caretaker, but the rest of the meadow was allowed to bloom with daffodils and golden rod and wild roses, just as it had when Fergus built his cabin in 1851.

By 1876 the Sioux no longer lived around Medicine Lake. They had gone north and west, some to meet Custer at the Little Bighorn, others to languish and die without honor on windy reservations. They were scarcely remembered and the 1862 massacre seemed almost a myth. By the time of the First World War very few of the ten thousand who lived in Golden Valley at that time knew anything about the martyr who had given their forefathers a famous ballad, a place of pilgrimage, and a town that had long since discarded its Foggy Meadow name and much of its history.

Birthing Babies

for Christine

It was Cristmas eve near to midnite when Cristobell got born. Daddy give her to Vernon and told him he had his heifer and he was to show he could take care of her. When she grew up all her milk would belong to Vernon. He would get the money from it. We both knew that Daddy wanted us to stay with the farm and was wanting to give us a start each with his own heifer. My turn would come when I got big like Vernon and was twelve. He drug Cristobell round to the other side of the stanchion so Beth could clean her up. Cow and calf look just alike both black mostly with white inside their legs. Cristobell she had a patch of white on her head that looked most like a keyhole like you could stick a skelton key in there and open up her head. Beth didn't have no patch on her forhead. Her raspy tongue give Cristobell a going over from head to tail and mooing in between so as the rest of the cows could know what she done. They knew. They was all reaching out as far as they could to sniff Cristobell. Some got in a lick or two of their own. So Cristobell had plenty of aunts to rub on in case she got up and wander down the manger. The church bells started ringing far off. We could hear them when the wind was blowing our way from Elk River. Daddy said it was time for Cristmas service. That was when Vernon named his heifer Cristobell cause of Cristmas and the bells.

Vernon got to stay behind and not go to church cause he had to milk Beth and get the colostrums for Cristobell. Beth kept kicking at him trying to push him off from milking her. Daddy told him to stay with it and use the hobbles if he had to. Vernon said he knows how to do it. So we left him there and went to thank Jesus for getting born, though I would ruther gone to bed.

When we got back Vernon he was still in the barn. Daddy told me to fetch him. I found him in the calf pen with Cristobell her head turned over her shoulder her feet and legs tucked up neat under her. Vernon hisself snuggle next to her sleeping. I covered them with straw and went back to the house. Daddy said that was a silly thing for Vernon to do, but to leave him be. I wanted to go sleep with them but wasn't let to.

It got awful cold after Cristmas. Broke some cold records below zero day after day. Hit fifty below on January one. The wind come on us hard from the northwest and dropped the tempature to eighty below. Nothing worked right. Tractors wouldnt start. Barn cleaner snapped a link ever time we tried to clean gutters. So we had to do it by hand. Shovel the gutters out and wheelbarow each load out the back door and make a pile. It was a two hour job and no fun at all, but it kept you warm. Some of the cows on the north end of the barn had frozen watercups. We had to pour hot water over the cups ever morning so to melt the ice. The cows they had to stay in their stanchions day after day which aint no good for cows. We put straw under them but some still got sores on their legs and some bigger ones needed help standing up. We would pull on their tails and push their butts with our shoulders and we would get them standing but as the cold wore on it got harder and harder to do. The cold got Cristobell too. She got newmonia. Which pretty much meant she was done for. Daddy said Vernon was to shoot her so as she wont suffer. But Vernon said he would make her better. He cried. So Daddy said maybe he didnt have to shoot her just yet but we never had a calf live through a winter newmonia. Daddy said it was good that they all died because he known of some what lived and they was sickly and growed up runts not able to breed and end up at Packerland anyway. But Vernon kept begging and crying. Mama rub his hair and give him hug and she got crying too. Daddy was going on and on about runts and bad lungs, trying not to look at Vernon or Mama. Cristobell would have to be done for eventually he said. Then I got blubbery to and that was all Daddy could stand. He went off to the other side of the barn and let us to hang all over each other and bawl about Cristobell.

That night after chores Vernon and me carried Cristobell into the house and put her in the basement next to the furnace. We give her plenty of straw and covered her with a blanket. She kept flopping over and laying flat out on her side. We knew that meant she was ready to die. Vernon kept pushing her back up and holding her, but as soon as he let go she flopped flat again. Daddy came down and said she was done for.

Maybe next time we would listen to him. He went upstairs to bed. Vernon was kicking the woodpile and saying bullshit bullshit. He had me help him make Cristobell stand up. Which was hard to do she was so unwilling. Her legs leaning this way and that like willow sticks. Finally we got her to stand still and Vernon got the calf bottle and made her to drink water, pinched her nose and forced it down. He said he put sugar and salt and baking soda in the water, which was what the vets did for calves when their hair got stiff like Cristobells. After she drunk it all, we made her to walk around the basement a bit. She was wobbly. I got sleepy and went to bed. Vernon was still talking to her late in the night. I could hear him through the vent in my room, talking soft to Cristobell, coaxing her to living.

In the morning he was still down there. He came out to the barn long enough to do his chores. Then he was back in the basement, making Cristobell to walk and drink. Daddy told Mama that by giving Cristobell to Vernon he wanted the boy to get the right kind of feeling about cows but this was going to far. Mama laff at Daddy and give him a kiss. They didnt make Vernon go to school that day. I wanted to stay with the calf to but no one took me serius. Mama walked me to the bus and told me if I didnt quit whining I would not get to help Vernon no more. Lot I cared. I was sore at Vernon all dam day.

Thats how it was for lots of days. Cristobell would be up and down, flat out near dead, hardly breathen at all. But Vernon wouldnt let her go. He would keep picking her up and make her to walk. He would stuff the nipple down her, make her to drink Beths milk, make her to drink the medicine water he made ever day. Vernon was looking a mess hisself. He got bony like Cristobell. His eyes black like a coon. Daddy kept swearing it was going to far, but Mama kept backing Vernon. Saying leave him be. She would bring his food down to the basement and feed him while he rubbed or walked Cristobell. She made him drink water. She told him he was doing good. She said she was proud that he had such spine in him. And of course he wasnt made to go to school. Which wasnt fair to me and I told them I should be let to stay and help keep the dam calf alive. But they wouldnt lissen none of it. Some days I got so mad I wished Cristobell would die. I even thought of killing her myself except Vernon was there so I didnt know how I would do it.

Then one day I come home from school and they all was happy and told me to go look see what was in the basement. I runned down and there was Cristobell up on her own. When she saw me she bawled and come over to suck on my jacket. I told her I wasnt her mama. I pet her head. Her hair wasnt all ruff and stiff like before. It laid down smooth so my hand slipped along like I was brushing new mowed grass. I could feel with my thumb where she was starting to get horns, just two teeny bumps I had felt on lots of calfs before. But on her they felt real special. Vernon come down and he like to hug the breath right out of her. Then he even give me a hug to. I didnt care no more about having to go to school without him. But Daddy he had to spoil it some. He said Cristobell would still be a runt and even if she werent she would probably not settle and even if she did settle she would not make much of a milker. He said he was sorry to say such things but we had to know and not count much on a calf that had been so sick. Cristobell runned across the floor and kicked up her hindlegs at us. Then she runned back and give Daddy a butt in the leg. He laff and play with her ears. He said she was ready to go back to the barn.

The rest of the winter wasnt so cold and Cristobell didnt get sick no more. Vernon and I both made sure she always had lots of good hay to eat. He fed her a pound of ten percent proteen grain same as the cows got ever day and she got fat and sassy. When the first green come to pasture Vernon had her outside and kept leading her to all the good spots that had early clover and trefoil. He made her to run up and down the pasture hollaring at her and clapping his hands so she would keep going even after she got blowing hard. When summer come he was still making her to run, only he got tired before she did. And sometimes she would be chasing him, making him run when he didnt want to. And thats how it went. She got better and better. But it is true she was behind all the other calfs in size and they could push her around. But Vernon he and me built her a leanto on the south side of the barn and kept her to herself so she didnt get bully much. Every chance he got he would wash and brush her down. She like it. She would hang her head till it almost touched her knees and she would close her eyes while he brushed and brushed and made her to shine like licorice.

She come through the next winter with no problem and by the

time she was fifteen months in March she was sized enough to breed. But Vernon wasnt for letting no bull have her. He wanted Cristobell to get bred artifishal. He looked through the magazeen of sires and picked one that fit what Cristobell had to offer. Vernon and Daddy went round and round about it. Daddy said Cristobell werent worth no fifteen dollar bull. She would probably not settle anyway. Vernon said the bull his name was Abel and he was just the right one to settle Cristobell and Abel was number one for calf ease. They argued round and up and down about it. Finally Vernon said he had the fifteen dollars hisself from helping Ed Liska fill silo last fall and Cristobell would have Abel and that was that. Daddy raised his hand to hit Vernon for being so sassy. Vernon stuck his chin out and said Cristobell was his wasnt she or did Daddy mean to take her back? Daddy drop his hand and shook his head. They didnt fight no more about it. Vernon called the breeder and Cristobell got Abel. She settled right away and was due to have her baby near December.

All summer Vernon he worked out for Ed Liska whenever Daddy didnt need him. Almost everything he made he spent on Cristobell. She got special vitamins and minrals and a special kind of sack feed cost ten a hundred. She got a half pound of grain ever day and the best hay in the barn. She was kept clean as a showcow and had her own little hut out back of the barn fenced off from the other heifers let to roam forty acres of woods and let to get pretty wild. But not Cristobell. She was most like a dog than a cow. She runned to Vernon when he come and put her head under his hand so he would pet her. She played with him, pushing him round and he pushing back with his shoulder, but she was to strong and always won the tussle. And sometimes he would hang on to her tail while she run him up and down the pasture and turn so sharp to whip him off and he go tumbling over the grass like a log. It would make me laff watching that. Mama and Daddy like to watch and laff to. Mama said how Cristobell should go to the fair and win a prize. But Daddy always said no she was still a runt and weak in the brisket.

When that summer got over and the fall came and December we started watching Cristobell real close. Vernon kept her in the leanto except then he closed it off so only the south side was open and she had an acre fenced around it. Vernon kept saying he was sure she was going to be alright cause she had fresh air and exersize and vitamins and she would come through the calfing and not get milkfever. He would keep saying the same thing over and over till Daddy or Mama would tell him yes he was right. Vernon he worried about everthing. He was reading books all the time about what might go wrong. Then doing what he could to keep it from happen. He did it all as right as he could but sometimes right is not enuff.

That dam Cristobell she got out when her time come and she disapeered in the woods. We come for chores one morning and she was gone, nocked the fence down cause Vernon he wouldnt use barbwire, so she just walk on over it. Vernon like to croak on the spot. He runned round the barn yelling her name looking high and low. I runned with him. Even Daddy was looking. We all ended up back at the leanto staring off at the woods. Sun was rising but it was still a bit dark. We could see the black trees and not much else and of course when we wanted snow to track there wasnt none but patches here and there. Daddy said it was certain she had gone to the woods to have the calf. He said go ask Liska for Husky and see if he could sniff Cristobell out. Vernon took off and come back with Husky in no time. Daddy give Vernon some baling twine and a knife and told him not to forget what he learned about helping a cow to calf, not to hinder but to help only if it was certain she was in troble. I went with Vernon and Husky. Daddy stayed for the milking.

We looked and looked and Husky he flushed out heifer after heifer, but they wasnt Cristobell. The sun come up high enuff to shine through the trees but it didn't make me warm. Even with all the walking and no wind, I was freezing cold. I told Vernon I want to go back to the barn, let dam old Cristobell have her baby and bring it on up when she got hungry. He got mad and yelled at me and wacked me on the ear which felt like it broke off. I couldnt help but bawl. Vernon grabbed me up and told me he was sorry but Cristobell might be dieing and need us and we couldnt just let her be in these goddam woods all alone. We just had to find her. It seemed no use to me but I said I would stay with him. My ear hurt quite a while but the wack made it feel warmer than the other ear. So I didnt mind much.

When Husky started barking again we hurried along the sound

of it and this time we found Cristobell. She was in a ring of trees and laid on her side, her big belly humped up like she had a boulder inside her. I said we best get Daddy. Vernon said no. Now that we found Cristobell everthing be alright. I said if we didnt get Daddy I bet Cristobell would die. Vernon almost hit me again but he stop hisself and told me to shut up. He took off his jacket and his shirt and laid down at the back of Cristobell. Husky and I sat down and watched him while he put his hand inside Cristobells woom. I didnt know how he could be so brave when it was so cold.

His arm was in her to the elbow and he said oh no, she was in troble for sure. The calf was backwards. Vernon had its butt in the palm of his hand. He pushed his arm all the way in saying he was gonna try to get a hindleg to pull up. He was pushing and grunting and given it all his might but it werent doing no good. Cristobell she look over her shoulder and give a moo. Like saying what you doing? Then she flop her head down and I thought she died. I said she was dead. Vernon pulled his arm out. He was bloody. Blood and gunk all up his arm and chest and his face. He was a sight. His chin was trembling. I dont know if it was just that he was cold or that he wanted to cry, but it wasnt a good time to cry. He stood up and put his arm round me and said I had to be a big boy and help him now. He said Cristobell was not dead but she would be if we didnt be smart and save her like we should. Husky come over and licked the blood on Vernons hand. He give Husky a kick and the dog yelp. Then give Vernon a look like alright for you and Husky took off for home. Vernon told me what I was to do. I was to get a stick about a foot long and put it in Cristobells mouth like it was a bit, and I was to sit on her neck and hold the stick and pull back on it hard, like I was pulling on reins ever time she tried to bear down, cause if we didnt get her to not bear down when Vernon push the calf forward he would never get the calfs legs up from under its belly and so he would never get it out and so Cristobell would wear herself out and die. So I did just what he said. We pick the stick together. A strong one about as big round as Vernons wrist. He set me on Cristobell's neck and shove the stick sideways in her mouth and I pulled on it best I could. He talked to me the whole time while he went behind her and put his hand up her woom. He told me he was trying to loop the twine round the calfs foot then he could pull the twine with his left hand and push the calfs butt forward with his right hand and maybe get one leg out at a time that way. I was glad to have Vernon tell me what sound like he new what he was doing. It give me hope alright. For the longest time he was trying to get that twine where he wanted it. He kept saying over and over, please God please God, and telling me to pull on that stick. Which I was doing till it like to pull my fingers off. And I told him so. But he kept saying pull harder. And then he was saying, yes God there he had the twine round a hoof and there he cinched it tight. Now he said I had to really pull cause he was gonna push the calf forward and pull the leg up at the same time and he could only do it if Cristobell werent pushing back. He yelled like he gone crazy, telling me to pull goddamit pull. I dug my heels in next to Cristobells nose and pulled like I never pulled on nothing before and I was saying please God and he was saying yes God and we was grunting like a pair of pigs. I couldnt of held out much longer. But then Vernon yelled it was coming. Then he yelled he got it. I let go the stick and looked back. There was a little yellow hoof showing out the back of Cristobell butt.

Vernon was laid on his back panting smoke and he was so full of blood all over he looked like he been shot. I slid down beside him, just all out of puff myself. But he made me to get right back up and put the stick in Cristobells mouth. Then we did the same thing again only there was more room and the second hoof come quicker. Which was sure a good thing cause I was pooped and could bearly hold back on the stick.

We rested a while after the second hoof was out, then we tied twine round both hoofs and we pulled and pulled. Cristobell look at us and saw something was finally going like it should. She took heart and started bearing down with all her might. We time our pulls with her pushs and here come the baby tail and then come the hips and when they passed through, the whole calf shot out slidding right into our laps and getting us more wet and right away start steaming and freezing. Vernon he laff and laff but I didnt see nothing funny. I was just thankful to have it over. Cristobell mooed and stood up and come round to lick her baby. The calf raise its head and look us over. You could tell it didnt know what was going on. I checked under its tail to see what was what. I told Vernon he had hisself nother heifer. That made him laff even more. The blood was freeze on his arm and chest, and I started flaking it off with my fingers. But he said leave it be and go tell Mama and Daddy what happened.

So thats what I did. I runned as fast as I could and I found them eaten breakfast and I told them everthing Vernon and I done. They kept hugging me and patting me when I told them how hard I pulled on that stick!

We all went out toward the woods to help Vernon bring the calf back. But before we got there here he come with the calf slung across his shoulders and Cristobell following behind bobbing her head up and down as she walked like she was saying yup thats my baby there yup I did it thats mine. Mama was telling Cristobell what a good girl she was. Vernon kept saying its a heifer! its a heifer! He set the calf down so Daddy could look her over. Daddy called her a real beauty, all black like a Cristobell twin with white inside the legs and a white keyhole on her forhead. Out on the road we hear the schoolbus honking. Mama said let it honk all it wanted, today was a holiday. Cristobell was still bobbing her head up and down like she agreed, yup yup. Vernon he slung the baby across his shoulders again and walked off toward the barn. Cristobell went with him.

I told Daddy I hope when I get my heifer she didnt pull none of that stuff on me like Cristobell done in the woods. I said I would ruther not have one if she was gonna act that way. Daddy said that was farming. Things just happen. But he figured I would change my mind once I was growed like Vernon. But I dont know. I dont know.

Incorrigible

Moving from Mankato to Golden Valley when he was fifteen didn't turn Peter Paul Pearson into a better version of himself. He kept getting into trouble. But not for stealing cars or threatening to kill his father. Mostly, he was in trouble for fighting. Pete was a kid running on adrenalin impulse anger. Experts today might give it a label other than *incorrigible*: call it post traumatic stress disorder from the many beatings his father and others had given him. Could be. But Pete didn't really know what was happening inside his head. Sometimes he thought maybe he was insane.

Pete lived with his aunt and uncle in Golden Valley for less than a month, before he got a job on a dairy farm near Elk River. He knew his aunt and uncle were glad to see him go and wouldn't want him back. He had heard them whispering, his aunt saying, What we got ourselves into with that kid? The uncle saying, We shoulda said no. The aunt adding, Wendy don't like him neither. Nobody does. He's scary.

The people who put him to work were named Joe and Rose Becker. Their son, Harvey, was engaged to Pete's cousin Wendy. Harvey took Pete out to the farm to help with the haying—cutting, raking, bailing, stacking. Pete fell in love with the place. It was 160 acres of corn and purple-flowered alfalfa and timothy and rolling pasture bordered by woods east and west. There was a huge white barn with a tile silo attached to its side. Forty yards away from the barn was a two-story frame house painted forest green and shaded by a towering elm. A large machine shed with a sliding door was near the house, followed by a chicken coop, a garage and a windmill tapping into an artesian spring running 100 feet below. The whirling windmill brought up the clearest, sweetest water Pete had ever known.

Old Joe Becker gave Pete a pair of work gloves, but he refused to wear them. He wanted calluses. He wanted thorn hands. Karate fighter hands. The hard work involved with hoisting hay bales onto the wagon, bringing full loads to the elevator, which carried the bales one by one, like miniature freight cars, up into the barn, stacking the hay in the loft, going back out with the wagon for another load, repeating the same routine all day long, plus doing morning and evening chores, feeding cows and milking forty of them and carrying five gallon stainless steel canisters of milk to the bulk tank, cleaning the cow gutters out with a scoop shovel— toughened Pete's hands, hardened his body, made him feel manly. Made him feel as if he were finally doing something useful.

Work makes a man a man, work gives you worth his mother had told him. Her haunting voice always in the back of his head urging him to measure up. Without work you're nothing. Without work the hero is zero.

When the haying was over, Pete asked Harvey to ask his folks to let him stay. Harvey no longer lived at the farm, so Pete could keep sleeping in Harvey's bed upstairs and help with the chores and harvesting the corn in the fall. Harvey told his parents that Pete ate like a bird and it wouldn't cost much to feed him. Pete didn't correct that impression. Truth is he had a gargantuan appetite and most nights he would sneak down to the milk house and fill glass after glass with milk. Drink it gluttonously.

Harvey's parents had the mistaken idea that Pete was a ward of the Minnesota court. They thought the state would pay compensation for keeping him, and since he was willing to work for room and board, the Beckers decided to let him hang on a while. By the time they learned there wasn't any money in it for them, Pete was already in school in Elk River. So they let him continue milking cows and doing chores and sleeping upstairs, at least until the school year was over. Then we'll see, Joe Becker said.

Pete also worked weekends for other farmers in the area who needed extra help with corn harvesting or making silage in autumn or piglet castrations or spreading manure or chopping cords of wood or stump pulling or combing newly disked fields with a stone boat and loading it with rocks left over from glaciers retreating ten thousand years ago. Those farmers paid a pittance for his labor, usually about five dollars a day, which gave him pocket money and made it possible for him to buy lunch at school. Lunch costing fifty cents. Fifty cents would get him a bowl of navy bean soup, a packet of crackers and a half pint of milk. Pete would cram the soup with crackers, relishing every salty bite.

The boy loved farming. He was a natural at it. He loved the dairy cows especially—called them *bovinities*. One or two of them were stinkers who might kick him or slash his face with a shit-soaked tail if he let his guard down. But most of them were gentle giants who reacted to soft words and affectionate currying by relaxing their bodies and letting their milk down. Pete would sing to them every morning and evening as he milked them and stroked them and pulled crusted manure off their flanks. His morning songs were usually something country: "In the Jailhouse Now" was one of his favorites. So was "Your Cheating Heart." At night he always sang "Blue Moon" and had a fancy the cows loved hearing him croon.

Joe Becker told Pete that he had a way with cows. Joe didn't know why Pete liked those contrary critters so much. Joe had been farming and messing with cows all his life and it showed in his stooped shoulders and twisted hands and the deep lines in his neck and face, a face that often looked haggard and worried. To him cows were machines, a means to an end. The milk checks he received once a month barely kept the farm going year round.

On the farm Pete was one type of person: industrious, mild-mannered, a person the Beckers could count on to do any kind of work, no matter how hard and exhausting it was. But at school the boy was intimidating. Being around other boys often brought out Pete's acids, the suffocating meanness and anger chewing his insides. So even with him wanting the Beckers to like him and hoping they would keep him, Pete kept creating problems the same as he had in Mankato, where, after he threatened the life of his father, the court authorities labeled him incorrigible. His father wanted him *out. Out of the house! Out of my life!* The powers that be had sent him north to his relatives as a last ditch attempt to rehabilitate him, save him from what seemed certain to be a life of crime and incarceration. The judge had said that Golden Valley was his last chance to redeem himself. Adding, If I ever see you in my courtroom again, son, it's a straight shot to the Industrial Boys School.

You won't see me again, the boy had replied.

Pete carried a push-button switchblade everywhere he went. He was always expecting someone to jump him. He had slashed a boy in Mankato in eighth grade. The boy was big. A bully. Always picking on kids half his size. When he started picking on Pete, there was no hesitation. Out came the knife, the blade flying open and lacerating the boy's palms, both of them thrown up to protect his face. The horrified look in his eyes was a thrilling sight to behold. The boy ran all the way home with Pete chasing him. Warning him at the door that if he said anything, I'll cut your fucking throat!

The bully wasn't a bully anymore. Whenever he saw Pete in the halls, he pivoted and went the other way.

This is the same blade Pete brought to his new school. The heft of it in his pocket making him feel safe. And dangerous. Pete would play with it when other kids were around. He would push the button and the blade would fly out and make everyone jump. Pete relished the fear his actions caused others. Their bulging eyes, their wonder. He knew his own eyes looked pitiless as pebbles. He had a prizefighter's wide jaw. It had taken countless punches from his father and other tough guys. No one had ever knocked Pete out. He was as solid as tamarack. Knuckles mean as marbles. He feared nothing but the judge in Mankato and the infamous reformatory.

One day Pete met a boy at school who wasn't scared of him at all. The kid's name was Tommy Keith. Tommy and Pete would play mumbley peg throwing the blade just outside each other's feet, making sure they stabbed the grass and not each other, seeing who could split his legs the farthest and touch the knife hilt with his foot without falling over. This was the game that got Pete in trouble when a teacher caught the boys playing it and took them to the principal's office. Pete confessed that the knife was his. The principal, Mr. Bergman, let Tommy Keith go. But kept Pete in his office and called the boy's probation officer. Pete was on the verge of being expelled, which, since his relatives had made it clear they didn't want him around, would have put him back in the hands of the court in Mankato. Pete's probation officer, a tall, slender fellow who always wore a light gray suit, a blue tie and a panama, its brim folding rakishly over his forehead, talked the principal out of the expulsion. Pete's knife was confiscated and he was given a two-week detention.

Pete had a Napoleon complex. He was generally shorter than other boys his age. Being short always bothered him. The farm work, haybucking, corn harvesting, making silage, chopping wood, the heavy barn chores had helped him gain ten or so pounds of hardcore muscle. He could do 100 pushups, thirty pull-ups (two with one arm) and 500 sit-ups without breaking a sweat. He weighed 155. Call him a middling middleweight. The boy never reached the coveted six feet his mother had wanted. Six feet being her measure of what a real man should be. Even though Pete willed his body to get taller, nature wouldn't cooperate. It wasn't until later that he understood why 5'9" was stretching the limits of what was possible for him. His mother had reached 5'5", his father 5'8". Do the genetics. But thanks to the shape he was in, and thanks to his father's *boxing lessons*, and the street fighting Pete had done, he was easily the bully of the ninth grade. Even sophomores, juniors and seniors were wary of him.

Pete picked on big guys, those big farmboys who had little idea how to use their fists or their feet. He never lost a fight while he was at Elk River High. Granted, Pete only fought four times, but they were all no contest. The chip on his shoulder didn't include anyone his size or smaller. Every big guy was fair game as far as Pete was concerned. If a boy was big, Pete automatically hated him and would start scheming on ways to hurt him, get him in trouble. Humiliate him. Most boys refused to fight Pete at all, though doubtless some of them could have done him harm if they had ever caught him in a bear hug or a chokehold or hammerlock. The ones that took Pete on lasted only seconds. When the fight was over, and Pete had calmed down, he felt sorry for what he had done to the other boy. But he soon got over it.

A certain intrepid tenth grader picked a fight with Pete one day. He was the second biggest kid in his class. His cousin, a guy who had backed down when Pete had tried to get him to rumble, was the biggest kid in school, well over six feet and wide as a combine. The fellow who challenged Pete was named Eugene. His cousin's humiliation was more than he could handle. He caught Pete off-guard in the hall, bumped him into the lockers and said he would meet him outside after school. Pete brooded about it all through history class and determined that waiting for school to end wasn't an option. When the bell rang Pete gave his books to Tommy Keith and asked him to hang onto them. Pete kept the history book. It was a fat thing. A heavy tome.

Spotting Eugene opening his locker, Pete walked up behind him and slammed the back of his head with the history book. When Eugene turned around, his hands holding his head as if trying to keep it from falling off, Pete smacked him in the face with the book. Aimed for his nose and bloodied it. In seconds Pete was on top of Eugene using the boy's hair as handles to pound his head into the linoleum. Pete was out of control, flames filling his brain, murder in his heart. A janitor and Principal Bergman grabbed Pete and hauled him away.

Again, the principal called the probation officer. Pete was overwrought and almost cried at the thought that there would be no more chances. This time they would take him to reform school for sure.

Through the door, Pete could hear the probation officer pleading for him. Story is that kid's mother hung herself Christmas Eve a year ago, he said. There was trouble between her and the kid's old man. They got in a fight, which from what I understand was pretty common with those two. Her husband run off in the car and when he come back the next morning, she was hanging frozen from a rafter in the garage. Pete was there trying to lift her up by her legs. Can you imagine that, Principal Bergman? What it must have done to that boy's mind? His old man beat him a lot, you know, and that type of rearing always causes damage of some sort. What I'm saying is Pete's a boy who needs to get his past behind him. A boy who needs time to get his head on straight. Inside, he's a good boy, got a good heart. And he's one hell of a worker the Beckers tell me. He's good to the cows, that's for sure. Sings to them to calm them. Curries them and croons. Makes me smile to think of it. Hard ass hooligan like that treating cows like they're all his big dumb pets. He's got them milking better than ever. The milk yields are way up. Look, I've been in this business twenty years, Principal Bergman, and what I know about truly bad boys is that the vast majority of them won't work hard for nobody, not even themselves. And none of them, by God not a damn one, would even think of singing to dairy cows for any reason whatever. Nope, bad boys wouldn't dream of it, Principal Bergman. This kid is special. I believe in him.

Pete was given detention the same as when his switchblade was confiscated. But this time instead of two weeks detention, it was two months. Every day, Monday through Thursday, Pete had to stay an hour after school and then hoof the six miles back to the farm. Always arriving in time for evening chores.

Pete wasn't allowed to just sit and vegetate during detention. He had to produce a page or two of writing for his English class: a theme or a story. He used the time to teach himself how to two-finger type on an old black Royal in the admin office. He pecked away and wrote about stealing cars and driving them like a moonshine smuggler. He wrote about hotwiring, giving instructions on how to do it. He wrote about the time he drove a Packard up a ramp at the golf range and split his head open when the car came down hard enough to break both front axles. The deep, vertical scar on his forehead was a memento of that moment.

Mrs. Johansen, an old educator with iron gray hair wrapping her head like a Nazi helmet, read Pete's efforts and corrected the spelling, punctuation, grammar. She was a no-nonsense teacher. Pete respected her and wanted to please her. She had one glass eye that often leaked lubricant. When she stared at Pete, the gooey fake eye wandered upward as if channeling heaven, while the good eye was always riveted on him fiercely red-rimmed. She was decent to Pete and encouraged his writing, though she tsked-tsked over much of what he wrote about. She told Pete that he should go into the service as soon as he was old enough. The service would straighten him, out, she insisted.

Pete knew Mrs. Johansen liked him all right. Almost certainly she was the only teacher who did. So he worked hard for her and got good grades for the first time in his life. Other teachers hated him. Some of them feared him. Only one ever dared confront Pete. He was the shop teacher, a rotund, bald-headed disciplinarian who despised Pete. Despised him so much that one day the teacher couldn't contain himself. Pete was talking to the boy sitting next to him when the teacher was lecturing and suddenly he leaped at Pete. Slapped his cheek and told him to SHUT UP! Pete had a T-square in his hand and raised it. The shop teacher said: Go ahead! Get yourself expelled! I'd like that, you ignoramus! You goon! Pete thought better of it. He set the T-square on his desk and shut his mouth. But Pete didn't forget. He knew there would come a time for payback.

Tommy Keith had a long, sharp chin. He had a beak of a nose—

Pete thought maybe he was Indian or Jewish. He worked on an egg ranch and used his beak and his whole agile body to imitate chickens: how they stabbed at the ground, scratched the earth, fluttered their wings and made pwaak-pwaak sounds. His chicken act was uncannily accurate. He and Pete had some things in common. Tommy's parents had split and he, living with his mother and sisters, started getting into trouble. Mostly burglary, petty theft. He was put in juvey until the authorities could find a place for him in the country. They put him on the egg ranch, paying the owners, Mr. and Mrs. Story, compensation to keep him.

Tommy was a wonderful singer. Listening to Tommy singing—*I hear that train a'comin, it's rollin round the bend* ... was magically Johnny Cash. Tommy and Pete practiced songs together and got pretty good at it. Tommy was never shy and would go into classrooms and sing for the students. One time he hauled Pete out of Mrs. Johansen's class (with her permission) and took him into another class and they sang "I Walk the Line." Their encore was "Live Fast Love Hard Die Young." Pete harmonized but mostly sang background noises. Dum-dum-waa-waa-dooby-doom. It was Tommy's show. Tommy had the voice. He said he was going places. That one day he was going to be a famous singer. Pete believed him, of course.

Harvey Becker and Pete's cousin Wendy got married in late April at the Catholic Church in the town of St. Michael's. Harvey had rented Pete a tuxedo and put him in the wedding as an usher. It was a perfect day, not a speck of cloud in the sky. Trees were budding, the grass flushing emerald green under the bright sun.

All good omens for the happy couple Rose Becker told Pete. Heaven shining on them, bless their hearts, she said, her voice tremulous.

Pete's aunt and uncle were there, but they didn't say a word to him. They avoided him, in fact. He wondered if maybe they thought by talking to him, they would be making a commitment again. Opening a door just in case he needed a place to stay. He told himself they needn't worry. Theirs was a door he wouldn't darken ever, no matter how much trouble he was in. He was sixteen now and he liked working for the Beckers and making his own decisions about what to do next with his life. Farming was just right for him. Maybe he would own a farm one day and then they would see what he was made of.

The reception afterward was at the little park next door to the church. There were sandwiches, pastries, sodas and beer.

The couple waltzed. Then Wendy danced with her father, while Harvey danced with his mother.

A few songs later, Wendy danced with Pete and told him she was glad for him, glad the Beckers had taken him in. She hoped he wouldn't ruin it by doing something stupid. Wendy was petite, a little bit of a thing, but her voice sounded ten feet tall. Pete told her, Yes, ma'am, I'm hoping they'll let me stick around at least until high school is over. Until I'm graduated, I mean.

He had every intention of behaving himself.

The music played on. Couples were swinging each other across the soft grass. People standing around under the trees chatting, drinking, smoking. Lots of laughter. Pete and Tommy enjoying themselves scheming on giggling girls who were eying them. It was fun, a fine party.

Until a shaggy-haired fellow came along who seemed to have arrived already drunk. His bleary eyes took a bead on Tommy Keith, who said *oh shit* when he saw him coming.

He got nose to nose with Tommy and growled, How come you a delinquent, Tommy Keith?

Tommy said, How come you a stinkin drunk, Tex?

I ain't no drunk, but you a goddamn delinquent, that's what I know.

I'd rather be a delinquent than a stinkin drunk, Tex.

You call me a drunk once more I'll hand you your goddamn head, you fuckin felon. Tex staggered a bit. He was wearing jeans with holes in the knees, a raggedy plaid shirt and cowboy boots down at the heels scuffing the grass. Do the chicken, Tommy Keith, he said. Pwaak, pawaak. Do the chicken, delinquent. C'mon, doo-doo!

How come you're here at all, Tex? Tommy said. No one invites you to these things. You just show up and crash every party so as you can get drunk and make a fool of yourself. Go on, get out of here fore I sic Harvey on you.

No one talks to Tex Ritter that a-way, said Tex, his chin jutting out as if daring Tommy to poke it.

But Tommy didn't want to poke it. C'mon, Tex, it's a goddamn wedding, man. Don't make trouble.

Tex was swaying. He backed up. Spat. Said, You the troublemaker, Tommy Keith. I been watchin you. You stole my kit. Piked it like the low-down dirty thief you is.

Tex lunged forward on legs thin as rails. He punched Tommy in the eye so hard he went down. Pete was somewhat drunk by then, his reflexes signaling slowly as he threw himself at Tex and swung the bottle, hitting Tex a glancing blow above his right ear hard enough to make him quit beating on Tommy. Tex was staggering trying to catch his balance. Holding a hand to his ear, he whirled to face a homicidal Pete.

Assassin! Tex hissed. Oinked me, he said. He started lurching from one watcher to another, mostly men happy for the diversion. Oinked me! I been oinked! He's a killer! A killer! Don't nobody care? A hand still pressed to the side of his head, Tex pointed an accusing finger at Pete. Officer, arrest that man! he commanded. Pete was in a crouch, his bottle ready for action. Harvey broke through the crowd and pushed Tex aside and told him, Time for you to leave, Tex Ritter! Get lost for I break you over my knee.

Tex stumbled toward the street grumbling, making noises. The only word Pete understood was Oinked! Harvey caught Pete by the arm and said, You goin home, kid. Get in the car. Pete tried to explain, but Harvey wouldn't hear it.

Treat you decent and you come here and try to ruin my wedding. Your cousin wants nothing to do with you. She wants you outta here and I do too. Pete's aunt and uncle were glaring at him, their faces saying, Told you so!

Harvey drove him back to the farm and had him take the tux off and put on chore clothes. Harvey took the tux and told Pete it was time to milk. Harvey went back to his bride and Pete went to the barn. He got the cows into their stanchions, filled the troughs with alfalfa. He got the De Lavals and milked the cows and sang to them. Sang—

Gonna live fast, love hard, die young and leave a beautiful mem-o-ry...

The school-year was flying fast. By the time it was nearly over, the Beckers had had enough of the principal calling to complain about Pete.

He made them worry and fret. They didn't know what to do with a kid like him. Their only compensation was the steadiness of Pete's work. Give him that, Joe Becker told Pete's probation officer, that kid is a hell of a hard worker. But we don't want to be liable for him. He damn near ruined Harvey and Wendy's wedding. Sorry, but he's got to go.

Pete understood why he had to go, but it still hurt that they wanted to be rid of him. If Pete had been in their place trying to deal with a sixteen-year-old public enemy, he would have wanted to be rid of him too. Joe Becker told the probation officer that Pete wasn't what they had expected at all. And of course, they thought they were going to get that state compensation for keeping him like the Storys got for Tommy Keith. The probation officer told them that Pete had been sent to close relatives. That was the difference.

In June when school let out, Pete would have to go back to Mankato and serve his time until his eighteenth birthday. It's his own fault, said Joe. Ain't no helpin a boy like that. Boy like that born for trouble. Life is hard enough without a boy like that giving me and Rosie ulcers.

On the last day of school, Pete found that he had flunked all his courses except Mrs. Johansen's English class. Not that he gave a damn about any of it. Pete's probation officer was waiting for him at the Becker farm to take him to the bus station, where an escort would accompany him to Mankato and make sure Pete was turned over to the authorities at the Industrial School for Boys. Pete's clothes were packed and ready to go. This very night he would begin serving his sentence. No one to blame but himself, of course.

When he said goodbye to Tommy Keith, they were standing outside next to the teachers' parking lot waiting for the school buses to arrive. Tommy said he would miss Pete and would never forget how he stepped in and clobbered Tex Ritter at the wedding reception.

He was hitting me and hitting me and suddenly he stopped when you bopped him with that bottle. You a forever-type friend, Pete. Tommy had a little present for him. Shake my hand, he said. When the two boys shook hands, Pete felt the hilt of a knife. It was his push button blade.

I stole it out of Bergman's desk, Tommy told him. I figure I owe you at least that much for what you done.

Pete stood a long moment staring down at the ebony handle. If I'd had this I'd a killed that Texan, Pete said. And then he said, Very cool, Tommy. I'll remember you, man. Tommy said he would remember Pete too and he hoped their paths would cross again. The buses came. Tommy got on his bus, a whole summer of freedom ahead of him.

Pete watched the buses fill. Watched them leave. He waved goodbye to Tommy Keith who gave him thumbs up. Finally, when it was quiet, nothing but a tranquil breeze teasing his hair, Pete walked through the lot to the shop teacher's unlocked Ford and hopped inside. Tore the wires from behind the ignition and stripped the plastic tips off with his knife. He twisted the power wires together and touched them with the starter wire. The engine turned over, started. Pete drove away, drove through Elk River.

Drove over the Mississippi Bridge toward Dayton. He felt lucky and unafraid. He had all the tools he needed to take on his father now. He'd slap him first the way his father had often slapped him. Pete had such thick calluses on his hands it would be like getting whacked with a brick. He had a sense of invincibility wearing him like chainmail. He had his trusty knife. He needed to cut a piece of someone's hose to use as a siphon for stealing gas. He had a few bucks for food. He would dump the car in Mankato after he got home and killed his father. Then he'd catch a ride south, east, west it didn't matter. Movement was what mattered. Someday he might come back and waste the shop teacher. But for the present he would hold his fury inside and simply follow his nose home and do what he had to do. Avenge his mother.

And then what? What about afterwards? There were farms out there. Work to be had. Work to make a man a man. Work to give a man worth. No way adding up to zero was happening to him. Not to this particular Pete who had miles and miles to go and was just getting started.

Tattooed

They drive through fog, while Dick tries to convince Virgil that every man should have at least one defining tattoo. He croons like a man in love with his own voice: "But it has to be the right one because a tattoo makes a statement, you see what I'm saying? A statement adding up to who you are. Who is Virgil Francis Foggy? *What* is he? *Why* is he? You see what I'm saying? It has to be a picture worth a thousand words summing up the bad motherfucker of Foggy Farm. The tough kid who can do it. You wannabe tough, kid? You wannabe a warrior like your brother and me? I've thought this shit through. I know what I'm talking about. What does my eagle and snake say about me right here on my arm? Why do I got *Semper Fi*? Why does this other arm have a ready-to-peck-your-eyes-out blackbird?

"I dunno."

"You dunno! Jesus, what a dodo. My tattoos say, RESPECT THIS MAN! They say, This man is always faithful to his cause and his country and the United States Marines. Do not fuck with me, motherfucker, that's what they say. I will mess you up! That's what they say. These be the tattoos of a warrior." He pounds the blackbird tattoo. "This is the tattoo of a *man*." Dick chuckles deep in his throat, velvet baritone rumblings. "I saw a guy had a tattoo of a duck on his chest. What the hell for? You shoot ducks from a blind. Sitting ducks, you've heard that. Who wants to have a sitting duck? You see what I'm saying? A duck makes a negative statement about you. Quack, quack, you're a quacker. Quackers and Quakers get no respect." He digs a finger into Virgil's ribs. Virgil squirms. "Saw another guy, he's got a worm on his forearm coming out of a hole. Two little round worm eyes looking out at the world like it don't know what's up. What's that say?"

"I dunno."

"You dunno. Plain as the nose on your face. The guy's a worm. A loser. He hides in a hole. He's afraid to come out. The world baffles him. Can't you make the connection? Worm. . . Hole . . . He has no confidence in his manhood. Manhood no bigger than my thumb. I seen em in Korea. They the ones who shit their pants when the shooting starts. *I wanna go home, I want my mommy!* Little worms disgracing the uniform. I seen em."

"Worm-hood," Virgil offers.

"Exactly! Worm-hood. Guys like that show their tattoos in a bar, you want to slug them. You see what I'm saying? Some bad motherfucker will insult a guy like that. Call him a worm or something worse. He's an asshole with worms up his ass. You tell him worms live in mud holes. Worms eat the dead. They eat corpses and grind them into topsoil. Tell him that! Fuck him if he don't like it! Maybe spit on his tattoo. Maybe kick his ass. And the asshole deserves it for being so ignorant! A real man wouldn't have no tattoo like that. Ducks and worms." Dick snorts. Repeats, "Ducks and worms. Bah, you see what you done? You got me in a bad mood all of a sudden. I'm in a ass-kicking mood now."

Nervously Virgil says, "But . . . but blackbirds are nice. They don't hurt nobody."

"Blackbirds kick ass," Dick says. "You ever watch them in the cattails zipping around like bats? Zipping around like badass thoughts is what they're doing. Zipping around like black arrows gonna kill somebody." Dick's hand zips here, zips there. The windshield wipers swipe at the fog. "What do you think they're doing? They're warriors making war! They're battling over territory. It's war! They kick the shit out of each other just like men do. They were made for it and so are we. Man is two things. Man is a war machine and a *fuck* machine. The baddest motherfuckers get the pussy and the territory too, you see what I'm saying? Whole lot of ass-kicking going on, whole lot of humping. It's the way of the world. Just look around, you'll see what I'm saying."

Dick's eyes narrow on the road ahead, the fog lying like a shroud over the farmland, trees, the numerous lakes. His eyes squinting so hard they're mere slits beneath his heavy brows. Frown lines weave across his forehead. His teeth worrying his lips. "Besides . . . you see what I'm saying? The new tattoo I'm getting is for your mother," he says. "I'm *not* going to be showing it around, you see what I'm saying? Our private tattoo, for her eyes only."

"I see."

"You see nothing. Something like that will make a woman fall all over your ass. It's the idea that you would brand yourself permanently for her. Her name right there on your chest." He slashes his finger over his heart where the tattoo will go. "When I'm in my grave rotting to ribbons, her name will be down there rotting with me. That's what women like to know. They like to know they got you even in death, that you won't get away from them even after you've bought the farm. Women are very possessive, kid. They want all of you. They want to rule you. Want you to be their property, another piece of furniture, an ornament sitting in the same spot where they can keep an eye on you, make sure you can't have any fun without them. You let them believe that's what they've got and they'll be content and won't fuck with your head so much. Busting balls is a woman's forte!" Dick is red in the face. His teeth tear at the air as he talks. "The bitches weigh you down with houses and kids and fucking bills and shit! Their plan from the beginning is to chain you to responsibilities and such. That's what happened to your dad. All that shit give him a heart attack. Worked so hard he dropped dead when he's only thirty-six. He did it all for her, to make her feel secure, you see what I'm saying? You slip on your mask for them—yes, dear, no dear, anything you say, dear, sweetheart, doll, I need you, I want you, I can't live without you, that's what they like to hear. Feed it to them like Bonbons. You do that and they'll take your bullshit because your bullshit makes them feel safe. That's what she wants, you at the entrance to the cave with a club in your hand and a hard-on for her anytime she wants to get laid. Never let them know what you really feel. Don't let them know they're smothering you!"

Dick continues chattering nonstop, telling Virgil all about those women who think they know you, and the wisdom of a man who knows how to play with that spot where she lives, play her instrument. He rolls his thumb round and round the tips of his first two fingers and throws a leer. "A woman lives at the fork," he says. "Same as a man who can't keep his hands off his cock. We're all just bare-forked animals, you know. Shakespeare said that. Shakespeare never told a lie."

Virgil is bored. He has heard it before and he yawns behind his hand. His eyes fidget, observing a patch of forest screened in fog. The fog wavering, like it can't make up its mind. The forest ending at an empty lot at the northern edges of Anoka. Paved streets passing by in a Puritan grid. Steep roofed, snow-shedding houses, bordered with poplars that chainsaws have spared so far.

"So, what you think, dodo? How about a eagle? You want a eagle? How about a hawk or a falcon? Just don't get the Minnesota state bird, for Christ's sake. A common loon. What numb nuts picked that one? So what'll it be, Virgil? Make your old uncle proud."

"I don't want one, sir."

Dick looks at the boy with pity. "You really, really don't want a tattoo?"

"N-no, sir."

"Fifteen years old and he doesn't want a tattoo. Kids his age dying for tattoos and he doesn't want one. There's something perverse about him, I say. Something perverse about my little nephew stepson who I'm trying to raise to be a man." Dick flashes a dimple. "Perverse, little monkey-shine. You spank your monkey all the time, betcha."

Virgil closes his eyes. Prays for the ride to be over.

"Don't slump so much. Get your shoulders straight," Dick orders. "You're getting round-shouldered, do you know that? Makes you look defeated. Walk proud, walk tall, what the hell's the matter with you?" He reaches over, clips the boy on the back of the head. "You always look like somebody's about to beat you. Look at your eyes, look how you stare with them suffering eyes. You've got your mother's eyes, basset hound. Why you got such big, sad eyes, anyway? You're not Italian."

"Mom's part Italian. Her dad was Italian."

"That old drunk? Yeah, I guess he was. But you're mostly Scot and Irish. Just like me and you should look like me because I look like your father. But you got them eyes instead. Moody things. Is it because your brother's dodging bullets in Vietnam?" Dick taps his chest. "I dodged em in Korea, it's his turn now. It's a rite of passage every man should experience. Milking cows is a rite of passage to looking old before your time and having a heart attack. I'm talkin about your dad workin himself to death."

"I miss my dad. I miss Vernon too. I wish they'd send him home."

Dick thrusts his face at Virgil, eyes teasing. Breath boozy. "You know what? You don't look a thing like your father. Vernon looks like him. Not you. You look like . . . like I don't know. Maybe the mailman. Ha! A cross between a stork and a round-eyed monkey and a baggy-eyed hound. Ha!"

Virgil tries to imagine what uncle-stepdad is seeing. Hound-monkey-stork.

"What do I look like?" Dick says.

"Hmm?"

"What kind of animal?"

"Dunno."

"Come on, everybody looks like some kind of animal."

Virgil looks at him hard and wonders *what does he look like? What would he like to hear?* "A sort of lion, I guess," Virgil tells him.

Dick grins. "A lion?" he says.

"A lion, definitely."

Dick roars, showing his nicotine teeth. "Fucking lions," he says. "I wish I could go to Africa like Hemingway and shoot me one with a major mane. Make him charge me and stand my ground and put a bullet in his mouth just as he leaps. Christ, what a picture!" Dick beaming at the idea, his conquering foot on a dead lion's neck. Dick is grinning as if someone is taking his picture. "Hey, you can quit staring at me now! Do you know you stare at people all the time? Yeah, you do. Even as a little kid sitting in your highchair, you stared and stared with them eyes. Are you a mind reader?"

"N-no sir."

"Hell no, you're not. Don't you know it's not polite to stare? Quit staring at me!"

"S-sorry."

"Like a round-eyed monkey," mutters Dick. "Like a goddamn hound." He curls his thumb and forefinger into the sign for asshole. "Eyes this big," he says, "big as a turd staring and staring like you got no manners." He peeks through his curled finger and thumb.

"A turd," Virgil repeats, thinking how turds come in all sizes.

"Like a deer in the headlights," says Dick. "You stare at people that way, it makes them self-conscious, you know? Nobody likes eyes that undress them."

"Undress?" Virgil says. He almost laughs

"It's a phase of speech," says Dick, waving him off. "Although by God in your case." He glances suspiciously. "You're at that sap stage of life. Getting hairy, getting horny. Spank the monkey. Everything growing and gawky and you don't know what to do with it. Who's there!" Dick reaches over and grabs Virgil's crotch.

"J-Jesus, Uncle Dick! Goddamn!"

Dick chortles. "Boy toy!" he says. "Virgil the virgin! Virgin Virgil!"

Heat flushes through him. Crossing his legs he squeezes against the door. Hands covering his lap. You dirty bastard, he says. But not aloud.

The car jerks back and forth as Dick maneuvers through traffic along Coon Rapids Boulevard in sight of the Mississippi. He goes left on 7th and pulls to the curb in front of:

TINA'S TATTOO PARLOR.
NOW UNDER NEW MANAGEMENT!
COME IN AND BROWSE

"R-E-G-I-N-A P-E-R-P-E-T-U-A," he spells. "It's a creative way to say that you and your woman are one. See what I'm saying? Women love that shit, it's romantic. Look here, a woman who don't love romance is a woman already dead. You understand?"

"Yessir."

"Might as well bury her. Her heart's a turnip. Romance makes a woman real. You see what I'm saying? You want a hotbox bitch, you give her romance and she'll open the cover and let you in. You get where I'm going with this?"

Virgil shakes his head. He's not really that stupid, though. He knows.

"Listen up. When you're in tight with a woman, you find ways to say her pussy's your god. You carve yourself with her name. See what I'm saying? Carve her into your flesh. Your mother's gorgeous when she wants to be. Except she's getting too fat carrying that kid. She needs to give birth and get her figure back. I never like em heavy. Too many creases where the dirt hides."

Dick eyes his own face in the rearview mirror. "You handsome dog," he says. And then he says, "You have to be careful, though, because what if you don't want her forever and you're stuck with her name needled on you like that? It happens all the time. You'd have to get it burned off. Burn her out of you. And it costs ten times more to take it off than to put it on." He sucks on his forefinger, wets his arching eyebrows. "No, I'd have it filled in. Turn it into a storm cloud and a lightning bolt firing down. Got it all worked out in my mind. He smiles abruptly and sings *"C'mon baby let the good times roll . . . c'mon baby let me feel your hole."*

Virgil considers getting out and hitching home. He can smell Dick's sweaty feet, a yeasty odor added to the sulfur of his breath. Dick reaches across him and Virgil flinches. "Hey, hey, cool it. I ain't gonna hurt you." Dick opens the glove box and grabs a pint of Old Crow. Twists the cap off. Takes a drink. His eyes are full of nasties that Virgil doesn't want to know about. Dick lights a cigarette. "Sooo . . . you getting any lately?" he says.

"Hmm?"

"You getting any nookie?"

"No sir." Virgil rolls down the window. The fog has lifted to treetop level.

"When I was your age I was getting nookie from sixteen year olds with perky little tits and tight little cunts. Nothing like a tight little cunt, you see what I'm saying? Wouldn't I like to be fourteen and go there again! Tastes like morning glories, baby. Ever suck the nectar out of a morning glory? That's what teenage pussy tastes like. Sonofa . . . phew, you know, there's just nothing like young-love. It's never the same again. You never get over young-love. It haunts you all your life. Women get mature and they get loose so that sometimes you hardly feel anything. Or they get dry and chafe you. And some old broads get smelly, the fat ones do, and they fart in bed and have bad breath and . . . bah, the honeymoon is over! But that young stuff, what wouldn't I give!"

Virgil looks away, closes his eyes. Breathe, Virgil. Breathe. Ohmmmm. His hand is on the door handle. He could cut and run. Two seconds and he would be out of reach. Get back to the farm, the barn. the cows, things that he knows.

"Boys have no ambition these days," Dick continues. "Wanna grow hair down to their bony asses and smoke pot and suck Mama's tit till they're twenty-nine. At your age I had already been screwed, blewed and tattooed and I ain't let up since. Being forty hasn't slowed me none. I'm a man, I'm a warrior. I wish I could get in that goddamn war. Vernon's lucky. He don't know how lucky he is. He don't know that this is the best-worst time of his life. Everything else is anticlimax after you come back from a war."

Dick pauses. Brooding. Then perks up instantly at a thought. He wolf-whistles. He blows himself a kiss. He cocks the mirror so it reflects Virgil. "So you deny any love interest, huh? You wouldn't lie to Unky Dick, would you?" He pokes a finger in Virgil's ribs again. "No, I guess not, poor stringy thing. You've been a mess since that dog had his way with you. Damn dog could've killed you. Glad I shot that fucker. But you'll grow out of it. Listen up. You should show those dog bites like badges of honor. Girls like that shit. They like scars. They like to feel sorry for your sufferings. Scars make them feel like you've got experience with the ways of the world. Don't hide them in long sleeves. How tall are you?"

"I don't know. Five-ten."

"You're getting there. Tall enough to make them curious about what you got. Girls equate height with size. Everybody knows that. Short guys are at a disadvantage, you see what I'm saying? Although, by gawd, I knew a guy in the Marines had a ten-inch crank and he was only five-foot seven. No shit. But be glad you're not going to be short, Virge. You picked your parents wisely. What you need now is *weight* that's what you need. A serious pair of biceps. More muscle on your ass. A muscled ass says ka-boom! You watch their eyes, they're just like us, don't kid yourself. They always go to your ass and your crotch when you ain't looking. Women's eyes are swift."

Small, ignorant, insignificant Virgil feels his thin bones close to his skin and the map of veins exposed on his chest and his heart beating fast and God, oh God he wants out! "I'm trying to eat more," he says.

Lingering pity in Dick's eyes.

"I guess I like Sandra Story some," Virgil adds hopefully.

"Sandy Story? Now you're talking. Good stuff. Great shitter on her. Yeah, like little bowling balls in her pants. She's a good choice, she's prime. Give her another year to mature those knockers and Roy Story will be beating you boys off with a stick. You need any pointers, let Dick know and he'll give you the word. She's right up my alley. I can tell you how to get some of that. I really can. It's easier than you think."

He lights another cigarette, stabs the butt of the smoked one in the ashtray and says, "Listen up, I got just the tattoo for you. We'll get you a red heart with a blue SS in the middle. We'll put it on your forearm there. That'd be cool. Very cool. You roll up your sleeve when you're with her and she sees her initials and her eyes bug out spring-loaded. She'll drop her drawers . . . guaranteed. Fourteen-year-old fur staring you in the face. Asking you to lunch. What're you gonna do? You gonna pass that up? What are you, a fool? Don't you know you only go around once? And look here, when you dump her, you get the tattoo filled in. Put a black arrow through it. You see what I'm saying?"

"Yessir."

Dick takes another pull at the bottle and says, "Ahh whoo! That'll put hair on your chest! Have a slug."

Virgil waves the bottle off. His stomach is queasy.

The blinking neon keeps calling:

TINA'S TATTOO PARLOR
UNDER NEW MANAGEMENT!
COME IN AND BROWSE

"All right, you don't want to be cool, fuck you," says Dick. He squeezes Virgil's knee. "Offering you the chance of a lifetime, but what the hell, you don't want one, I ain't gonna make you. But Jesus Christ, you're such a punk. When I was your age . . . aww, forget it."

Dick puts the booze back in the glove box. Gets out of the car. Swaggers across the sidewalk hitching his pants. Disappears inside the door. People go by. People dressed for rain. Some hold umbrellas over their shoulders. In cities— Minneapolis, New York, Chicago, Milwaukee, Detroit—thousands more going by in a hurry, eyes fixed on cement, fleeting glimpses of her or him. Don't stare. Cars nosing along, nudging each other throughout Anoka. Get out of the way, you moron! You're the moron, buddy!

Virgil rolls a smoke. Lights it. Calls up the image of Sandra Story in faded jeans. Grabs her shoulders from behind, pivots her around and shows her the red heart tattoo with SS inside.

She melts.

What next?

Down go her pants.

She invites him to lunch at the Y.

Would she really?

Would he?

Hard to believe people do. They'll go to hell for that. Sandy is the only girl he has ever tried anything with. Which wasn't much. Years ago on the playground he asked her for a kiss and she spit in the snow.

"That's when I fell in love with her," he reminds himself.

Looking toward the parlor, the heart tattoo with SS inside is suddenly more appealing. He leaves the car and stands outside the parlor door taking deep breaths. He steps on his cigarette and twists his toe. Then goes inside.

There is a waiting room with three chairs. An end table sloppy with magazines. On the walls are illustrations of tattoos: birds and butterflies, dragonflies and bees and scorpions and black widows with red hourglass bellies, and there are wolves, bears, moose, elk and blushing skunks, flirting rabbits, chipmunks and cats, and every kind of dog, and lots of snakes banded red-on-yellow-kill-a-fellow, or diamond-backed, or drooling Gila monsters, and hula girls, and totally naked girls showing happy breasts, happy lips, poofy hair, ball and chain earrings dangling on their necks, there are knives and Thor's hammer and hearts with arrows, MOTHER or MOM or HER NAME HERE and rosebuds and roses flushing full, yellow daisy and yellow daffodil, a lavender iris open-mouthed, its bubbled base looking like curvy hips. Beneath a cross are words announcing COMMITTED FOREVER.

Down the hallway he can hear a buzzing sound behind a glass-bead curtain. Peeking through he sees Dick in a barber chair, leaning back, eyes closed. A woman is bending over him, working on his bare chest with an electric needle. The woman looks Spanish. She is wearing a tight black skirt. The skirt is moving as if some animal is burrowing in it. A moment passes before it registers what he is seeing. At the bottom of the skirt is an elbow.

In a deep, dreamy voice Dick says, "Whoa, Tina, you're so soapy."

She chuckles and says, "When I get done, you'll be the soapy one."

Virgil starts to back away and she spots him. She starts slapping at Dick's arm. He pulls it out. "Can I help you, sonny?" she says.

"I . . . I . . . wa-want a tattoo."

Dick glares. The woman looks impatient.

"A heart," Virgil says. Looking at Dick. "With SS inside?"

"Do you know him?" she asks Dick.

"Never seen him before in my life. Go away, kid, can't you see she's busy? Snoopy little sneak."

"You're too young for a tattoo," she says. "I'd have to have your parents' permission."

"Yes, ma'am."

He leaves quickly, his fingers blindly groping the wall as he hears Dick saying, "Eyes like a monkey, you notice that? You notice his eyes?"

"He was scared," she says. "You looked like you were going to eat him."

Chased by laughter, Virgil hurries outside and heads for the highway, where he can hitch a ride home. In his mind he sees his uncle's hand rummaging between the woman's legs. Virgil wonders if she was writing his mother's name while his stepfather's fingers were reaming her.

Revelation: His eyes saw what they saw, but he knows for certain he will keep his mouth shut about it ever and ever.

Maybe . . .

Maybe not.

Ways of Looking at a Blackbird

The engine starts sputtering as he's entering Owatonna on Interstate 35 north. Pete figures it's an overheating coil. He could fix it but he doesn't have the money or the tools. In desperation he takes the 218 leading him into the southern part of the city. The car is gasping. He nurses it another mile, until it dies at the turn onto Austin Road.

"Hunk of junk," he says. "Chrysler products: fuck em."

He walks his attitude through the environs. The sky is drizzling. In his pocket he fingers his switchblade. He needs money. He's going to get some. He sees a Casey's Pizza and Southpark Lanes & Lounge in the distance. Continuing north checking out cars, houses, escape routes, he goes left on East Park, finds a cluster of very old houses, nineteenth century probably. Everything looks easy-pickings. Dripping trees line the terraces. Stray leaves whirling over summer-green lawns. Street gutters edged in scaly cement. Blackish mold in the seams of the sidewalks. Along the curbs cars call to him, *Steal me! Steal me!* The rain is a slow soaker, half mist, half fog. He comes upon a black Ford pickup, a key in the ignition. Overhanging the sidewalk are blackbirds on the limbs of a white birch. Their tails jerking. Yellow eyes filled with evil intentions. *Here comes one, get ready.*

"Watch out!" warns a voice nearby.

White home, brown trim, rock chimney, an old man sitting on the porch, his belly resting heavily on his thighs. He has silver hair, a silver beard. Rosy cheeks. He looks like Santa Claus. He chuckles and says, "There are thirteen ways of looking at a blackbird, you know."

"There are?" Pete glances again at the birds. Their wings ballooning like umbrellas.

"You're all wet," says Santa. "Come up here. The rain'll blow over. Keep an old man company. C'mon."

Pete shrugs why not. He climbs the wooden steps dented with age. Takes refuge underneath the eave, removes his cap, shakes the water off. Then squares it neatly on his head again. The old man's bulk flows over a plastic lawn chair. His hair and beard are a mass of tight curls. His nose is very large and laced with tiny red veins. Next to him is a plastic end table. On top are a Meerschaum pipe and a book entitled *Latin at Your Fingertips.*" There are two more plastic chairs on the porch. Pete smells sweet marijuana. He looks at the pipe and wonders if he might get a hit. He sniffs moldy wood, rain-soaked earth, unwashed old man. It registers that this guy is probably poor. More easy pickings, but nothing worth stealing. Except that pickup parked at the curb.

Eyes smiling, mouth seeming about to laugh ho, ho, ho, the old man says, "I'm *the* George Foggy, retired entrepreneur and acknowledged genius gifted in arts—literary arts, sculpting arts, tap dance and ballet choreography, poetry and mime and anything else you care to name that has to do with artistic endeavor. No doubt you've heard of me. I've devoured whole libraries in my time and there's nothing I don't know about Shakespeare. Shakespeare on film is child's play to me. Go on ask me a question. The answer is . . . cogitating, cogitating . . . the answer is *Quem di diligunt adulescens moritur, dum valet sentit sapit.* He whom the gods love dies young, while he still has strength and sense and wits. You can look me up in the annuals of Owatonna. I lived the American Dream. Before I got old. *Senectus ipsa morbus est.* Old age itself a sickness. You may wonder why I talk so cultured. I'm learning Latin to keep my mind from deteriorating. It's either Latin or math or crossword puzzles. Remember that when you get my age, sonny."

"Don't believe a word he's saying!" declares a querulous voice behind the screen door. Pete can't make out if the voice belongs to a man or a woman. George Foggy smiles, jerks his head toward the screen.

"Jesus freak," he says. "Get old, get Jesus, become a cliché." He beckons Pete closer and whispers, "He didn't used to be this way." Suddenly he yells—"Honk! Shut it, Honk!" A tic quivers below his right eye. His whole cheek getting into the act. A corner of his mouth jumps as if an ant is biting it. Followed by his right shoulder. Everything jerking. Is he having a fit?

"Yes, Jesus!" hoots Honk behind the screen.

Pete notices a HELP WANTED sign in the window next to where George Foggy is sitting. Spattered over the front of the old man's shirt are ashes. Some of the ashes falling like dirty snow as he holds out his hand and says, "You look, you know, remarkably familiar. What's your name, my love?"

Pete takes the offered hand, shakes it. The hand is huge, dry, powerful. "I'm Pete."

"Pete?"

"Peter Paul Pearson."

"Triphilia Pete? Three in one Pete? *To impose upon the nations the code of peace* Pete?" George Foggy leans his head toward the screen. "Hims Trinity, Honk!"

"Trinity whom?" says Honk.

"I'm Peter Paul Pearson."

George Foggy's hands fly to his heart. "P.P.P!" he shouts. "Triphilia, what did I just say?" He presses his chest as if his lungs are bursting. "Where have you been. P.P.P.?"

"Where has he been?" Honk inquires.

"You've changed," says Foggy. "Your eyes so dark. Your mouth so angry. What big teeth you have. Has someone been mean to you, my love?"

Pete slides toward the steps, ready to vamoose. George Foggy is in tears, sobbing, his fat shoulders fat gut heaving.

"An uncivilized world! Nothing's what it used to be!" he cries. "P.P.P., P.P.P., Foggy has missed you so—"The crying jag cuts off abruptly and he shouts, "Shit! Fuck! Crap!" Then pulls a hanky from his pocket and blows his monstrous nose. He keeps eyeing the boy as if he's a mirage.

A frail old man with two canes comes out on the porch and watches Foggy with callous eyes. Behind him is a woman. She looks to be less than five feet tall. Her blue-black hair gathered in a knot on top of her head. Her face scribes a circle. She reminds Pete of Lucy in the *Peanuts* cartoon.

"Told him God would get him," says the frail old man. He shakes one of the canes at Foggy. "I said—told him God would get him!"

Foggy ignores the outburst and raises teary eyes to Pete. "Don't go away just because Honk is crazy, P.P.P. We've got to talk, we've got to work it out. Sit down, my love. Please stay. Let's chat."

"I gotta go," Pete tells him. "I'm not who you think."

"You need a job?" asks Foggy. He points to the sign. "Some gardening, some leaf raking, lawn mowing, a little caretaking is all, some cupboard doors need tightening, hinges need oil. You can paint the porch, maybe? The garbage disposer won't work. We need a little help around here. We're old."

"Can you cook?" asks Honk.

"I cook!" shrieks the midget woman.

"Swing that door, Honk. Show him how it squeaks."

Honk swings the door, but it doesn't squeak.

"Humidity," Pete says. "The rain."

"Smart as ever, P.P.P.," says Foggy. "Come here, my love. Let me look at you. Sit by me. We've got catching up to do."

"I don't know you, old man. We never met."

Foggy starts to speak, but doesn't. He looks puzzled. The tic in his eye keeps firing, forcing him to wink, wink, wink.

"I'm Peter Paul Pearson, I'm Pete ..."

Foggy nods. "Of course," he says. "In my head you are. But in my heart you're the image of what I'm missing. Are you fifteen?"

"Sixteen now."

"He would be older," says Foggy. "That was back in . . . that was years ago when ... He's gone. Why don't he come back? Me no understand."

"Was he your son?"

"The son of my soul, the son of my heart, the son of . . ." His voice trails off. His eyes stare at something distant. Then he says, "Of the way things used to be. Of course you're not him. Don't try to fool me. I'm not senile. Old as sin, but not senile. Where do the years go? How do they happen?"

"You know what?" interrupts Honk. One hand thrusts a cane out like a rapier. The voice repeats itself, "You know what? Do you know what I'm going to tell you? Do you know what I'm going to say? Beware the blackbird." He points to the birds cluttering the birch. "Carriers of diseased thoughts," he says. He stabs at George Foggy. "Him! Him! Get away from him! He be crazy fat old man!!"

"I got to go before those heavy clouds let loose," says Pete pointing to the sky. He hurries down the steps. He eyes the Ford pickup again.

"Heavy heart, heavy," says George Foggy. Then he shouts, "Wait!"

"Nice to meet you!" Pete yells.

"But you'll come back, won't you? I want to talk to you about something!"

"Jesus is the way!" says Honk. "Stay away from this old junky! He smokes Turk!"

"You're the one!" says George Foggy. "Hash man!"

"Both of them!" shouts the woman. "Is dope fiends!"

"I have neuritis neuralgia!" Honk says to Foggy. "I have rheumatoid arthritis and high blood pressure and gout. What's your excuse?"

"Heart condition, stomach and lung cancer, varicose veins, hyperten—"

"Hypochondria extraordinaire," interjects Honk. "You're healthy as a horse. Never sick a day in your life. I, on the other hand—"

The woman is making faces. Pete bets she has heard their one-upmanship a million times. He can see now that she is very old, maybe seventy-five, maybe older. "Shut up! Shut up!" she orders. "Look what you doing! Frightened him away, you windy braggers!"

And Pete thinks, *Jesus Christ, I hope I never get old like them! Live fast, love hard, die young!*

"P.P.P.! . . . P.P.P.!" bleats George Foggy.

The boy stops a few feet from the birch. The blackbirds waiting like assassins. The boy looks at Foggy's winking eye, feverish cheeks, trembling lips, shivering beard, big belly shaking as he stands up and says, "Don't you want to know the thirteen ways of looking at a blackbird?"

"Sure."

"Do you want to know?

"Yeah, what are they?"

On a snowy field a black dart.
Black fig shimmering on a limb.
A sooty leaf whirling.

A beady-eyed baby in a black beret.
The curse of a man who has hammered his thumb.
Caliginous jealousy in a woman's heart.
In the wind of a whistle searching for a mate.
Where two black rhythms fold into one.
A midnight circle of lovers sowing seeds.
Black plum falling on a brittle lawn.
In the sinful heart of the heart of humankind.
Fish leaping in front of the moon at night.
The black breath of a liar.

"So, is that copasetic or what, my love?"

"Cool," says Pete. "But . . . but what does it mean?"

"If you come back, I'll tell you," says Foggy. He fingers the top of his head. Carefully, tenderly adjusting his hair. Instantly his forehead is higher, broader.

Pete steps off. Waves at him. "See you!"

"When?"

Behind his back he hears Foggy saying, "Was he a chimera? Do I wake or sleep?"

Pete jogs back to the 218. Cars swishing by splatter him. He looks northwest and sees infinite clouds. The rain is falling harder now. To his right is a baseball field, a parking lot, industrial buildings. Hunching into his jacket he walks the edge of the road and thinks about the old man and thirteen ways of looking at a blackbird. He tries to memorize them.

In the sinful heart of the heart of humankind.
Fish leaping in front of the moon at night.
The black breath of a liar.

A fish could look like a blackbird, yes. The black breath of a liar. Adding *nevermore* would be poetic. Vanishing in the night like ink into ink, that's what blackbirds do. "Black scarf blowing over fields of snow," he says, testing out a way of looking at a blackbird. He doesn't admire it especially, but maybe it works.

Closing his eyes he sees white fields, a dot of blackbird swooping. Raisin floating in a bowl of milk. Blackberry hanging from a vine.

"Shit, this is easy! I'm onto something," he says. Looking over his shoulder toward downtown Owatonna, he can still see the end of Austin Road spilling water into the vacant lot. A block west is the CHAMBER OF COMMERCE VISITORS CENTER, and not far away a white church, its bell tower taller than the trees hemming it in.

Bird thing: It's got to be black or feathery or winged or bird connected somehow. Black figs in—no, no, no! Foggy used figs. What about . . . what about black coffee in a red cup? Black truth pecking at white lies? Black finger feathers drawing graffiti on a whitewashed wall? Who are they, really? Black woman's breasts bared nipples.

The wind blows his cap off. He chases it and thinks—black cap winging east. Catching the cap he crams it back on his head. Black wing nesting on black hair.   The old man was sitting there bloated with knowledge: Buddha. Yes, and he wept like Jesus. Old fat fart pregnant with learning. Maybe a message from some other world. A dark angel? One who smokes pot? Or was that a joke? No, the aroma in the air was unmistakable. That Meerschaum on the table. Yes, the old crocks are potheads. They need to soften reality. Who doesn't? Pete fingers his knife. He could soften their reality. What do they have in that house? Poor as they look, you never know. Money hidden in the closet in a shoe. Wrapped in plastic in the freezer. He knows all their stupid tricks.

Pete searches the sky. Rain licking his face as he mutters, "Is the old man Santa Claus? Naw. He wanted me to be his son that he lost. He wanted me to pretend. Yeah, I could do that easy."

The rain falling harder. The wind gusting. He pivots back, goes to the church, tries the door. The door is locked. He has always believed that churches never locked their doors. In case there were homeless boys like him needing shelter. In case a lost soul needed to pray in God's house. In case a broken heart needed some comfort. In case the suicide wanted God to talk him out of it. Pete shows his finger to the church and jogs on.

The chair where the old man sat is empty. The *Latin at Your Fingertips* is gone. The pipe gone too. The porch lonely. Scattered leaves on the steps look arthritic. Pete hesitates. He chaffs his palms. He's awfully wet. He's getting cold.

"Who is this come to us?" says Foggy as he opens the door. He yells over his shoulder, "It's P.P.P.! Come in, come in! So good to see you, my love. Have you come back for the job?" Foggy's face twitches, his shoulders jerk. Curly beard shaking like its saying *boogie woogie*.

"I could help out," says Pete.

Foggy puts a massive arm around him. "Room and board. Ten dollars a day. We're no trouble, no trouble at all."

Pete enters a stifling house smelling of canned pumpkin. The temperature must be over eighty degrees. A pounding noise comes from somewhere down the hall. It sounds like someone is driving a spike into a railroad tie. *Clunk!* Foggy's forehead is lower now, hair cocked to the side. He ushers the boy into the living room.

Books and papers are piled everywhere, on shelving, on the mantel, on end tables, on a roll-top desk. On a coffee table is a black vase filled with dead flowers, petals long ago morphing into moribund beetles. The flower heads are using scattered books for pillows. The chairs and a sagging couch give just enough room for Foggy's belly to squeeze by. Books are on the floor as well, strewn under tables, propped against the sides of furniture. Some books climb corners. Titles: *Samuel Johnson's Dictionary of the English Language, The Life of Savage, Rasselas, Miscellaneous Observations on the Tragedy of Macbeth, The Vanity of Human Wishes.* The room smells of marijuana, burning birch, dusty human skin. Like an idling engine, flames hum in the fireplace. On television is *American Bandstand.* The music playing is "Tequila." On a chair in front of the TV sits the pie-faced Lucy from the Peanuts cartoon. She is so small that her boots levitate three inches above the rug. The overstuffed chair is swallowing her.

"Fix the disposer," she orders, lifting her eyes to Pete. She wears cherry lipstick and heavy mascara. She has a wattle beneath her chin a rooster might envy. Her neck is thin and long.

"It's P.P.P.," says Foggy. "He's come for the job."

"Get to work!" The old lady snaps to attention, narrows her eyes. "Sweet boy. Come to Gerty, give kisses, smoochy, smoochy."

Her arms go out and he obliges, bending down, trying to peck her

72

cheek, but she pulls his mouth around to hers and locks their lips.

"Gerty," says Foggy. "Let him go. You'll scare him off again!"

She struggles with him. He breaks away. She lifts a bit of hem and wiggles an elephant stump.

Pete retreats frantically toward Foggy.

"Come on," Foggy says, "Honk's in the kitchen."

As they go down the hall, Foggy adjusts his hair, fluffs his beard. The smell of pumpkin gets stronger. They enter the kitchen and Pete sees Honk in a wheelchair with a wrench in his hand. He is beating the garbage disposal under the sink and flicking a switch on and off. With each clank of the wrench, each flick of the switch, he says, "Demon disposer."

"P.P.P.'s come back to do business!" says Foggy. "I hired him to run the joint!"

"Hunh!" Honk jerks a wheel of the chair and looks at Pete. "Don't sell him the Turkey shit! Give him the Minnesota domestic."

"What's wrong with your disposer?" Pete asks.

"It's possessed!" says Honk. He waves the wrench as if threatening Pete.

Pete looks into the mouth of the disposer. Puts a hand in it and tries to spin the wheel. It's frozen. "How long has it been like this?"

"Since numb nuts put egg shells, coffee grounds, and potato peel down it," says Honk, his eyes scowling at Foggy. "The man's a menace!"

"*Moi?*" says Foggy. "*Curas hominum. Quantum est in rebus inane.*"

"Yeah, you!" says Honk.

"What did he say?" asks Pete.

"You don't know French?" says Honk. "Don't they teach you anything in school these days?"

"Actually, no," the boy replies.

Foggy puts a hand over his heart. The other hand is vertical. "Human cares. How much futility in the world." Foggy winks, pets his bulbous nose and looks proud. "I won't go doddery into that good night."

Pumpkin meat in a bowl. Crisco, sugar, eggs, flour, cinnamon and nutmeg, a pie crust waiting on the table. Pete sees a broom by the back door. Fetching the broom, he tells Foggy that he came to say there are twenty-five ways of looking at a blackbird.

"Twenty-five!" shrieks the old man. "But that will never do, my love. Oh, no, no, no, no, no, no, no. Twenty-five is not divisible by three. You must come up with twenty-seven ways!"

"I wanted to tell you the ones I made up." And he does.

Foggy covers his ears. "Don't end on twenty-five," he whines.

Pete shoves the broom handle down the throat of the disposal, catching the end of the handle on a blade and pulling backward. The broom bends. He eases up, repositions the handle and tries again. The wheel breaks loose. He flicks the switch and the motor whirrs. He runs water.

"What a smart boy." Honk peeks over the edge of the sink, watching the water swirling. "What a smart boy," he repeats.

"Twenty-five ways," says Foggy. "God help us! Come on. Out with another, come on, hurry up, no time to lose. Bad luck is sticky. Here's five dollars." Digging in his pocket Foggy pulls out a dollar bill and thrusts it at Pete. "Your first day's pay."

Pete takes the bill, starts to say it's a one not a five and he was promised ten. But he shrugs and says instead, "I can't make them up just like that," snapping his fingers. "They come to me out of nowhere. Out of something my mind wraps around, you know?"

"I like this boy," says Honk. He rolls to the table and starts mixing ingredients in the bowl.

From the living room comes the theme song for *American Bandstand*—"Bandstand Boogie."

Pete recalls the dead flowers on the coffee table.

"Dead flowers drooping from a black vase: twenty-six ways."

"It'll do, it'll do. Do one more and divide by three and we're safe."

"You come up with one."

"*Moi?*"

"A genius should be able to pop one out like nothing."

"Too true, too true. It is the burden I carry, thrust on me by superior bloodlines. Knowing everything is very hard, my love. But I've already done thirteen." His head and shoulders keep twitching.

"So have I. Come on, go for it. Twenty-seven divided by three is nine."

Foggy grumbles, burps, winks, sniffs and bursts forth, "Lord is my shepherd, ack! foo! Don't believe it!"

"That's a way of looking at a blackbird?"

"If your brain's on straight and can encompass the cosmos the way mine can. I am large. I contain multitudes. All right, never mind. Stand by. Genius cogitating." He plops in a chair. The chair groans. He folds his arms over his belly. His eyes roll up. His cheeks glisten. Forehead reddening dangerously.

"Geez, don't kill yourself," Pete tells him.

Foggy shakes his head as if shaking off a mood. He pulls the makings from his pocket and stuffs the pipe. Lights it. Drags deep.

Holds.

Blows.

Honk takes a hit and hands the pipe to Pete. He tokes and passes it back to Foggy. Shreds of sweet pot sprinkling over mashed pumpkin, cinnamon, vanilla odors blending as Honk pours the mixture into a pie pan. And into the oven. He holds out a gooey finger and offers Pete a lick.

"No, thanks."

Honk pops the finger into his own mouth and cleans it. "Lick the bowl?" he asks.

"Not really."

"Lick her myself then. You kids today don't know what's good."

Something tells Pete this ain't gonna work. He wishes the rain would stop. Old people are way too *whoa*.

"Veni, vidi, vici sitting on a fence. Along flew bird beaks and bit em on the cocktail, ginger ale, five cents a glass, if you don't like the flavor, cram it up your—ask me no questions, I'll tell you no lies, if you ever get hit with a bucket of shit, remember to close your eyes: twenty-seven ways of looking at a blackbird."

Smiling brightly Foggy fills his lungs, holds while smoke curly cues over the pipe. Honk waving the smoke toward his mouth inhaling.

Pete ruminates the twenty-seventh way and says, "I don't know about that."

"Veni, vidi, vici sitting on a fence? What more could you possibly ask, my love?"

75

"Hmm," hums Pete.

"Muddled, that's what it is," says Honk. "Muddled, muddled."

"*Et tu Brute?*"

"It's got to feel black and bird-like in some sort of way, don't it?" Pete says.

"But . . . but it does!" says Foggy. "*Along flew bird beaks and bit em on the* … Who started this anyway? Who knows what he's talking about? Me and Wallace Stevens. *Casual flocks of blackbirds make ambiguous undulations as they sink downward to darkness on extended wings.*"

"Okay," Pete says, not willing to argue since he has no idea what the man just said or who Wallace Stevens is. "But really it should be more like Gerty in her black dress and black hair and black boots. Redwing mouth. She could be a blackbird, Gerty could."

"Too much lipstick, too much rouge. It's not real hair either." Putting his hand sideways shielding his lips from those with big ears he says, "Bald as a cue ball. Poor thing. Cancer of the bungus. Chemo, you know."

"Lipstick and rouge could be the shoulder whatchacallems," says Pete.

"Epaulettes," says Foggy.

"That's it."

While Foggy and Honk pass the pipe back and forth, Pete paces the floor with the broom. The broom and the gray light hitting the window give him: "Witch on broomstick bursting through boiling clouds."

"It was right on the tip of his tongue," says Honk.

"Look what you've done!" freaks Foggy. "Now we've got to go for thirty! Divide by three and we're home free. Go for it!"

"Why we got to go for thirty?" Pete says. "Your first thirteen don't divide by three."

"What? What?"

"You said it must divide by three."

"Three, yes, the Trinity of genius. Three is in thirteen! As long as three is in there it's okay, my love. Thirty-three is, however, the perfect number. Divides by three into a prime number that can only be divided equally by itself. Get it? Come up with thirty-three blackbirds and your life will be pumpkin pie forever. Maybe you'll never die. I mean it. It's magic."

"Give him the signs," says Honk.

"These are the signs," says Foggy. He rubs his nose, winks, sniffs, shouts, "If you're dying it won't do any good to whine! Tuck the fuck up!" He pets his nose lovingly, burps, jerks. Stabs a finger at the boy. (Pete has heard of this behavior, a medical condition, but he can't think of the name of it.) "Listen," continues Foggy, "I'll only repeat this several times: birdphilia, biblophilia, triphilia—the Trinity signs of genius." He rocks a little in his chair. Hands folded on his placid belly.

"But what does it mean?" asks Pete.

Foggy ticks each meaning off on his fingers. "One, do you love birds?"

"I spose."

"Two, do you love books?"

"I've read a couple."

"Three, do you love the number three?"

"It's okay."

"I rest my case."

"Does that mean I'm a genius?"

"The signs are there, the rest is up to you. Let me speak Newton. This is how it works—Ork!"

Honk switches the mixer on.

"Noise!" Foggy shouts. He rumbles out of the kitchen.

A syndrome, remembers Pete. *Some kind of syndrome.* He is feeling spacey. Maybe they're setting him up to eat him. Pete baked in a pie. Four and twenty blackbirds. *Their shit making me paranoid. That's what's happening. You gotta gets the fuck outta here, man!*

Pete weaves slowly slovenly toward the front door. Foggy grabs him by the sleeve. "We have no wills of our own," he says, licking his lips as if he wants to smooch. "We are like mercury in a barometer rising and falling according to the pressure surrounding us. As sure as there are canals on Mars, my love, does the naked eye lie? Crap! Snork! Fink!" His eyes roll.

Pete looks round the corner into the living room. Gerty sitting with arms on the armrests. Face frozen. Hypnotized by the dancers.

77

"Now listen," says Foggy. "Females are busily choking their maternal instincts as fast as they can." His forefinger seals his lips. "Shh." Wink, wink goes the eye. "Marriage and motherhood are companions keeping company, but there's nothing necessary about them, don't you see? Children are brother and sister to their mothers. We are devolving toward ultimate entropy. Do you know what will save us?"

Pete shakes his head.

Foggy's dilated eyes hovering like glossy soap bubbles.

Pete offers up—"Outer space?"

"The ant dome," Foggy says. "All for one and one for all, the perfect society built on the number thirty-three. Mark me, mark this! Wait! Unk, crap, shit! All striving must become a ritual for the good of our country. Individualism must vanish. Fall in line. Quote cliches. Note how happy conformists are! Float the flag. Quack the duck. Be a triple good duckspeaker. Fly the ways of the blackbird. Eeek a freak."

Pete blinks and goes blind for a second.

Foggy's voice rushes on the path to "Do you believe it?"

"Sure, if you say so." Pete eyeing the door, hearing the rain tapping the porch. But fuck the rain! The knife in his pocket pulls at him like chaos. If he stabbed the old man, the blade would find six inches of fat first.

"Grounded, I say, in reason and belief in a rational life. I may make a mistake, but no—no brag just fact—it is exceedingly rare. Doubtless I'm a seer, a living interpreter of the cosmos. I can't help it! I am what I am. E equals MC squared is tinkertoys for me. Formulas impregnate my pores. I can unify the field theory. Make plain the abstruse connections between weak and strong forces and their influence on gravity and electricity. They had no beginning and will never end. *Ergo*! Shit! Unk! Tuck! We float and reconnect with ourselves eternally. We've had this conversation a million times before. It's a simple formula manifested in spherephilia. Do you understand now?"

"Fuck no."

"Roundness, my love, roundness. Everything comes back around. We are doomed to repeat ourselves. What goes round, comes round. Roundness everywhere. Circles within circles within circles. Read your Emerson."

Honk wheels from the kitchen. He stares at them, his eyes a pair of opaque tunnels.

"Go away, I'm talking," says Foggy.

"Giving you spherephilia?" says Honk.

Foggy's shoulder jumps. Followed by head jerks, hair slippage.

"Roundness!" says Pete.

"My balls," says Honk, "are round."

Foggy squeezes his head between his palms. "Ook, ook, my mind is like an impassioned eel! You hold it down in one place, it coils round you in another. Listen to me, you need fat, not sugar, to protect you from frostbite. Ask the Eskimo. Don't go out there, my love!"

"He's always this way when he smokes Turk," says Honk. "Pay him no mind, no matter."

"Is it an attack?" says Pete. "I've heard of a syndrome—"

"Passionate eel?" says Foggy.

"That too," says Pete.

"Ook! Like your brain wants to come out your ears and say hello?"

"Ooo-*kay.*"

Foggy coughs wetly. Starts to say something more, but bends over and has a coughing fit that threatens to blow a hole in the floor. When he has his breath back he says, "Cancer. The Big C. Crap! Dork! Days are numbered. If you're dying it won't do any good to whine. Dive! Dive! Tuck the fuck up!"

Honk is grinning. He has taken his teeth out and put them in his pocket. His mouth looks like the wrinkled version of a baby reaching for a nipple.

Gerty shouts, "I'm hungry. Make that pie!"

"It's baking!" says Honk. "Can't you smell it?"

Foggy says, "I've got enlargement of the heart and arrhythmia and what else? Flat feet. Toenail fungus. Every organ in my body is failing. Only my philias have kept me going. Threes have kept my brain in balance with the Trinity. I'm like a juggler with three balls in the air. My physical life has been radically wretched. The only thing worth living for is my unmatched mind—my sacred lotus." He caresses his head lovingly. His hair slips. He adjusts it.

"How about hypochondria-philia?" says Honk.

"Pay no mind to such a one! He's a cartoon," says Foggy. "Just remember this. There are thirty-three ways of looking at a blackbird and all you have to do is find them and report back to me and all your troubles will be over. Nirvana in the palm of your hand. A child shall lead them. Go!"

Pete opens the door. He feels like his face is wrinkling. His spine curving. There are pains in his knees and hips. He can't breathe deep enough. Old people have heatphilia. How does anyone stand them? It's like a house full of babbling toddlers!

"You leave a radiant trail!" Foggy calls out. "Don't stay away too long, I've lots to teach you, my love! Where, by the way, are you going? Don't you want the job? Room and board. Five bucks a week."

"Five? You said . . . neh, never mind, I gotta get. Way too hot in there."

"We'll write a paper. Sell it to *Scientific American Psychology Today.* 'Heat and the Elderly'." Foggy is flexing his fingers, limbering up.

"Pete tells him, "I'm heading—"

"Where?"

"I don't fucking know."

"Is that near Kansas City? Going to Kansas City, Kansas City here I come ... crazy little women there and I wish you'd stay, my love!"

"Get a grip, old man! Take your meds!"

"He'll calm down tomorrow!" says Honk. "He'll wake up sober, a seer! You'll learn lots if you stay. He'll nourish your mind and I'll save your soul."

"Oh fuck yeah, that's what I want."

He searches the sky, but the ways have vanished gray on gray. Where did the assassins go? Lurking. Hope hurls him toward the Ford pickup. Behind him he can hear George Foggy wailing.

Getting old is insane. Whoever invented it should have his fucking throat cut. No way will Pete let it happen.

The hood looks like a beak. *Black beak reflecting bright bullets of rain.*

Divided by three makes one down, more to go.

Going Gay

The widow who owned the egg ranch was named Ellen Story. She was fifty. She was short, petite, almost elfin. Hard work had kept her shapely, filling her tight jeans as well as any woman her age could. Her face was heavily lined, probably from working outdoors most of her life. Behind the mist of wrinkles, Eddie Turner could see the beauty she had been in her youth. Whenever she got dolled up to go dancing, she looked years younger. Her earthy brown hair combed out long and falling. Bright lipstick, rouge, eye shadow, a silky green dress, pearls. Eddie loved the illusion. First time he saw her looking like that he did a double take. She caught him checking her out and said, "So what you think, kid?"

"Cool," he said. Pausing before adding, "Pretty."

She smiled at him, her teeth so white so perfect he wondered if they were real. His mother had teeth like that. One night, years ago, when he was a little boy, he had seen her coming out of the bathroom, a glass of pale blue water and grinning teeth in hand. The sight of her collapsed mouth had shocked him. She was only thirty at the time, but she had looked way older to Eddie. He learned later that a terrible gum disease had made her teeth fall out when she was only twenty. The knowledge had made him fanatical about his own teeth. He flossed and brushed them after every meal. He used two different formulas of mouthwash, the minty one in the morning, the harsh one at night. He always had a toothpick in his mouth. He had never had a cavity in his life.

One afternoon, just as Eddie put the last rack of eggs in the incubator and was about to knock off for the day, Ellen came in and said, "Kid, how'd you like to go to Edina with me tonight?"

"Edina?"

"Arthur Murray's. I'm a member. I'll give you some lessons. No pressure, no obligation to join, but if you do I get my next four visits free. Whaddya say? Wanna go?" She shuffled her feet and twirled.

He told her he'd like that, but all he had to wear were his work clothes and old boots. "I wouldn't look too good next to you, Mrs. Story," he said.

"My ole man was tall and lanky like you," she said. "Let me see what I can do."

A few minutes later, she showed up at Eddie's trailer with some of her dead husband's clothes—a Hawaiian sport shirt that Eddie didn't much care for, black slacks, loafers. Everything fit well enough.

There were lots of couples at the studio that night. Some of them looked professional on the floor making moves Eddie admired and envied. Watching them made him feel shy. He stood back while Ellen was doing her stuff with a thin, little guy who was so graceful he seemed to glide like an ice skater leading Ellen through several amazingly intricate turns.

After the music ended, she walked over to Eddie and told him to stop being a wallflower. She forced him out on the floor and taught him to waltz and do the tango (sort of). He was at least two heads taller than Ellen and at one point while they were waltzing she leaned back and said, "How's the weather up there, Shorty?" Eddie had heard it before, but he laughed anyway. Picking her up, he gave her a squeeze and was startled when she nibbled his ear. He enjoyed himself and after the night was over, he signed a contract for six months worth of lessons.

A week later, after his first lesson, Eddie and Ellen turned their moves on the dance floor into moves in the bedroom. They went to the trailer and drank beer. She sat on his lap and kissed him. Ellen hadn't fucked in years and had gotten tight and dry and had to use Vaseline. The jar of Vaseline reminded him of eighteen-year-old Charlie Sugarland wanting Eddie to masturbate him. Eddie was twelve at the time, so tall for his age he was given the nickname Too Tall Turner. Charlie paid for the handjob with his '48 Mercury convertible, letting Eddie drive it around Mankato showing off for the girls.

Unlike Charlie Sugarland, Ellen needed a lot of kissing and foreplay to get her ready. It was also a lot of work to give her an orgasm, which only happened if he used his fingers on her while doing her spoon style. She taught Eddie exactly where to rub her. But, like Charlie, she never touched Eddie himself. Which he kind of minded. Did she think touching him there was too nasty? Eddie had stopped doing Charlie when he said, "Only queers give handjobs. So next I guess you want this bad boy in your mouth, hey Too Tall?"

One night after making love, Eddie went to the bathroom. When he came back, Ellen, her head propped on pillows, was bathed in moonlight shining through the window. Gazing at her, Eddie had a vision of how she must have looked when she was younger. The violet air had washed away the facial lines and given her the appearance of a reclining pin-up out of *Penthouse* or *Playboy*. The elfin curves of her body could have been the curves of a nubile teenager. When Eddie told her what she looked like, she burst into tears and said: "Don't turn no lights on. Come back to bed, honey." When he snuggled up to her, she cried in the hollow of his neck and told him no one had ever said anything so sweet in her entire life, not even her husband. She said she was thankful and she hoped it was how Eddie would remember her when things were over. He told her things didn't ever have to be over. But she said, "It'll happen, Eddie. You're just a baby. You've got a lot of living to do. But let's make this last at least to my next birthday. Promise?"

Ellen hired an immigrant German couple to work for her. She installed them in the old two-bedroom house near the corner of her ranch where the roads crossed. She had lived there with her husband long ago before they built the house she and her mother lived in now. It was only a year after moving into the new place that the husband stroked out and died. She told Eddie that not long before the stroke her husband had gotten into porno. He wanted to experiment. "He wanted to do filthy things," she said, "but I refused to go that far. You step over a certain line and you're not you anymore, you're a pervert." On their first night together, Ellen had told Eddie she didn't give head and she didn't want head and if he wanted that sort of stuff they couldn't be lovers. He told her it didn't matter at all. He wasn't into that stuff either.

Ellen's mother was seventy-something. Tiny. Gnomish. Her face imploding with far more and deeper wrinkles than Ellen had. She would sit on the covered porch in her chair knitting and not saying a word. Whenever Eddie saw her there, he would wave and say hi. But she always ignored him. Maybe she had had enough of men by then.

The German couple Ellen hired had a ten-year-old girl who looked a lot like her blue-eyed, blond father, a guy who rarely spoke and never smiled, at least not when Eddie was there. The daughter, Karin, loved for Eddie to swing her round and round and hoist her overhead and down through his legs and back up again. Eddie liked playing with her, liked hearing her squealing and laughing. Eddie would carry the little girl around on his back pretending to be a galloping horse. Karin told Eddie: "Papa never plays with me like you do. Papa's always sad. You're never sad. You make me laugh, Eddie." Every afternoon, after jumping off the school bus and changing her clothes, the girl would come looking for Eddie, wanting to do whatever he was doing.

Karin helped him gather eggs and fill the feed troughs, even though she feared the black widow spiders that hung from the wooden rafters of the long rows of chicken pens. The spiders never bothered Eddie or Karin, but there was always the chance that a crazed spider would drop down and bite one of them on the neck. People died from black widow bites. Karin wanted to know how something so small could be so mean, so poisonous. Eddie figured it was Satan's doing. "All bad things on this earth were invented by Satan," he said.

Whenever Eddie would wheelbarrow a pile of dead chickens to the capped well at the edge of the property line, Karin always wanted to go too. Eddie would lift the iron lid and the blast furnace odor of death would assail them. They would hold their breaths and throw the bodies down the well. There must have been thousands of chicken carcasses down there, but they couldn't see them, only smell them. Karin would look into the black pit with eyes both terrified and fascinated. She told Eddie the well scared her more than the black widows. Eddie admitted it scared him too.

And he said, "If either of us accidentally slipped and fell in, it would be over in seconds smothered by rotting chicken feathers and guts and gunk, a horrible way to go, no doubt about it." When Eddie closed the clanging lid he would shout, "Run, Karin, run!" and they would run as if Death had scaled the stench and was after them.

The girl's mother, Elizabeth, lost the keys to their car on a day she was going shopping for groceries. The car was a 40s vintage, decrepit old Ford that looked as if it had come straight from a junkyard. Eddie hotwired it for her. He screwed the wires out of the ignition and clamped them together with a vise grip and hit the starter button. Elizabeth called him amazing. She said her husband would never have figured out how to get the car started. But she was still afraid it might stall and she would be stranded, so she asked Eddie to drive her to the store in Elk River.

On the way, he asked her what life was like in Germany during the war. Did any of her relatives die? She told him she had lost her parents and grandparents. Her brother died in the Navy. She was barely eleven when the war ended. There was nothing to eat. She and her older sister had to depend a lot on the kindness of American soldiers. The soldiers taught them English. Some would give them food for free. Others wanted to touch them. Given their situation, having sex with soldiers didn't seem bad to her or her sister. The girls lived in an abandoned house. There were dozens to choose from. They took what they wanted from other houses or apartments and furnished their place so that it was almost as nice as where they had lived with their parents before planes bombed them. She had been in school that day. The teachers and children had hidden in the basement. A bomb hit the school and many of the children and teachers were killed. She and her sister were trapped in the rubble for lots and lots of hours. Elizabeth was sure she was going to die. She would always remember the children crying out for mommies and daddies. The moaning of the dying. The pitiful voices asking for water.

"Vor," she said. "Neywer go to vor, Edee. No gud. "

The soldiers would give her cigarettes, which she would sell to other Germans. Occasionally she had enough food rations to help feed starving neighbors. It was mainly bartering. A can of lima beans and ham might be worth a coat or a pair of gloves or boots.

They lived that way until Elizabeth met Kurt and moved with him to Munich. Her sister married a soldier and went to America, to Anoka, Minnesota. Kurt was a cabinetmaker. They lived hand to mouth for many years before her sister and brother-in-law offered to sponsor them. Ellen had befriended the sister and wrote a letter to immigration promising that Kurt and Elizabeth would have jobs and a place to stay on the egg ranch.

"So vee here," she said. "Vy vee not dead don't know. Strange, eh? You life strange, Edee?"

"For sure not strange like yours."

He told Elizabeth how he had worked all over Minnesota as a

dishwasher, a carpenter's helper, a hod carrier, a ditch digger, a dump truck driver, a backhoe operator. He was good with his hands. Big for his age, he had no trouble going into bars and drinking with his older buddies. He talked about answering Ellen's ad in the paper and hitching a ride out the same day. She hired him when she saw how well he could run all the equipment, the tractor, the frontend loader, the bobtail. "Don't tell her but I'm only seventeen. She thinks I'm twenty-one."

"I neywer tell," said Elizabeth. "I thirty-nine. Karin ten. Kurt forty-seywen. Vee loosing our first babby. She vould been you age, Edee. Vhooping cough, poor babby." Elizabeth looked away. Eddie saw a tear trickle down her cheek. She lifted her baggy skirt and blew her nose on it. "Ya. Neywer goes avay," she said tapping her temple.

After getting groceries and stopping at the salvage yard to buy an ignition for the car and installing it for her, Eddie asked Elizabeth to teach him some German cuss words. She said it was naughty and why would he want to know bad words? He told her he liked cuss words in all languages. She laughed at him. She said he was cute and funny. She said Kurt was never cute and funny. She said he might smile now and then, but you would rarely hear him laugh. She said she loved laughing. And she said: "I teach it you nice vurds. I teach it you: *Ich liebe dich.*" She translated it as I love you. She said he should say it to the girl he loves. Eddie said he wasn't in love with anyone. She batted her eyes and asked him if he was sure. He kept goading her for cuss words and finally she gave him some: *Sacramento* and *scheisse* and *Gott verdammen.* She said she couldn't really translate the first word. There was no English equivalent, but it was a very bad word and Eddie shouldn't use it around Karin. To Eddie, *Sacramento* sounded like cussing the sacraments of the Church, so that's how he thought of it; the second bad word simply said shit; the third was God damn.

"How do you say stupid chicken?" he asked.

"*Dummes huhn.*"

"Shithead."

"*Scheissekopf.*"

"Asshole."

"*Arschloch.* No more, Edee. Naughty, naughty."

He repeated the cuss words over and over, "*Sacramento, Gott verdammen, dummes huhn, scheissekopf, arschloch,"* and had her shrieking with laughter at his accent.

"You fonny Edee. I neywer so ohh, ohh."

The next thing Eddie knew she had put her hand on his thigh. He thought about pulling over, kissing her, maybe doing more if she wanted. Elizabeth had so-so looks, nothing to jerkoff over—thin, heartshaped face with a broad forehead, pointy chin, slim jaw. She had popping round brown eyes and dishwater blond hair. She was also slightly bucktoothed. But she had sexy rosebud lips and respectable breasts and capacious hips. Eddie waited for her to move her hand higher, hoping she would grip him. But the hand stayed still. He could feel the warmth of her palm soaking through his pant leg. Maybe she was waiting for him to move her hand onto his partner. Maybe that's how the soldiers who groped her in Germany had done it. Or maybe her hand on his leg was just a friendly gesture. The rest of the way home, both of them remained silent. She moved her hand from his leg as he pulled into the driveway.

While Elizabeth put the groceries away, Eddie went to the egg room where he buffed and graded eggs and packed them. He was in the cooler stacking cartons of eggs when she came in and closed the door. Took Eddie in her arms and kissed him while she rubbed her crotch up and down his crotch. Any second someone, maybe her husband, could have opened the door for whatever reason and they would be caught. But the kissing and the rubbing had put them both beyond the border of caution. She backed Eddie against a wall and dry fucked him. Until he turned her to the wall and hoisted her skirt. She had already taken off her underwear. She was sloppy-ready and wiggling so much it was hard to stay in her. She had her orgasm in what couldn't have been more than twenty seconds. Almost immediately she fled back to her house.

Fucking her became a daily thing whenever Karin was at school and Kurt and Ellen were off working with the chickens. Usually they fucked in Eddie's trailer. Sometimes in the kitchen against a wall or bent over the counter or the table.

A few weeks after starting his affair with Ellen, and then with Elizabeth, Eddie found a car for sale nearby, a '49 Ford convertible not in bad shape for its age. He asked Ellen to front him the money ($200) and she did. Taking her money made Eddie feel like a gigolo. He promised to pay her $25 a month. He made the first two payments. But then he started driving to Anoka nearly every night and drinking up most of his money with his cronies at Bee Jays. When he missed a payment, Ellen didn't say anything. Eddie continued to see both women, but Elizabeth was the one he really went for. She was so passionate! And she didn't take any greasing or foreplay. It was always quick with her, a minute or two and Eddie would be on his way.

This can't last, Eddie kept telling himself.

When he missed another payment, Ellen quit taking him to dances and stopped slipping into his bed at night. He quit making payments on his lessons at Arthur Murray's. They sent him letters, but he threw them away. He still had Elizabeth who couldn't get enough of him. Sneaking around and screwing whenever they could was more exciting than anything he had ever done before. He had it in his mind that maybe she would leave her husband and daughter and run off with him. He wondered if she was crazy enough to do that. Just the two of them like man and wife. Maybe Karin could come later and they would become a regular family. He would go back into construction. He had already talked to some of the boys at Bee Jays and knew there was plenty of work in Minneapolis. High-rise stuff. He would have to join the Ironworkers Union. He daydreamed and planned and told himself *why not?* She's crazy about me. Sexy thing. Nympho.

Ellen came into his trailer early one morning and woke him and said he smelled like a brewery. "I'm too old to put up with this shit, Eddie," she said. "You got my money?" He shook his head and told her he was sorry. "You think I've paid you to fuck me?" she said. "I didn't buy that car for you. It was a loan. Your credit's no good here anymore, Eddie. Pack your duds and go."

"But ... but I'm broke, Ellen."

"Where's all your money going?"

"Well, I bought tires and changed the oil and I got new jeans and a couple shirts and skivvies and socks. New boots and work gloves. The car's not running so good. I gotta get a tune-up or something."

"And you're drinking with your pals. And you're buying rounds.

And you're burning gas. Maybe picking up prostitutes, who knows? Does that about cover it, Eddie?"

"No prostitutes," he said. "Honest, Ellen, no girls."

"What about Elizabeth? What about you and her? I can't have that shit here." She stared at him a long time, looking into his eyes as if she might find the truth there. Finally, she said, "Yeah, truth is, Eddie, Kurt works twice as hard as you and I don't want to lose him because you can't keep your pecker in your pants. Don't think I'm jealous, because I'm sure as hell *not* jealous. I'm too old to be jealous!" Her voice kept rising. Soon she was yelling two inches from his face. Her hand was up and abruptly she slapped him. It stung, but he didn't move.

"I'm sorry," he said. "She come after me. I didn't start it, honest."

Ellen slapped him again as she shrieked, "Who gives a flying fuck?" Next thing he knew she bit him on the cheek. Jesus it hurt! Made him holler, "What the fuck!" She whirled in a circle wiping her palm over her mouth. When she faced him again, her voice was shaky. "Listen, whore-boy, I'm just carrying you along because … well, because. But I can't afford it no more. Not emotionally." She reached into her shirt pocket and pulled out two twenties and tossed them on the bed. "That's about all a whore like you is worth. Now get!"

"That's no way to treat me," Eddie said. "You … you capitalist."

Ellen laughed coolly as she said, "You are so fucking fired, boy."

She went out slamming the door. Eddie rubbed the bite mark. It hurt but she hadn't broken the skin. He told himself, "You're lucky she didn't have a gun, Too Tall. What a spitfire."

He didn't know what to do. The last thing he wanted was to go back home to his mother in Mankato. She would welcome him, but the thought of her breathing down his neck all the time telling him to grow up, telling him to get an education, make something of himself, if he didn't want to end up a bum like his father, was more than Eddie could stand. No, he would rather be homeless. And then he thought:

Scheisse, what about Elizabeth?

What about her, Arschloch? Nothing I can do about her now. Karin neither. I like them a lot, but what the hell? I gotta look out for number one now.

He thought maybe he'd come back for them someday. But

knowing how way leads to way, Eddie Turner knew pretty much that this part of his life was over.

He packed what few clothes he had, leaving the dead husband's ugly Hawaiian shirt, the loafers and pants on the bed.

When he tried to start his car, it wouldn't start. He had to ask Kurt to give him a shove with the tractor. Kurt said nothing. He climbed onto the tractor and gave Eddie's car a push. He put the Chevy in second gear and let in the clutch. The engine fired and Eddie drove down the dirt road leading away from the Story egg ranch. He waved at Kurt, but Kurt didn't wave back. Eddie looked for Elizabeth as he cruised past the corner house. He honked his horn as he turned at the end of the driveway. No Elizabeth.

§

Eddie Too Tall Turner drove to Anoka and stopped at McDonald's for a burger, fries and a chocolate milk shake. He parked next to the Rum River. After eating he went down to the water with his toothbrush and paste and brushed his teeth savagely. He washed his face as well, being very careful not to agitate the bite wound Ellen had given him. It felt like someone had punched him. He sat on the bank holding a wet handkerchief to the bruise and watching the river go by just as it had done for years beyond counting. Everything comes and everything goes he told himself. "What's next, Too Tall? Get a job."

Later, he lay back in the shade of a tree and slept. When he woke, the sun was far west and fading.

Eddie got back in his car and drove to Bee Jays on Third Avenue. By ten o'clock he was drunk and slurring his words. He was in a booth talking to one of the regulars, Lewin, a soft-spoken, older, slightly pudgy, round-shouldered fellow, with short curly brown hair and a furry mustache that looked as if it was dyed. Lewin was buying pitchers of beer and filling Eddie's mug as soon as it was empty. Eddie had unloaded his sad tale, and Lewin couldn't have been more sympathetic.

"Called me a whore and bit me, Lewin."

"She's the whore, my boy. Fifty years old? She took advantage of you."

"Yeah, van-ish."

Lewin pointed to Eddie's cheek. "Wouldn't surprise me if that leaves a smudge you won't get rid of, my boy. We'll call it your dueling wound."

"Yeah dueling."

"Let me get something for it." Lewin went to the bar. He talked to the bartender, while pointing at Eddie. The bartender went into the back room and returned with a big round bandaid and a disinfectant wipe.

Lewin tended to Eddie's wound while saying, "What I'm saying is that bitch seduced you. You didn't seduce her. The same with that nymphomaniac Elizabeth. She jumped your bones. You didn't know what hit you, my boy."

"Yeah."

"That's pussy for you. Pussy never takes the blame. It's always someone else's fault. You got burned by both those bitches."

"Yeah. Burned. Yeah. Bitches. Yeah." Eddie leaned forward and said in Lewin's ear, "I'm so fucking fucked, man. I got no money, no job, no roof. I could go back to Mankato and live with my mom, but fuck I'd rather cut my throat."

Lewin patted Eddie's hand, squeezed it. "You can crash at my pad. I'll help you get on your feet."

"You'd do that? You put me up?"

"It'd be my honor."

Eddie's vision was fuzzy, but he could see well enough Lewin meant what he said. Kindly eyes, fatherly, compassionate smile. Very clean cut for his age, which Eddie guessed was mid-forties, maybe fifty.

"You not married, Lewin?"

"Never been married. Women. Can't trust them."

"Thas right. You put your finger on it, Lewin. Can't truss em."

When Eddie had to get up and go pee, Lewin went with him, the two of them standing at the urinals, Lewin talking, talking. Telling Eddie, "I was born in Miami. Moved up here thirty years ago and never looked back."

He worked in Minneapolis at a wholesale house that sold car radios and speakers. Early in life he had been a mechanic. His family—

mother, father, three sisters still lived in Florida. Lewin hadn't seen them in years.

"The more you're away from your people, the less you miss them. We were never close, my boy. My mother and sisters liked me all right. But my old man couldn't stand me. He said I shamed the family. Last time I went for a visit, I brought a friend. The old man wouldn't let us in. Can you believe that?"

"Why not, Lewin?"

"Because he's a bitch, Eddie, that's why. So what the hell, I cut my losses. That's what you gotta do. Cut your losses and make a new life. You hear what I'm saying? Let's go get your car and you follow me to my pad."

Eddie couldn't get his car started, so he left it in the lot and Lewin drove him to some part of town Eddie had never seen before. It was one a.m. when they got upstairs. Lewin mixed Eddie a vodka tonic and started unbuttoning his shirt.

"Wass doin, Lewin?"

"You need a shower, my boy. We both need one. I been sweating all night. The humidity. Muggy, muggy, muggy."

"Yeah."

"Drink up, drink up."

"Yeah." Eddie downed his drink in two swallows.

In the shower Lewin soaped himself and then soaped Eddie and told him he had a beautiful body, so tall and slim. Solid muscles.

"Yeah."

Eddie closed his eyes when Lewin kissed him. The boy wanted so much to fall on a bed and sleep, but Lewin kept rubbing their soapy bodies together. He reached down and pulled on Eddie's partner. Despite how tired he was, Eddie felt himself responding. Next thing he knew Lewin was on his knees giving him a blow job. Lewin's mustache looked like pubic hair.

The rest of the night was a blur. Everything hazy. Everything draped in shadows.

Vaguely, Eddie remembered mutual masturbation and oral sex.

He didn't wake until noon. He had an odd, musty taste in his mouth. He went into the bathroom and brushed his teeth and gargled.

The bandaid had fallen off and the bite was swollen. It was sore. It was deep blue. He hoped it wasn't infected. He had heard that human bites were poisonous. There was a terrycloth robe hanging from a hook on the back of the door. Eddie put it on and went into the kitchen, where he found a note on the table:

My boy,

You were a wetdream come true last night. I pray you'll stick around awhile. I'll take you to dinner at GayLords tonight. I promise you'll like it. I'm going to talk to a foreman I know at McMillan Construction. I'm pretty sure I can get you on there. It might not be what you're looking for, but it will be a start and give you an income. Believe me when I say you're welcome to stay here as long as you like. We'll get your car as soon as I get home. Look for me half past 5:00.
With great gratitude,
Your Own Lewin
PS – I think I'm in LOVE.

Eddie got dressed and had a bowl of Grape Nuts cereal and a slice of toast thick with butter and honey. He explored Lewin's apartment and found one room filled with bookshelves floor to ceiling. In his entire life, Eddie had never seen so many books owned by one person. There was a comfy-looking overstuffed chair. There was an ottoman. There was a lamp on a little table next to the chair. Eddie sat down, put his feet up and stared at the hundreds of books. Had Lewin read all of them? Eddie hadn't even finished high school. The only book he ever read when he was a kid was *Charlotte's Web*. And now he couldn't even remember what it was about. Charlotte was a spider, wasn't she? Was she poisonous? What happened to her? Didn't she die?

Eddie closed his eyes and napped. He dreamed of spiders dropping from the rafters one by one. He was swinging Karin. She kissed him hard on the mouth.

That evening Eddie and Lewin went back to Bee Jay's and pushed the dead Chevy. It just wouldn't start. Lewin diagnosed carburetor problems. He said he would get a kit and teach Eddie how to rebuild the carburetor.

Lewin drove him to GayLords in Minneapolis on Hennepin. The place was packed. Music so loud people were shouting at each other. Eddie didn't know the song or the singer. Lewin told him the singer was The Divine Miss M. Lewin took him to a dining hall up a winding staircase, where it was somewhat quieter. The Headwaiter sat them at a table and gave them menus.

"Bette Midler," said Lewin. "It's from her first album."

"Oh," said Eddie. He had no idea who Lewin was talking about.

"She's all the rage," Lewin told him. "What do you want to order?"

Eddie ate breaded walleye with garlic mashed potatoes and salad with blue cheese dressing. He drank his first martini ever. Then drank two. Then three.

Men kept coming to the table and hugging Lewin and kissing him. He introduced Eddie to so many names he couldn't keep track. Most of the guys were fairly young, slim, good-looking. Eddie thought they seemed … sleek. When they shook his hand, their palms were soft. Some gripped him hard. But the majority of the handshakes were limp, gentle, almost tender. Lewin appeared to know everyone in the dining room. Downstairs laughter and music floated upward, now and then becoming a roar.

"They know how to have fun, ey!" said Eddie, smiling and happy because everyone else was smiling and happy.

"Booze," said Lewin. "Plenty of coke as well. You want some coke? I'll fix you up."

"No thanks. I'll stick with this. Putting sugary Coke on top of it would probably make me sick."

After dinner they danced. Lewin was full of compliments. Eddie told him about the lessons at Arthur Murray's, and Lewin said, "Money well spent. Look at you. Tall guys are usually awkward on the floor, but not you. You're smooth."

Eddie waved Lewin's words away. "Ain't much, not really," he said.

They sat at the table again and ordered more drinks. Another friend of Lewin's came over. He sat down. His smile was dazzling as he stared at Eddie and then said to Lewin, "I don't know how you do it, you old bitch, but he's absolutely gorgeous."

"This is Lance," said Lewin. "This is Eddie Turner."

"Lovely to meet you, Eddie Turner. Did Lewin give you that bruise? Does Lewin beat you? You into rough trade?" Lance laughed as he patted Eddie's knee under the table.

"What's rough trade?"

"Lord, you are a sweetheart!"

"He's sweet and he's taken, Lance. Don't paw him."

Lance had light reddish hair. It was so long it brushed his shoulders. His hair made him really stand out. All the other men Eddie saw around the dining room had short hair nicely trimmed, impeccably neat. Lance wore a red shirt silky, glittery. It clung to his torso as if tailor made. He was talking. He was saying to Lewin, "You're coming to my party for Chuck and Dale in June, right? And of course you're bringing this hunka-hunka too. Tell me you are."

"I are," said Lewin.

"Dale and Chuck are getting married at my place mid-June, Eddie. Everyone who is anyone will be there. Lots of booze, lots of banging. It'll be fun. You coming?"

"Sure, I guess."

"Bitchin!" Lance stood up. "I've got a friend waiting for me at the bar. Nice to meet you, Eddie."

"A pleasure, Lance."

When Lance disappeared, Eddie said to Lewin, "That guy's got some terrific teeth. You see how white they are?"

Lewin shook his head, leaned over and told Eddie, "Lance had all his teeth pulled, so he could give better blowjobs, my boy. Some fags do that. The crazy ones. Be careful of that guy."

"Had em pulled, really? That's fuckin nuts, man!"

Lewin talked with his friends until midnight. He drank but didn't seem to get drunk. Eddie, on the other hand, was staggering by the time they left for the car. Lewin put his arm around him—propping him, guiding him.

When they got home, Eddie fell into bed. Lewin came in later and woke Eddie by rubbing the boy's belly round and round. Then Eddie felt him go down. "You're packing an accordion. It just keeps inflating," Lewin said. The last thoughts Eddie had before passing out were: *Shit, Too Tall, you didn't brush your teeth.* And: *What means packing an accordion?*

Lewin bought the rebuild kit and showed Eddie how to break

down the carburetor and put it back together with the new parts. Lewin also showed him how to clean and re-gap the plugs and points and how to reset the timing. By the time they were done the flathead V8 was purring like it had just come off a car lot. Eddie was very impressed.

"So this is what you used to do, Lewin."

"It was my métier. My old man was a mechanic too. He said I was born for it. He wanted us to have our own shop: ACCELERATUS INCREDILUS is what he wanted to call it. But I ended up hating the grind. That and the busted knuckles and grease under my nails. It's a hard life. I wouldn't wish it on anybody. Shit, I wanted to go to college, not fix fucking cars. The old man never got over it when I said no. I was a bookworm. I loved school. He said only fairies loved books and school. When he said it, a light went on in his eyes. The look he gave me is one I'll remember as long as I live. He was ALL MAN, you see. So when he realized I wasn't, he wanted nothing more to do with me. That's the way it goes. Let's check this baby out. You drive, my boy. This baby gonna have *acceleratus incredilus*! Let's see what she can do."

They stayed home that night. After dinner they drank beer and Lewin as usual talked and talked. He would go into his library and bring out books he wanted Eddie to read. He said the only thing the boy was lacking was a real education, but he could do as Lewin had done and read himself to at least the equivalent of a college degree. Eddie would leaf through the many books, but he wasn't really interested. Looking at all the words filling up page after page made him dizzy. He asked himself: What's it all mean? What's the point?

Lewin said baffling things: "There are no parameters you can put your finger on that will tell you absolutely who you are. Not really. We're all in a state of continual flux. So much in life depends on how much mental and physical energy you've got. Beware of losing it. And dullness. Beware of dullness, my boy. You have to keep inventing yourself, unless you're a psychopath."

Eddie had no clue as to what the man was talking about. He nodded his head and went along and that seemed to be what Lewin wanted. It encouraged him.

"You know what Thoreau said about it."

"What?"

"The mass of men lead lives of quiet desperation."

"Gee, that's depressing, Lewin."

"But it's true, my boy. And you don't want that, do you."

"Nuh-uh."

"Thoreau also said that he didn't want to come to the end of his life and find out he hadn't really lived. I can't think of anything worse. Keep inventing yourself. Whatever thy hand finds to do, do it with all thy might."

"Okay."

"You know what you and I have here. What we have is called Greek love. Pederasty. You know what it means?"

"Nuh-uh."

"The elder teaching the younger. It's not all about sex. My role is to enlighten you. It's a noble role practiced from time immemorial. Ten years down this road we're on, you'll be as well-read as any scholar with a master's. Listen to your elder. Try to take this in. Try to understand the basic notion that to a large degree our minds create the world we live in. Every eye sees that world differently. Your mind creates the world you see. Four billion people see four billion separate worlds. It's why our species can't get along, why it's so hard to see someone else's point of view. We're all too self-contained and isolated and too often superficial in our relationships. Intimate, yes, but essentially cut off from one another. A No Man's Land between us. Do you understand?"

"My head's spinning, Lewin."

Lewin laughed large. "That's what I love about you. No pretense. What you see is what you get." From the pile on the coffee table, he pulled out *Walden's Pond* and *Love Has Its Reasons That Reason Knows Nothing Of.* "Read these by next week and we'll talk about them."

Eddie said he would try.

Over the course of the week, he read *Love Has Its Reasons.* The story was about a gay guy who loves a straight guy. The gay guy doesn't want to do anything to scare the straight guy away. They become good friends and rent an apartment together. One night the straight guy takes a shower. Then the gay guy takes a shower and uses the straight guy's towel to dry off. The gay guy feels the straight guy's body impressions buried in the towel. Gay guy melts with rapture at the thought of this. Eddie found himself pulling for them to consummate their feelings for each other, but the story ended with the straight guy getting married to his girlfriend.

For Eddie the towel scene epitomized the agony and ecstasy of erotic love.

"Next he tried reading *Walden,* but it was beyond him. What did the book mean when it said people began digging their graves as soon as they were born? What kind of talk was that? Eddie Turner wasn't digging no grave.

Lewin got him on at McMillan Construction as a laborer cleaning up behind drywallers and tapers at a new housing project on the outskirts of Golden Valley. Eddie and a paunchy forty-something named Carl would haul out the scraps of drywall and tape, load it all on a dump truck, run full loads to the dump, return to the project and scrape and sweep the floors. Moving on to the next blur of houses day after day. It was mindless work, but Eddie didn't care. He had money in his pocket. He was earning his way, which is what all good Americans who loved God and their country were doing.

Mid-June finally arrived. It was cloudy and dark when Eddie and Lewin walked around the corner to Lance's apartment to celebrate the marriage of Chuck and Dale. The apartment was cluttered with guys swapping tales, flirting, drinking. The music was something south sea exotic jungle sounding, whistling birds and drums dominated by a piano. Lewin said it was Martin Denny music. Which meant nothing to Eddie except it was sexy.

As the hours passed, Eddie moved through the apartment hearing now and then snippets of poetry and opinions of this or that novel or writer. There was talk about politics and movies and painters and famous people and discrimination against gays. The unfair world: no justice no peace. Evil everywhere. And he, listening, told himself: *What large minds they have! Their minds know the answers to all the riddles and puzzles.*

Later, as everyone drank more and more, Eddie heard stories about cruising and rough trade and threesomes and foursomes. A guy named Ken told about bringing home a bitch who gave him the clap. The same bitch spread it around to other gays living close by. That bitch's name was Bruce the bitch of all bitches. He was a beautiful rogue, said Ken. He had hair piled in a high wave surging back tightly over his ears and tied in a ponytail. He wore tight outfits that showed his curves. "He had a shapely ass that any woman would die for," said Ken. "But that bitch's pussy was an abyss."

Eddie asked Lewin what Ken meant by an abyss. "Overused," said Lewin. "Loose."

At midnight the happy couple took a bath together, the door open so everyone could come by and congratulate them. Lewin said a shared bath meant they were married now and going on their honeymoon. The honeymoon was a noisy romp in the bedroom, loud music, laughter, moaning and groaning.

Lance caught Eddie on the balcony getting some air and kissed him and asked him if he was still a virgin. "I know Lewin never does anal," he said.

"Me neither," said Eddie.

Lance told him he had no idea what he was missing. Told him he would feel things he could never imagine. Told him there were fabulous sensations to experience, sensations to be had nowhere else but in the arms of a skillful lover like himself. Told him that every boy Eddie's age was anal in his heart of hearts.

Eddie said, "I'm not really gay, Lance."

"Just slumming?"

"No, I really like Lewin, but I'm not really gay. At least I don't think I am. None of this feels real to me. Feels like I'm dreaming my life."

Lance said, "The first time I looked into your eyes I saw a flaming gay bursting to come out and tell the world."

Lance told Eddie that a man lived only once and he shouldn't waste time on the small stuff, the mundane going-through-the-motions of ordinary people who lived and died and were soon forgotten. Told him that Andrew Marvell was right: Time's winged chariot is hurrying near. Told him it wouldn't hurt anything to give Lance-love a try. "Come on, Eddie, why not. Come on, Eddie, what the hell?"

Eddie saw heavy eyes, a mobile mouth with its weird pinkish

lipstick, intermittent flashes of divine teeth.

Music. Wine. Handsome hard-charging homoerotic Lance.

Was Eddie tempted?

Lewin broke it up by stepping onto the balcony and saying: "Not gonna happen, bitch." Said it nicely enough, but Lance knew he meant it. He looked at Eddie sadly and shook his head. "Gorgeous is missing a world-class experience he'd remember the rest of his life. How about the three of us? Would that work, Lewin? C'mon." They stared at each other until finally Lance shrugged and said: "If you ever change your mind."

Lewin pulled Eddie back inside. The party was winding down. "Let's go home. Things are going south now," said Lewin. "I can smell an orgy coming on."

As they were walking back to Lewin's place, he told Eddie, "Believe me you don't want to have sex with him."

They had rounded the corner. Eddie could see his car. He also saw four men walking through a blue haze of streetlight.

"Oh-oh," whispered Lewin.

They stepped aside for the four to go by.

A second after they passed one of the men yelled, "Hey! Where you think you gone, faggots?"

"Run, my boy, run!" prompted Lewin.

"What for," said Eddie. "I ain't done nuthin." He turned round and said, "What's up, guys?"

"You queers?" said the one on the far left.

"You a couple of fairies?" said the one on the far right closest to Eddie. He saw psychotic eyes. He saw the tattoo of a cross on the man's forehead. There were also tattoos on his neck. The tattoos had bled together and Eddie couldn't make out any images. "Fruitfuck, I'm talkin to you."

"Eddie, let's go," murmured Lewin out the side of his mouth. "The house is right behind us. Make a run for the door."

"You asking if I'm gay? I'm not gay, *scheissekopf*."

"Shy what?" said one of them.

"*He's* gay for sure," another said pointing at Lewin. "He pick you up in a bar? Taking you home to suck you off?"

"Why you talking like that? What's the matter with you *arschlochs*?"

"You cussing us, dick-lick? What language is that?"

"Look, me and my buddy are minding our own business."

Eddie had a lot of booze in him, but not enough to keep him from feeling a tide of fear rising inside when he heard:

"Nuthin we hate more than filthy queer cocksuckers."

"Let's kill them."

Lewin held out his wallet. "Take it," he said. "I got eighty-four dollars in here. Take it and leave us alone, *please*. We just want to go home."

"Sure thing," said the one on the far left. He stepped forward, snatched the wallet and punched Lewin's jaw. Lewin went down. When Eddie tried to pick him up, the man with the tattoos and wild eyes kicked him in the head. Eddie went over with Lewin under him. He felt kicks and punches landing all over his body. A hard-booted toe caught him in his left eye and the light went out of it. The kicking continued for what seemed hours, but was probably only a few seconds. Eddie's mouth was filled with blood. His teeth were shattered and dropping like Chiclets. He was barely conscious when the men stopped beating him and walked away laughing. Dimly he heard Lewin yelling for help. Heard him sobbing and saying, "My boy, my boy! Oh God! God!"

Mercifully, Eddie went under.

He woke in a hospital eighteen days later. The first person he saw was his mother. Oh no, thought Eddie. Oh no. "I think he's awake," he heard her saying. "Get the doctor. Squeeze my hand, son. Squeeze my hand. It's your mother. Mama's here, baby boy. Mama's here."

He felt as if his head was wrapped in a turban. His left eye was bandaged. His tongue told him that all of his front teeth were missing top and bottom. His gums were ragged and raw. He heard a machine gurgling beeping wheezing. His mother's voice kept calling.

I'm dreaming. Wake up, Too Tall, you're dreaming.

Eddie had no idea how many days went by after he regained consciousness. He was getting morphine and drifting away from his mother's voice. He remembered her telling him: "None of this would have happened if you had listened to me, son. I'm taking you home. I won't take no for an answer. You're gonna get well and go to school and make something of yourself. Listen to your mother, listen to your mother."

He remembered her telling him that she had four life insurance policies and he was the beneficiary. "When I'm gone you'll be fixed for life, son. But first you have to come home. You have to live with me and get an education. You have to make your mother proud. Eddie, I've done it all for you, for your future."

A detective questioned him about the four assailants, but all Eddie could tell him was that the one who kicked him first had a tattoo of a cross on his forehead. Everything else was muddled. "Talk to Lewin," he said. The detective said Lewin had described the attackers, but the police had no leads to go on.

Lewin came by and mostly moaned about how sorry he was. He kept breaking down, weeping so often it got on Eddie's nerves. The crying and his mother's continual demands made Eddie long for his morphine.

It was August before the bandages came off for good. A doctor told Eddie there was nothing to be done about his left eye. The retina was detached, shattered. "But the rest of you healed up pretty well," the doctor added. "That's youth for you. Youth is resilient. You'll need to see a dentist and get a bridge. Or maybe just get dentures. I think that's what I would do." He patted Eddie's arm and said, "You're one tough kid."

That night Eddie got out of bed, got dressed and snuck down the hall to the stairs. He walked all the way to Lewin's place. Lewin burst into tears when he saw Eddie standing at the door. "Now everything will be good again, he said. "All will be well, I promise."

He gave Eddie the bed and slept on the couch.

Eddie rose the next morning, showered. He gummed a bowl of toast soaked in milk. Then dressed and packed up, stuffing all of he had in a pillowcase. He left a note on the kitchen table.

Dear Lewin, being gay is to dangerous to way scarey. I know you love me but I got to go, Lewin. You a good guy. You will find someone else. Don't cry no more. Sincere Eddie.

The car's battery was dead. Eddie had to take it out and carry it to a gas station two blocks away to get it charged. Later, he drove to McMillan's in Golden Valley. The boss gave him his job back and gave him an advance and told him where there was a room to rent just around the corner from Piggly Wiggly.

§

Seven years passed and Eddie Too Tall Turner still lived in the same place. He continued to work for McMillan Construction. He wore a black patch over his left eye. When bar buddies asked him about it, he told them he was an ex-prizefighter who had fought in Florida under the name Too Tall Turner. He had lost his eye to his last opponent who used the thumb of the glove to gouge Eddie's eye out because he, the opponent, was losing and it was the tenth round and this guy was meaner than Sonny Liston. Invariably whoever heard Eddie's story commiserated, saying things like, "Dirty bastard, rotten thing to do. Sorry, Champ."

"No problem," Eddie always said. "I get around just fine. You know, there's one good thing about losing this eye."

"What's that, Champ?"

"I only see half the ugly in front of me."

This would always get some laughs and usually another round of free beer. Occasionally, one of the men might say to the others that he had heard of Too Tall Turner. Had heard, in fact, that Turner was thought to be a heavyweight championship prospect. Eddie would shake his head modestly and say, "That was in another life."

Winter came and Minnesota had record snows by mid-January. A portion of Elk River High School's roof couldn't hold the weight. It caved and a thirty foot section of the school had to be closed. McMillan's was given the contract to do the repairs. Eddie was part of the crew.

His first job was to haul school desks to a storage unit set up at the curb. He was out there the next morning when the buses arrived. Eddie was watching the students leaving the buses when he spotted a girl taking off her stocking cap and putting it into her coat pocket. Her hair looked like it was packed with sunbeams. She turned her head Eddie's way for a moment, looked at him. He saw confusion wrinkling her brow. He had a feeling that somehow or other he knew her. Students were passing by tromping up the walk to the school's main door. A boy put his arm around her waist, kissed her cheek. She smiled at him. She said something Eddie couldn't hear, but now he knew who she was. Karin. Karin seven years older now. Same brilliant hair. Same lovely smile. He closed the door to the storage unit and headed round to the back of the school. He hurried. The thought of Karin recognizing him filled him with anguish.

He almost reached the door before he heard footsteps crunching across the snow behind him, her voice saying: "Is it really you?"

Eddie hesitated. "Yeah," he said, looking at her. The boy who had hugged her waist was hanging back, hands in pockets, eyes jealous.

"You're so tall I couldn't miss you if I tried," she said. "How have you been, Eddie? Why you wearing that patch? What happened to your eye?"

"Just a accident, Karin. Do I look like a pirate?" His hand covered his mouth while he chuckled. Hoping she would laugh too.

But what he saw was pity in her eyes. It made him wince.

"Poor Eddie," she said. "Your poor face." Tears welling in her eyes.

"No, no, I'm fine," he said. "I'm working for McMillan's. Making good money. Things could be worse. And you? You must be a senior by now."

Karin, blinking back tears, took a deep breath, coughed, cleared her throat. Said, "I graduate in June. You live round here? You ever see Ellen?"

Eddie shook his head. He asked about Karin's mother. Found out she left Kurt and was working as a waitress in Dayton. Karin and Elizabeth shared a little house not far from the Mississippi. In winter with the leaves gone, she could see the river from her living room window.

"She and Kurt broke up?" said Eddie. "After all they been through? Wow, hard to believe."

Karin said it was not long after Eddie took off. Her parents were fighting all the time, and finally one day she packed up and left with Karin in tow. Kurt was living with Ellen now in the main house. When Ellen's mother died he moved in. Karin hadn't seen her father in years.

"Just being around him made me sad," she said. "He never got over the war. What it did to him and Mama and their families. But we're okay now, me and Mama. Life is a lot calmer. I hated the yelling."

The warning bell sounded. "Five minutes," the boy called out.

"I'm coming," she said.

"That's your boyfriend," said Eddie.

"That's Kevin," she said. "We're gone on each other."

"Good for you."

"Gotta go, Eddie. Gosh, it was good seeing you. Remember how you used to twirl me round and round and swoop me through your legs and back up again? Remember those spiders? God, they scared me. Remember the death well? I wish you had stayed, Eddie. I never understood why you left us."

"Ellen didn't need me no more. She said your father made two of me. Yeah, I was getting bored anyway. Sorry I didn't say goodbye. It was better to leave fast, I think."

Karin looked down and shrugged. "Who knows?" she said. Then added, "I hope you'll drop by and see Mama. She works at the Bar and Grill on Robinson. Can't miss it."

"Maybe I'll do that."

"I know she'd loved to see you. We talk about you sometimes. Those days. And how you fixed that crummy old car. And—"

"Good to see you, Karin. You growed up real nice."

She waved and ran back around the corner with Kevin.

Was she real?

Was anything?

When his shift was over he drove out to Dayton and parked a block from the Dayton Bar & Grill. The sky was low and heavy. Promising snow. Eddie looked in the café's window and saw her. She had only two customers, two men. One had a winter jacket on. The back of it said McALPINE WELL DRILLING. Elizabeth was pouring coffee for them. She looked a little heavier in the hips. Thicker ankles. Fuller face. She had dyed her hair a lighter shade of blond. *Blond as butter*, thought Eddie. He caught his reflection in the glass, the ravaged left side of his face. He looked like a man split down the middle. A Jekyll and Hyde. Lewin's voice entered his head, Lewin saying, "You have to keep inventing yourself, unless you're a psychopath." Snow started falling, tapping at his hair, getting his attention. Saying:

105

Don't stir things up. Don't surprise her. You want to see Karin's pity in her mother's eyes? Fuck that!

Walking back to his car, he reminisced about her, about how she loved to make love. Those were good times. The good times come, they go. She had told him once that he completed her in a way Kurt never could.

He had come a long way since then, lived a life full of encounters that should have taught him lots and lots about human nature, but he still had no idea what Elizabeth or any of those encounters meant.

Lifting his face to the sky he said, "What's it all for? What's it all mean?" Eddie opened his mouth, felt the cold air rushing over his gums as he caught snowflakes on his tongue. Each flake a dream vanishing. He told himself that maybe it's an age thing and one day you just wake up knowing.

Behind the Green Door

For the wake Pete buys a white shirt, a green tie, a new pair of jeans. He would wear a suit to show Alice respect, but he can't afford to buy a suit. He wears Nikes cleaned in Amy's washing machine. He and Amy walk to Askold's restaurant. It's a drizzly morning, typical May weather, and Amy's arthritis is bad. She's limping. She's having trouble with her weight. In five years of renting a room from her, he's never seen her looking quite so gimpy, so flabby. Pete curses the gloom overhead. It's Alice's last day above ground and there will be no sun to warm her coffin.

"Fucking Minnesota weather," he says. "You'd think we were going to a funeral." He smiles at Amy, but she doesn't smile back. Her brow is crinkled. She is only forty-two, but looks sixty-two. There is a wrinkle running like the shadow of a lightning bolt from her hairline to the space between her brows. Sunglasses hide her grief-stricken eyes. She is wearing a dark blue dress with blue pumps, low-heeled. Varicose veins show through her nylons. A Celtic cross hangs from her neck, its nexus connecting future-present-past. She has a Bible in one hand. In her pocket is a prescription bottle filled with nitro.

Before she and Pete step off the curb, she takes another pill from the bottle, slips it under her tongue. Her breathing is heavy. She presses a hand to her chest. Her face contorts as she fights to control the pain. Amy has told Pete she doesn't know how she will stand it. For days she has felt anxious about seeing her sister for the last time ever. Dead just four years after Helen (breast cancer) and their mother (breast cancer) and Harry, Alice's husband who died in a car accident, all three dying within a few months of each other. Their deaths put Amy into a downhill spiral from which she hasn't recovered. And now this third loss from breast cancer. Amy said it runs in the family. She said she should get her breasts lopped off before it's too late. "I'd do it," she said, "except my dickey heart would probably explode."

Pete has tried to reassure her about the wake. He gave her Askold's speech about celebrating the life of Alice—"We'll give her a party! Booze, music, friends, the last hurrah for Alice Becker!"

Amy had agreed a celebration was the way to go: "But just like Helen, Alice will be dead tomorrow and the next day after that, and so on forever. It's the forever part I can't stand. I miss my sisters. I miss my mom. I want all this shit to end."

When they enter the restaurant there is nothing of the party atmosphere Pete had hoped to see. The place is crowded. Mourners slumped in booths talking in whispers. A few of Alice's friends are filing by the pale green coffin. Many of the people are strangers to Pete. He recognizes only her regulars, the ones who were always quick to tease her, the ones whose names she knew, the ones she would pause to chat with and call them honey or dear.

Amy's breath quickens as Pete walks her toward the coffin. She grips his hand so tightly it hurts. Her hand is damp and icy. A sign on the wall says—

BON VOYAGE ALICE BECKER WE WILL MISS YOU!

"Do you want to go home?" Pete whispers.

Amy shakes her head. She lets go of his hand and starts to maneuver her way through the crowd. The coffin sits on two café tables and is centered below the aperture where Alice used to place her orders on the carousel. The coffin lid is snug beneath the tables. It looks like a dugout canoe. There is walking space around it. An overhead light shines on her. A ceiling fan rotates slowly, sending cool air over the corpse and stirring curls of white crepe that Pete had hung the night before when he and Askold had decorated the place.

Pete follows behind Amy, keeping his eyes on her meticulous braid. The braid is mostly gray with brunette reminders here and there. They arrive at the coffin and peek inside. Amy takes off her sunglasses. She pulls back. Then looks again. Pulls back once more. She shields her eyes from the overhead light and looks a final time. Her face crumbles. She whispers, "My God, what a cruel joke."

Even though Pete has known all week that Alice is dead, and even though he has imagined what she will look like in her coffin, he is as shocked as Amy to see the waxen face, the manipulated hair, the clownish spots of rouge on her cheeks, the red gash of her mouth, the thin smile. "She looks like a clown," he says. "I ought to kick that mortician's ass."

"Like a clown!" Amy echoes. "She wouldn't have wanted us to see this. I should have gone to the undertaker myself and not left it up to Askold. But I just couldn't make myself go. I've been sick, you know."

Yes, Pete knows. Five years ago Amy had looked good for someone her age, someone sticking to her diet and exercise plan. But then with three deaths to deal with in the space of one year, Amy and her plan went all to hell, and Pete became more than just a boarder. He was her caregiver. Like a son taking care of his mother. She quit her job and went on disability, while Pete worked for Askold as a dishwasher and busboy. In his spare time he took care of Amy's rooming house, doing repairs and the gardening, while watching boarders come and go. The boarders she has now were his friends yesterday, but today he hates them. He believes they are Satanists. He wants Amy to kick them out.

"At least it's a nice dress," she says, stroking Alice's sleeve.

"Yeah, that ain't so bad," says Pete.

Alice is wearing a white dress, smooth, satiny, with a gauzy green frill at the waistband. Pete thinks it's a dress a bride might wear to her wedding.

The bags beneath Amy's eyes redden. They sag like pockets of loose change and he is afraid she is going to start blubbering again. He puts his arm around her, supporting her and supporting himself as well. He thinks he knows what she is thinking, she who very nearly died of a heart attack, she who could, in fact, die any second, even now standing in front of the coffin, she, Amy Story, is seeing her future, seeing the sign on the wall saying BON VOYAGE AMY STORY WE WILL MISS YOU. Trembling fingers play with Alice's sleeve. Trembling fingers touch her shoulder, her chin. Amy bends, kisses Alice's forehead.

"Goodbye, sweet sis," she says. "You and Helen and Mom in the arms of Jesus. Soon I'll be with you." She pats Alice's folded hands and adds, "Cold. So cold." She shudders. She puts her sunglasses back on and says in a firm voice, "No viewing, Pete. You make sure they keep the lid on. Promise? No viewing."

"Whatever you want, Amy."

At the corners of the coffin the shamrock balloons move like bobbers on water. The balloons are tied to the brass handles. Pete wishes there were enough of them to lift her up and out the door, a straight shot to heaven, the Golden Gates.

The bells tinkle. Pete sees Artie entering wearing his black turtleneck and gold chains. His hair slicked back and curling on his neck. Behind him comes Keyes with his guitar and Marilyn. Pete stares at Marilyn, willing her to look at him, but she won't. Her eyes search the ceiling. She looks at the fan, watches the crepe paper and balloons dance. Pete bites his lip. He doesn't know what to say to them, especially to her. He sees them naked again, the three of them on Amy's queen-sized bed, there in the red lights, sprawled across each other, their mouths open, breathing, snoring. Between Marilyn's naked thighs is an empty bottle of White Horse. On its tri-pod at the foot of the bed, the eye of the camera watches everything. The camera's motor is still running, making a ticking sound. The expended film slapping inside its canister as the gears whirr. Pages of the script look like confetti strewn over the floor.

Pete had *not* been shocked to see them. In fact, he had half expected it, even though a part of him had hoped she would fool him and be in his bed as usual waiting for him to come home from his shift. But she is a poet, an actress, a model—in one word an artist. And (as she has told him) artists must have experiences. They have to know all sides of the human condition. When he saw the three of them, he decided he would not blame or hate Marilyn for what she did. In the large scheme of things, her betrayal was not worth the jealousy he had felt. Nothing near the pain of Alice's death or what the loss of Amy Story would cause him. He recalls Amy lying in a similar sprawl a few weeks ago, almost dead from her heart attack. Marilyn had looked uncannily like a younger version of Amy last night—used, abused, not long for this world. The room had reeked of stale orgy, a smell reminding him of cat spray.

Pete smiles cynically at the memory of Artie saying how the porno industry would make them filthy rich. *You will be kissing my feet everyday for letting you in on the ground floor,* he had said, *this thing's gonna be bigger than 44-D's: Behind the Green Door, what a cool fucking title!* He said he would make it into a series like Sergio Leone did with spaghetti westerns.

"There they are," says Amy.

"Yeah," says Pete, "Satan's disciples."

Amy cocks an eyebrow. "Is the pot calling the kettle black?"

"It's evil what they done. I'm not the pot or the kettle. You the one got me baptized and born-again, Amy. God has opened my eyes. So now I know evil when I see it."

"You were going to be in it, Pete. You were going to be the Stud." She titters and covers her mouth.

"Yeah, but the difference is I backed out. I couldn't be part of that shit. Marilyn could, though. I don't hate her, but she disgusts me."

"They were drunk."

"Sin-sin-sin."

"Pete, what the hell does it matter, really?" She nods her head toward Alice.

He whispers, "I thought about that too. But Jesus, Amy, Alice is dead and they're having an orgy? That just ain't right!"

"They were making a movie, trying on an art form. Life goes on, you know. Art helps life go on."

"What's got into you? Porno ain't fuckin art, Amy." He closes his eyes a second. Takes a deep breath. "But yeah, you're right, who gives a fuck? I sure as hell don't. I refuse to care. I didn't feel anything when I saw them."

Pete wonders how he could have been so calm, how he could have seen them like that and not taken out his switchblade and sliced them up. The old not-born-again Pete would have done that. But no hard feelings he keeps telling himself. No hard feelings and who cares? He will not be moved. No sir, he is not moved. Can't move him. Forget it.

When he left the naked trio and went into the living room he found Amy asleep in her recliner, forced to sleep at an angle like that because if she tried to lie flat she wouldn't be able to breathe. Her Bible was on the floor, open to Psalms. *The prayer of a believing heart* underlined. The cats were draped around her like a shawl. With each breath she took he could hear mucus gurgling.

He went to his room and laid awake most of the night thinking about Artie's offer. Initially he had told him "Yeah, I guess I'll be your stud." And they had laughed about it. But Pete had been drinking that night. And the next day he said, "No way, Artie. That's some fucking sick shit you're up to." But Pete wondered if he had been wise to back out. In the light of day, the whole thing had seemed stupid, but truth be told, porno was making money faster than any other genre of film on the planet. He had thought about how making a killing would give him enough in the bank to afford a real college, instead of the two classes he was taking a semester at night school, crawling his way toward a G.E.D. Hey, there were worse ways than porno of getting there, weren't there? The means would justify the ends. Or is it the ends justify the means? Porn is not armed robbery, after all. It's not murder. Hell, why not join in with Artie and Keyes and Marilyn? It was only sex after all. He thought about the commercial she did for Ivory soap, how pure she seemed holding that naked baby in her arms and saying, "Gentle enough for my baby's bottom. Ivory soap. Ninety-nine and forty-four one hundred's percent pure." Marilyn the model morphing into Marilyn the porn star? It didn't compute. Nothing made sense anymore.

When he got up in the morning, she and the two men were gone, and so there was no action needing to be taken, until now, seeing her there at the entrance holding Keyes' horny black hand and refusing to look in Pete's direction. The action, he knows, will come later if at all. Maybe he will slide by and whisper, "Screw you, Marilyn." Or maybe he'll say, "Okay, Marilyn, you win, I'm in." But hey what the hell? Death is in the room. Alice Becker a clown-faced corpse. Everything else can wait.

There is a keg of beer on the counter, and next to it are bottles of vodka, scotch, bourbon, gin. The mourners rotate from tables to counter refilling their drinks. Keyes sits on the counter, his feet on a stool, guitar in his lap. He plays something jazzy kinda blue.

Askold enters wearing a suit and tie. He has Alice's twins with him. And he is already drunk. "What kind of wake is this!" he roars. Raising a bottle of beer he says, "Here's to Alice Becker!"

Glasses go up, people shout "Alice Becker!"

Askold takes out a handkerchief, blows his nose. He looks at the children. "Orphans," he says, "Orphans." From his pocket he extracts some notes. He tells the crowd that Alice Becker was born May 27, 1932, in Saint Paul, Minnesota.

He pauses. Clears his throat. Continues: "She died on her birthday, May 27, 1972. Her husband Harry died two years ago in a car accident. Alice is survived by these little ones here, her twins—Harry Junior and Hart aged seven. Both now legally under my guardianship. My last and most sacred promise given to Alice was to raise these babies as if they were my own. I'm their daddy now."

Again he pauses. He wipes at his eyes. "And she comes to work for me eight years ago. The best waitress I ever had. Pregnant and on her feet all day, she works right up to the time of her labor. Three days after she gives birth to these kids, she's back at work again. An amazing woman. This is a first-rate hero we are honoring here. Things were tough for Alice. It's a mean world. Her mother and sister and husband die, one right after the other, boom boom boom, but Alice's courage, her energy doesn't wane. When the money gets tight, she gets a second job. Later she's dealing with breast cancer. She never complains. She never wanted anyone's pity. She had the heart of a pioneer. She is what we mean by good American stock."

Askold blows his nose before adding, "And so, how bitter and tragic it was when cancer come on top of everything else. It was then I had her marry me, so I could take care of her and the kids. The weeks, the months, a couple of years go by, and me, I watch her decline day to day, until she couldn't work no more or take care of her children and had to go into hospice. Such experiences make us very humble, make us appreciate the blessings we have." He hiccups. Waits several seconds holding his breath until the hiccups are gone. And then he says, "When Alice Becker died, she did so without fuss or bother. Like a candle guttering out. The world is poorer without her. The world needs her energy, her toughness, her humor, her goodness, her honesty. I'm going to miss my Alice, and I know all of you will miss her too, especially her sister Amy. But it's the damn way of things and there is no arguing with *the way*." Askold puts his notes back in his pocket and says, "*Even the weariest river winds somewhere safe to sea*. Rest in peace, baby. R. I. P. So be it. Amen."

There are a few echoing amens and lifted glasses. The atmosphere is painful. Askold bends over, whispers to the children, "Orphans, orphans.

Come give Daddy Askold loves." They hug him. He cries while they look over his shoulders. Their eyes are large. Their eyes saying *what's going on?*

"Well shit," says Artie, "are we partying for the babe or not? Are we gonna make a celebration of her life or make a tragedy? Goddammit, Keyes, make noise on them strings, tickle that guitar. Marilyn, c'mon sweet stuff sing, c'mon! Pass the booze! Let's get this show on the road! Gimme some vodka! Play, Keyes, play for Alice."

Keyes plays while the liquor flows. The place fills with party noises. "Starting to sound like an Irish wake!" someone yells.

Artie leads some of the mourners in a bunny-hop around the coffin. The jukebox is blaring now. Keyes is dancing close with Marilyn, his long-fingered hand on her ass. They do a lot of groin grinding and Pete gets jealous and starts downing shots of gin warm in his glass. Askold is dancing too. On his shoulders is Harry Junior hanging on to Askold''s ears. The little girl holds Askold's hands and hops around giggling. Pete thinks there is enough noise to wake the dead. He fantasizes Alice sitting up and ordering a beer. He wishes she could. He would lift her out of the coffin and dance with her. He would dance wild. He would show Marilyn and Keyes a thing or two.

Later, Artie takes Pete by the arm and leads him into the kitchen and talks to him about how bad the movie is going without him as the leading man and what does Artie have to do to make things right? "I need a good-lookin cat like you in my movie," he says. "That fuckin Keyes, he ain't no actor. He's not photogenic like you, baby. With all those teeth crowding his mouth he can't do nothing but mumble."

"No way, Artie," says Pete.

"It will make your fortune!"

"No way."

"It's Keyes' fault you're mad at us. We was just gonna do a dry run, you see, just practice our moves. A rehearsal with no penetration. Not till you come. That's what I said, 'Not till Pete shows up.' But that goddamn Keyes, he got us all drinkin and after awhile, no one knew what we was doin. Listen, Artie would never betray his best pal, not for a million bucks. But when booze steals your mind, what you gonna do, huh? Jesus Christ almighty, once little Marilyn gets wound up, she really goes wild,

114

I'm tellin you. C'mon baby, don't you wanna be her Romeo? C'mon, baby, say it's so."

"Nuts," says Pete.

Artie pours him another drink and spins scenes of rising to the top of the industry, endless sex and tubs of money, fast cars, yachts, champagne baths with nymphomaniacs. And he says, "What red-blooded American male heterosexual don't want some of that? Is you normal or not, honey?"

"Nuts," says Pete. His head is wobbling. And his knees. There is a feeling that his brain is full of iron filings.

"Look, here, honey, I'll drop Keyes like a ton of shit, you just give the word, I'll send him packing. He's no good for us, he's no good for the future of you and me and Marilyn." Artie drapes an arm over Pete's shoulders, kisses his cheek, reaches down and pats his butt.

Pete's head is getting heavier and heavier. He is very confused. Maybe he should be a porno star, maybe he should. Does anything matter? Nothing matters. "I want to be a better person," he says. "I wanna go to heaven, see Jesus. Get a college degree. Be somebody. No more gangsta and gangbanging. I want God to love me."

"Say what?" says tearful Artie. "You got God and college in your pocket, baby. Oh, baby, baby, you're the most righteous, smartest child in the world. You're good as gold. Artie never loved nobody like he loves you. Don't you wanna go to California? It's where I'm takin this show. San Francisco here we come! Now, goddammit, do what I say, you fucker! Let me show you something. Jesus, the things I have to do to spread a little lightenment!"

Artie drags Pete back to the coffin. "No second chances for her," he says, pointing at Alice. "What you spose she would do now if she could come back and get a chance like I'm givin you? Fame and fortune, think she'd turn that down now she's been on the other side of the great divide floatin in that creepy world? Hell no, baby. She'd open up, she'd go for it! 'Don't miss your chance,' she would say. And look there, look over there. That's your Marilyn and Keyes like white and black Siameses. Practically tooling your broad right in front of you with that big black cock of his. Ain't he got no shame? If that was my broad I'd kick his ass. You understand my meaning, baby?"

"Dirty bastard," says Pete. He watches Marilyn and Keyes dry humping to the music. She is Keyes girl now. "Stole her right under my nose."

"That's right. Some pal he is. Listen, baby, that mumbler can't speak the words trippingly on the tongue. He ain't no true artist like you, baby. If I make the movie with him, I ain't gonna let him talk at all. He can't talk, you know what I'm sayin?"

"She's my girl, she's mine," says Pete.

"Hallelujah," says Artie.

"I'll straighten him out," says Pete. "I need my blade. If I had my blade … I shouldn't have left it home."

"Sic em, baby, sic em."

When Marilyn puts Keyes' finger in her mouth, Pete goes nuts. He shouts, "Dog of the hair that bit you, you bastard." He rushes toward Keyes. Leaps. Finds himself on the floor. Next moment Keyes is kneeling next to him, cradling his head.

"Motherfucka, Pete, you my man. Whass up?" Keyes says.

Pete closes one eye so he can focus. "You stole my girl."

"It wasn't like that. It was the movie and liquor and we all went nuts. If it makes you feel any better, I don't even remember what me and Marilyn done, not none of it, Pete. The whole night's a hole of Calcutta. Look here, I don't want to pick bones, but if you had come on as the star like you spose to, none of this woulda happened."

"So it's my fault."

"Not exactly, but—"

Pete looks up and sees Marilyn. She looks concerned. "Marilyn, do you still love me or not?"

Her eyes are remorseful. "I love you, Pete. But I love Keyes more."

"See, I knew it," says Pete.

"Get away from him," says Artie. "You is outta my movie, Keyes. And I'll replace you too, Marilyn, if you go with him. Kiss your fame goodbye, baby. I'll run you two out of the industry." Artie kicks Keyes in the leg and says, "I said get away!"

"Don't you dare kick me, you motherfucka! I will kick your ass for that!" says Keyes.

He jumps up and the two men start pounding each other. Everyone backs off to give them room. Blood flows from Keyes' nose. Artie's mouth is bloody too. The two men start wrestling. Artie drives Keyes backward into the coffin and it spills, pitching sideways and ejecting the corpse. There are screams as the coffin makes a complete roll and deposits Alice on the floor face down, nose against the tile, the split in her dress showing her attitude to the world.

"Stop that music!" Askold shouts. "Jesus Joseph, look at this mess! Look what you did, look at her! And in front of her kids! You're exiled! I want you out!"

In the silence that follows, Keyes and Artie are panting hoarsely and looking at Alice with guilty expressions. Her exposed ass seems to be making a final statement. The kids are standing on chairs gawking at their mother. Harry Junior points and his mouth moves, but he doesn't say anything.

"Someone should film this," whispers Marilyn. "Run get the camera, Pete."

"That's evil, that's an evil thought," he says.

"Art knows no evil," she says stiffly. "You and that Christian crap, evil's all you ever see since you got Jesus. Evil my ass."

"Your ass *is* evil, Marilyn."

"It is? Well, you've been screwing it for the last six months. So what does that make you?"

He sees her with the naked baby bathed with suds, the purity intertwined. *Gentle enough for my baby's bottom. Ivory Soap.*

"Neither of you have any respect for anything," says Askold to the exhausted fighters. "That's the trouble with you, you don't even respect the dead."

Gently the three men roll Alice over and put her back in the coffin. They leave the coffin on the floor and move the tables out of the way and stand the lid against the wall. When she is tidy once more, Askold asks what started the fight.

Artie points at Keyes. "Playin with Marilyn's ass," he says. "Right in front of poor Pete."

117

Keyes is holding a wad of napkins to his nose. "We're dona det married," he says.

"Both of you is outta my movie!"

"My movie as much as yours, mudderfucka. My money's in it tew. Me and Marilyn wanna finish it, don't we, Marilyn. It's our investment togedder." He blows and blows, trying to clear his nostrils. The napkins are soaked with blood.

"We've come this far, we might as well go all the way," she says. "What's some sex between friends, anyway? We're all clean."

"Behaving this way at a funeral," says Amy, shaking her sunglasses at Marilyn. "Marilyn, how could you?"

"It's not my fault, Amy. I can't help it if I've fallen in love."

Amy rolls her eyes. "Hello," she says. "Anybody home?"

"What?"

"I want you out of my house. You and Keyes and Artie go room somewhere else. Just Pete gets to keep his room. He's the only sane one of you all."

"But Amy—"

"No buts! Out! I want you out!" Amy looks at Pete. "Not a brain in her head. What the hell do you see in her?"

"Ivory Soap."

Amy blinks.

Artie says to Keyes, "Give the gal back to him."

"She's not mine to give, motherfucka. So back off."

"Lousy actor."

"Stupid director."

Artie tells Pete to sock Keyes and take Marilyn back. "Women respect that in a man," he says.

"I don't want her," says Pete. He looks at Marilyn and feels nauseated.

"Screw you," she says, "you . . . you loser!"

Artie slides up next to Amy. "Honey baby," he says, "we gots to stick together. You don't really want me to leave, do you? You're not kicking Artie out, hey? Not yet. Gimmee a month. I'm goin to California next month. Got some backers lined up."

"Out," she says. "You bunch of heathens. God will get you, you'll see."

"Naw, you don't mean that, honey. You'll change your mind. I'm fun, you need me around. Let Keyes go, but not Artie. Banish not Artie your company. Banish Artie and banish all the world!"

"Get away from me! Don't you know I'm dying, you self-centered cretin! I've no time for this. I need the Lord, not you!"

"Baby, how could you speak that way to me? Don't you know I love you?"

Amy takes Pete's hand. "We're going home," she says. "Get me out of this madhouse. I don't feel so good." There is a bluish ring around Amy's mouth. Her skin looks gray and clammy. Pete no longer feels very drunk. No longer feels anything for Marilyn either. What was that all about? Her and her putrid poetry. Her film star aspirations. It was her poetry that had pulled him in at first, the two of them on the bed that night and her sweet voice singing poetry to him. Jesus, who wouldn't fall in love? And then they were going to make a movie and become stars. Only it wasn't porno, it was *Romeo and Juliet* until Artie came along with his schemes. And it was beautiful once and she was too. But there comes a point—

"Let's go," he says, making his way through the mourners, who don't look very mournful now.

"Last chance," says Artie. "San Francisco here we come!"

Outside in the cool air, Pete and Amy walk hand and hand toward home. The clouds are still there and the air is vaguely weeping. Their faces are damp. They cross Hennepin and go by two derelicts leaning against GayLord's Bar. One holds out his hand and says, "Change?"

The other says, "Vietnam vets."

Pete fishes in his pockets and gives them all the change he's got.

"God bless you, brother," says one of the men.

A bus roars, the smell of diesel, traffic humming this way that. A hearse pulls up in front of ASKOLD'S STEAKHOUSE. Pete points. Says, "Here to get her."

Amy slips a pill under her tongue. She's clutching the Bible to her heart. "Go slow," she says. "Thank God it's over and we can slow down now."

"What about Artie and Keyes and Marilyn?" asks Pete. "What we gonna do?"

Amy squeezes his hand. "Throw all their cameras and shit out on the porch. If they come to the door, don't let them in," she says. She hesitates, her brow furrowing. "Fighting like that at Alice's funeral, those fools. God forgive them." A second later she is murmuring, "Men used to fight over me, you know. It was always exciting. It never failed to put my heart in gear, let me tell you." She chuckles softly.

"Funny, ain't it?" says Pete. "They were panting like dogs, their tongues out."

"Yeah."

"You miss it sometimes, I bet. Being fought over."

"Yeah. I miss a lot of things. Marilyn's got nothing on me but youth."

Her color improves as the pill takes effect. Pete feels fine again, relieved. He has come to love Amy and he knows her death will devastate him worse than when his own mother hanged herself eight years ago. But he won't think about that right now. Because there is only now, this day and Amy beside him urging him to go slow. She is going to make it home, he can tell. The house is just around the corner. And the cats and the recliner and the calm life she needs. He's going to fix her some chicken soup. But first he's going to toss all that movie junk and their belongings on the porch and lock the doors. In the window he'll hang the VACANCY sign. The next boarders who want rooms will have to go through Pete. He will interview them. He will ask for references. Whoever they are, he's going to make sure they are God-fearing Christians. He's going to make sure they shun evil and live clean.

Lives of the Cougar

It is 1999, a Friday and there is no way she can know that leaving Lariat's with him will determine her future.

Thrilling though, hugging his back, cheek on his shoulder, blond hair flying behind her, the roar of the engine throbbing like a direct link to the core of everything primitive.

This is living!

LARGE—

Long lanky luscious.

And Karin loves it.

It's 1999, a Friday. The sky is cluttered with stars crowding each other as the Harley leaves Anoka chasing a moonless landscape. Cows at pasture lumpish as black boulders haphazardly scattered. Black trees fanning beyond them. A farm house in the distance, light on the second floor a beacon. Maybe someone reading in bed? It's 1999 and not quite midnight. The motorcycle weaving curve to curve. Hills up, down. The headlamp searching for whatever is waiting.

Karin is thrillingly frightened. She loves his scary Harley. She's been in love with danger since her husband died and freed her. She doesn't really believe anything bad will happen. The way Mike handles the bike is masterful. She thinks of home and him in her bed again. She thinks about her two children, her twelve-year-old son, her fifteen-year-old daughter sleeping, the TV on for company. She and Mike had locked the house down and left her kids oblivious. The drone of television masking their mother's absence. She knows if they wake, it won't be a problem. She's trained them. They're used to Friday nights without the mommy. She and Mike will be home when the kids wake in the morning. She will make them breakfast.

She's on the verge of raising her mouth to Mike's ear telling him to turn around and take her back. I want you in bed, she'll tell him. If he wants to. What if he doesn't want to?

Don't be silly, he wants to. All men want to.

"Mike," she says, "let's go back, it's late. You can—"

The headlight spears an Angus the size of an SUV blocking the road. Mike leans hard, the pavement mere inches from her knee before the bike straightens and rockets into and through a row of rural mailboxes. Karin flying. She is upside down and where did Mike go? Karin has no time to look for him, her head and arms hit gravel, the rest of her crumbling, tumbling, bones breaking, liver bursting. All of her instantly painless.

No thoughts. Nothing.

§

It's 1999, Friday night. Karin's legs are weary from so much dancing with this slow swinger named Mike Cavuto. Pleasantly tired, pleasantly buzzed. Mike asks if she wants a breath of fresh air. Minutes later he is pressing her against her car in the parking lot. His hands caressing her butt, tugging her groin into what feels like a warm sausage. It's almost midnight and she knows lovemaking would be the right ending to such an uninhibited night. Lovemaking to soothe her, all wound up as she is from drinking and flirting. Legs gliding over the dance floor.

Mike is dry-humping her. She knows he is close to two decades younger, twenty-one, twenty-two. Twenty-four at the most. Too young for her forty-six years, but she can handle him. She handles all of them fine, all the men she handles them.

"How about I take you for a spin?" He points to his motorcycle.

She thinks she might. But then she thinks not. Already way too horny to wait. "Follow me, come home with me," she whispers, breathing the words into his ear as he nuzzles her neck and presses himself into her belly.

Caressing her hair, he smells it and says, "I heard a rumor natural blonds are nymphos in bed."

"Follow me. It's just around the corner, not far," she tells him.

He hesitates. He's staring at his hands in her hair and hesitating. "Sexy hair," he murmurs. "I like it long like this. Pixie hair is a turn off."

"Are you married?" she asks him.

"Never fear," he tells her. "Lead the way, babe."

She doesn't like the word *babe*, but for now she doesn't say anything.

At home, while Mike goes to the bathroom, she checks on the kids and notes how sweet they look sleeping, cheeks flushed, mouths lazy. Cathy's hair spreading over the pillow, blond streaks caught in a glimmer of brightness from the open door. Liam's thin, pale arms lie outside the covers, ghostly hands folding over his chest, fingers layered. He reminds her of his father, the way his father used to sleep, hands guarding his stomach. The same way he looked in his coffin.

Mike is behind her. Puts a hand on her shoulder.

Whispering she tells him, "Cathy and Liam."

"Beauties," says Mike. "How old are they?"

She gives him their ages as she leads him to the bedroom, the bed.

§

The lovemaking is as good as she thought it would be. Nothing like a young-younger man who can stay the course several times over with no prompting. Her husband had been that way when they first got together, high school sweethearts wrestling in the backseat of his parents' Buick. It was 1971, the two of them exploring the mystery. The two of them bursting with body fluids.

When they graduated, he joined the Army, planning to make a career of it and marry her. By late 1972 he was playing a war that was nearly over. She waited for him. She waited faithfully. In 1973 he was discharged with a medical something wrong with his lungs. The effects of Agent Orange, he told her. He learned to function as a bookkeeper at the Ford dealership. But he never got over the exfoliate kicked up in the dust by his boots, sprinkling down his neck from dying vegetation above, breathed in with every breath he took. He functioned as a man battling numerous ailments, a surfeit that aged him. Always tired. Always cranky. He sued the Army.

And lost.

Dead two years now. Leukemia. Army insisting Agent Orange had nothing to do with it, not this late in the game. It was 1997 when she buried him. Six months later she went to Lariat's. And scored.

Easily.

She wakes with the sun, but Mike is already gone. She has no idea what time he left. Maybe he's one of those guys who don't like staying all night. Fearing, perhaps, that waking in the morning cuddling a woman puts her on the inside, giving her a claim on him. Or maybe he just had to go to work early and was being polite, tip-toeing around so he wouldn't wake her. If it were that she'd be fine, no problem. Mike, come and go as you please. Where does he work? Didn't he say something about construction? A carpenter.

He did tell her he would meet her at Lariat's Friday, didn't he?

§

It's 1999, Friday night and Karin has her table, the one Arthur set aside for her between the bar, the barstools, and the curving edge of the dance floor, narrow pillars to the right and left of her, more tables leading to the side wall and the entrance behind her. She can see it over her right shoulder. The band, Deadly Virtue, is playing "Did I Shave my Legs for This?" Karin sips beer and hums along. The clock says 9:50. The place is lively. Couples chatting laughing. Friends crowding the booths, the tables. Every barstool full. Waitresses scurrying. Arthur and Jason filling orders.

Karin feels happy sitting in the midst of it all. She keeps glancing towards the door. Lots of people tumbling in arm and arm, or holding hands, following each other searching for places to sit. She recognizes some of them. For a moment she thinks one of the men is Mike Cavuto. But nope.

Soon the dancing starts again. The floor is jumping. The music stirring her in a pleasurably sexual way. She closes her eyes and listens to—fiddles, guitars, drums, piano. It takes a moment to recognize Deadly Virtue is playing "Old Enough to Know Better." She closes her eyes. She daydreams.

This night she has arranged to have the whole house to herself. She's left the kids with her mother in Dayton. She's bought a case of Budweiser. She's bought chips and three kinds of dip.

124

She'll coax him into taking her home early. She'll make him comfy on the couch. Put on a CD. Something sexy to hotwire him, set a wild mood before changing to slow romantic "Strawberry Wine." They'll dance to that, sweet swaying, no need to move much, just rhythmically letting his hands work, letting their lips touch. Gluey lips, slippery tongues. The vision of it rises like copulating phantoms inside her. Young stuff. Fresh, not all used up.

"Care to dance, pretty lady?"

She opens her eyes. No, it's not Mike. Some teenage cowpoke with a beer-drinker's belly looking ten weeks pregnant. But attractive enough otherwise, firm beardless jaw, clear eyes youthful blue. Are they blue? Hard to tell beneath the multi-colored lighting.

"Oh, I'm sorry," she says. "I'm waiting for someone."

The young man looks around. Says, "If you was my gal, I'd never leave you sittin alone in a joint like this."

"He got held up," she says, hoping the guy won't try to engage her, hoping he'll take the hint and leave. He tips his Stetson and tries his luck elsewhere. It isn't long before she sees him with a woman whose jeans are so tight across her ass the seams are separating. He has his hands on her hips. She has her hands around his neck. Actually, he's a graceful dancer, carrying his belly almost as if it isn't there.

The door keeps opening. More people arriving. Some are leaving. She looks at the halo clock hanging high over the register. Where did the time go? Thirty minutes after eleven. But surely he'll come. He will come. Won't he? She doesn't recall if they set a time.

It was: Friday night. Lariat's.

It was: I'll be there.

It was: I'll be there if you will, babe.

Time riding the earth while Deadly Virtue plays on and on. The couples on the floor look sweat-drenched. All of them feverish.

Somehow the men know not to ask her to dance. She sits isolated, feeling like a leper. She switches from beer to bourbon with waterback.

Almost before she knows it, there are five glasses of water crowding her table. Five shot glasses and she's drunk. She didn't mean to get drunk. She wonders if she can walk. She wonders if she can drive her

125

car.

It's after 1:00 before she tries to get up.

Plop goes her fanny back on the chair.

Nope no way.

Another shot of something amber appears in front of her. She looks at the waitress who says, "Arthur on the house."

It's Arthur who gets her home after he locks up. It's Arthur, big-shouldered and bald who ends up in bed with her.

He rises at noon. He showers and dresses, kisses her on the lips and says, "Whoa, babe, you got dragon breath."

"My head," she says, rolling over.

He chuckles. She feels him patting her sore ass. She hears the door open and close. "Water," she croaks. But he's already gone.

§

It's 1971, an easy summer after basic training and Kevin can't seem to get enough of her. Five times already and the other couple knocking on the motel door asking if they want to go eat. "Later," Kevin hollers. "Sex addicts," says the muffled voice of his boot-camp buddy Billy. Kevin goes back to working on her. Kissing her, licking her, half his fist inside her while he says how much he missed her, how much he thought about her every night and couldn't keep from kissing his pillow. Couldn't keep from masturbating.

"All those guys in the shower, all those butts everywhere, some of em very fine, so feminine you even start thinking about going anal. At our age, you're a slave to your hormones. Can't help it."

She can't talk. She listens to him. She's all sexed-up, the core of her radiating heat from the top of her head to her toes. They've been fucking so long and hard she's getting sore, but she doesn't want to stop anymore than he does. He keeps whispering, "God, I wanted you so badly, Karin I went a little crazy, I think. Boot camp was like being in stir."

It was an amazing time and then he had to go back to camp and they didn't see each other until after he came home from the war.

126

§

It is 1973. The war is over and Kevin is no longer a horny boy. A man with jittery hands now. A man with night sweats and bad dreams and impotence. He tells her he should never have gone into the Army. He says one wrong move ruined his life. He says he's a martyr to American Imperialism. He says there is no going back to correct the mistakes we make. Determinism, not God, rules everyone, everything, he says. He emphasizes it, telling her *Determinism rules!* Once you go off-course, you're off-course forever, he says. No going back, no starting over.

It takes him six months and three shots of vodka and a lot of oral sex before he finally gets it up enough to make love to her. She hopes with a little help they can duplicate that day and night in the motel a little over a year ago. But he is only good for one round before he crashes, his damp head on her breasts. His heavy breathing transforming into childish whimpering that makes her feel repulsion. She wants to help. She wants to be the courageous woman who stays by his side. She wants to be a heroine.

§

And she is. She stays with him. They marry in 1973. Many barren years go by, until at last in 1985, she is pregnant with Cathy. Kevin on Ativan by then, enough to get him through the day. Ativan is thought to be the reason he coughs so much when he wakes in the morning.

Three years later she is pregnant once more. They are trying for a boy. They are trying for Liam.

Liam grows up nervous-tetchy like his father. Always anxious about school. Picked on. Beaten. Unable to obey his father's command to fight back. Every black eye, bloody nose, split lip his father takes personally. His father takes the boy by the hair and shakes him back and forth and yells. "No son of mine is a coward! I'm a war vet, goddammit!"

"Tomorrow you go up to that bully and punch him in the nose!"

"When you see him, go after him, Liam! Knock his teeth down his throat!"

"Liam, a coward dies a thousand deaths, the brave dies but one!"

"Kick him in the balls, Liam!

"Stab him!"

"Take a bat and bash his head in, Liam!"

"Why can't you be a warrior like your old man? Kick some ass!"

Liam never kicks ass. He hides out behind the bleachers in the gym. He hides out in the bathroom in the stalls, his feet on the toilet seat, his eyes now and then above the rim of the door spying, worrying about his enemies finding him.

By the time he is ten and his father dies, Liam is a wreck who is flunking everything and needs not only tranquillizers but therapy. He is diagnosed with attention deficit and given lithium. He is sent to a school for autistics and retards.

§

It's 1999, a Friday night at Lariat's. Karin is sitting at her favorite table waiting for Mike Cavuto and listening to country music. She is watching the dancers. She sips a slow-gin fizz, sweet enough to make her tongue restless. She closes her eyes. She dreams of his body. If he comes tonight, she'll let him rocket her to the stars.

"Care to dance, pretty lady?"

She opens her eyes. No, it's not Mike. Some teenaged cowpoke with a beer-drinker's belly looking ten weeks pregnant. But attractive enough otherwise, firm beardless jaw, clear eyes youthful blue. Are they blue? She darts a look over her shoulder. She looks at the clock. He ain't coming, she tells herself.

"Sure, why not?" she says.

Possessively, he supports the small of her back as he moves her to the floor. He spins her. He grasps her hips. She puts her hands on his shoulders. They dance and she likes his dancing. Pot belly be damned, he's fluid.

"How old are you?" she says.

"Old enough," he says.

"Barely legal, I'd say."

"My name's Bodie," he drawls, smiling. His teeth looking like

128

baby teeth.

"Karin O'Leary," she says.

"Irish."

"German. My folks came here on work visas years ago after the war. I married an O'Leary."

"Divorced?"

"He died in Vietnam," she lies. "Died in battle. He was a hero. A Silver Star."

"Wow."

They dance. They drink. She wonders why he wasn't carded. "Eighteen?" she says. "Nineteen?"

"Does it matter?"

She considers his question. She shakes her head. She says, "Except you could probably be my son."

"Now that's a thought," he says. "You got a son?"

She tells him about Liam and Cathy.

"Twelve and fifteen, huh? So you married again?"

She lies again. She says, "He left me, so I took my first husband's name back for the sake of the kids. Less confusing."

"Yeah, I get it."

Bodie orders another round. "Chugalug," he says.

Time measures their conversation, their coordination. *Blue ain't the word* ... twangs the guitar.

The door opens and Mike strolls in, same jeans, same leather vest, same silver-toed cowboy boots. He spots her, comes over, says, "Bike broke down, babe. Sorry." Looking at his greasy hands he says. "I gotta wash up."

While Mike is washing up, Bodie asks, "Is that the cowboy you waitin on?"

"I was."

"Past tense?"

She tries to think it over, but her mind is cloudy. "I feel foggy," she says.

"C'mon," he says and leads her back to the dance floor.

Over his shoulder she sees Mike regarding her. Her impulse is to go to him. Her impulse is to say, "Excuse me, Bodie," and go to Mike's arms. But before she can do that, he pivots on his heel. He leaves Lariat's.

A moment later she hears the Harley wrapping—Wrap! Wrap!—as if it's saying: Get your ass out here!

Two in the morning, Bodie escorts her to her car, says he was dropped off, asks her for a ride. They end up at her house. She looking in on the kids with him standing beside her, his hand on her ass, kneading it. She says to herself, she says, Karin O'Leary, you are sooo easy.

The sex is quick. The sex is over in a minute, maybe two, with Karin hardly feeling anything. Did she? Did she not? He keeps kissing her, touching her, trying to light her fire again, but she is fading. The last thing she feels is Bodie against her hip getting hard again.

"Not now, Mike," she says. "Morning."

"Mike?" says Bodie. "I'm Bodie, not fuckin Mike."

"Rain check," she says. "Catch you in the morning."

She passes out. Vaguely she feels rubbing, she feels probing.

Soon she feels …

Nothing.

Until she wakes hearing someone screaming, shouting. It's Cathy's voice, some man's voice saying "Oh baby oh baby." On fragmenting feet, Karin careers down the hall into walls into the bedroom, where she sees him naked on top of her pumping away, his ass rising and falling. Liam comes in the door holding a kitchen knife, flashing by her, stabbing the man named Bodie, stabbing him twice. Karin snatches the knife from his hand. Bodie rises. He turns on her, trying to take the knife away. She slashes his hands. He stumbles out of the room, stumbling over the floor, stumbling out the front door. Where he starts yelling, "Help! Help! Murder! Help!" Naked man (bare ass, pot belly and all) staggering toward the road. His cries weakening. His legs caving under him. Rises once to his knees. Falls onto his side heavily, a thump like raw dough hitting a breadboard.

§

It is 1999. Liam's mother brings a man home whose name is Mike Cavuto. Liam has seen a lot of men come and go, but Mike isn't one of them. He is a lot younger than Liam's mother, but in some ways he seems older, seems like a man in charge. He is a carpenter. He is mechanical. He can do electrical work. He can fix the plumbing. Over the course of several weeks, he and Liam work together getting the house in apple-pie order.

One Friday night Liam hears his mother and Mike talking in the kitchen. She's all dolled up in her Harley outfit. They're going to Lariat's, but right now they are sitting at the table and she says, "No, Mike, it wouldn't work. I'm too old for you. There's twenty years between us, honey."

"As if that means anything," he says. "Age is only a number. I've been looking for you all my life, Karin. And I'm thinking you been looking for me too."

Liam hears his mother sobbing softly. He hears her say, "Oh Mike, oh Mike, if only it could be. Why didn't you come along years ago? Why is time so merciless?"

"It's not only if it could be, babe, it is! I love you. I love your kids. That boy of yours, he's crazy about me. He doesn't say much, but he's always hanging around. He wants to watch what I'm doing. He wants to hand me tools. I taught him how to adjust the valves on the Harley today. I tell you if I get time with that kid, he'll make liars out of everyone who says he's retarded, those who call him autistic. That's bullshit, babe. There's nothing wrong with that kid except the world won't give him a break."

"Cathy won't like it, Mike. Cathy resents you already. She says you're more her age than mine."

"Ah Cathy, don't sweat her, Karin. She's just a mental case like all teens are for a while. I was, wasn't you? She'll come around. I'll charm her, you'll see. Too bad she doesn't like motorcycles. I told her I'd take her for a spin, but she said no way." Liam hears him laughing. Whenever Mike laughs, Liam's heart swells so much he fears it might bust.

There is a long pause and then Mike says, "Look at it this way, babe. She's gonna grow up and find someone and leave you just like you left your mother. And so will your son. Ten, maybe twelve years down the road, they'll be out of here and only me and you left, only each other. What we do now will determine what comes after, so you gotta think careful. This will determine your future, babe. This will determine *our* future. Okay, we don't have to get married. I don't care about that. But let's just say it's like we're married. We'll be faithful. We'll be long-time commitment lovers. Only problem I can see is your mom. Since I ain't got none, it's all about you, babe. You'd have to persuade her. I think she likes me a little, don't you?"

"Well enough," she says. "Mom called me Cougar the other day. I think she's a little jealous. Yeah, well, she did ask me if I thought you'd stick around. I said it seemed like you wanted to, but I learned with my husband not to count on anyone being the same everyday for the rest of their lives. Something happens and people change. The difference between the old Kevin and the postwar Kevin was night and day. But I wanted to be the noble woman. I wanted to sacrifice myself for a good cause."

They quit talking. Liam peeks around the corner. Mike is leaning across the table kissing her, his hand cupping her breast. After a long moment, he pulls back and says, "I won't change on you, Karin. There's no night and day. There's just me."

She nods her head, smiles. Then she says, "Let's go have that drink."

Liam knows something.

He knows what his mother sees in Mike. A good man. Dependable. Thoughtful. Good with his hands. No doubt a great kisser as well. Quivering love runs through the boy's body. He understands how important her decision is. He understands that her decision will make or break him. He understands his mother and Mike are determining his future.

The Go to Girl

Judy Turner closed her office door. She went behind her steel desk and adjusted the nameplate that said DR. JUDY TURNER DIRECTOR OF ENGLISH, aiming it at a forty-five degree angle facing the hallway. She straightened the In box and the Out box, making sure they were in line with the brushed chrome edging of her desk. She looked at the beige walls surrounding her and knew she was where she belonged. Minutes passed as she tidied papers, re-alphabetizing the pesky books on the bookshelves, which somehow always got out of order. From a bottom drawer she took out a feather duster and dusted the mahogany framed banner quoting Elaine Showalter:

> ONLY THE JEREMIAHS OF THE FEMINIST CRITIQUE CAN LEAD US OUT OF THE EGYPT OF FEMALE SERVITUDE TO THE PROMISED LAND OF THE FEMINIST VISION.

She turned to the wall behind her and feathered Sandra Gilbert and Susan Guber's title: NO MAN'S LAND. She sang as she cleaned:

> *The feet could not stop . . .*
> *They could not listen.*
> *What they did was the death dance.*
> *What they did would do them in.*

Her quick feet quibbled with the floor and her little buns twitched inside her pencil-thin Prada skirt.

She was puffing from her efforts, and finally there was nothing left to do but sit in her captain's chair, get down to business, read the grievance from that malcontent Mason.

"Okay," she said, "Calm down, Judy Turner, get centered. You don't want to, but darn it you have to. When you're in charge, you have to be a soldier and charge right in. You've got to get the job done. I'm doing the best I can! I know, I know. But no one else really understands how hard you're working and that's to be expected from the likes of them. Pack of prima donnas. It's killing me! Buck up now, Judy Turner. No complaints, no whining. Yes, you're right. Go on now, read it, read this moronic criticism of yourself."

She reached into the In box and grabbed the letter of grievance. As she read the flaming words, her cheeks flushed, her heart raced.

The paper shook in her hands. Her mouth got dry. "I did not," she muttered. "Oh, what a lie. Listen to her. As if I had the power to do that! What a trouble-maker!" Thoughts hissed in her head—such things she would do to Mason, karate chop words that would silence her cackling tongue. Judy Turner let go of the grievance and stifled the impulse to crush it. She turned Mason's words face down and decided it was pointless to read such drivel, such lies. She told herself: "When anger rises, think of the consequences."

The door opened and a cadaverous face peeked around the corner, frogeyes shining like dollops of syrup.

"Sit down, Howie, look at this," said Judy Turner. She handed him Mason's letter. "She names you too. She calls us—" Judy Turner hesitated. "Well, you'll see."

Howie read what Martha Mason thought of him and Judy Turner. His ears reddened. The redness spreading to his jaw and throat. His mouth pressed together in a dry line. His nostrils quivered. "The little nit-twit," he whispered.

Judy Turner found herself wondering if Howie was Jewish. Howard Planter, what kind of name was that? Planter. English? Such big nostrils you have. She was thankful for the delicate Asian nose she had inherited from her Vietnamese mother, her full, sensuous lips, her flawless teeth only very slightly tea-stained. She was going to have them whitened soon.

"It's a lie," said Howie, his voice as high and thin as a whistle. He threw the paper into the air. It oscillated down, down. "Where did she get the idea that I was trying to steal her Sacred Books course? Did I ever tell you I wanted it? All I said was she doesn't have a degree in it, that's all I said. I never said I wanted to teach it. Stealing it, my foot. There's no such thing as stealing classes. How absurd."

"But we have no one to teach it now, that's the problem," said Judy Turner. She squirmed in the chair. Her ass itched.

"Oh, don't worry, boss, I'll teach it," said Howie. "But I didn't steal it from her. I'm just filling a need." He gestured with his hands as if throwing off something sticky. "I mean, honestly, it's one of our most popular courses and someone's got to offer it. We can't let the students down."

"Heaven forbid!" said Judy Turner.

"It's a lot of prep work, though," said Howie. He scratched his neck, leaving red trails next to his jugular. "I'll be burning the midnight oil for weeks," he added. He bowed his head and his bottom lip pouted and his hair drooped diagonally over one eye.

You old pirate, thought Judy Turner. She knew that Howie had had the course ready for months. She smiled at him and he smiled back.

"She calls us conniving and mean-spirited, huh?" he said, glancing at the grievance. "And she includes the dean! What a dumb mistake. Oh, I would have liked to have seen Vita's face when she read that!"

"You know Vita, Howie. She just smiled politely and said she would smooth the way for Martha and be sure she got everything she wanted."

Howie said, "A one-way ticket out the door." He glared at the letter and said, "She brought it on herself. You're not to feel guilty, Judy."

And Judy Turner said, "Martha has spread it all over the university email."

"That putrid bitch! What a rotten thing to do." Howie gave the grievance a kick but couldn't get it to move. He stepped on it, leaving a shoe smear across one corner.

"Yes, but she's cooked her goose and we're still here and people forget things like this," said Judy Turner. "It's sour grapes and nastiness, everyone will see that."

"Vindictiveness," added Howie. "Mean-spirited vindictiveness."

"That's right. Our colleagues will see it for what it is. No one will stick up for her, no way." Her absolute triumph over Martha Mason filled

Judy Turner's heart with pity. "The poor thing," she said. "Her own dumb mouth did her in."

"That's right. It was her big mouth and her arrogance."

"Her arrogance," Judy Turner echoed. "Yes, she was too good to teach freshman comp. She said she had taught freshman comp for fifteen years and she wasn't going back to it. Teaching it was a step backward, she said."

"She blamed it on you."

"I told her and told her it wasn't me, it was the dean. What can you do when the dean wants more writing classes offered? You give her what she wants! The dean is the dean after all."

"Martha could never get it through her thick skull that she was only part-time. Did she really think—"

"Well, that's the trouble right there. You let these part-timers stick around for so many years they start thinking they're entitled." Judy Turner frowned. Then remembered how repulsive her lips looked frowning, so she forged a bright smile. "Believe me," she continued, "the dean has the right idea on that. The union can't help them if they don't go beyond two years."

"Oh, that's just so right on," said Howie. "Don't let them get entrenched."

Judy Turner sighed. She felt the weight of responsibility on her shoulders. She wanted to shrug it off. But then again she didn't really want to. "I never wanted this job," she said. "They begged me to take it. Who in her right mind would want all this responsibility?" She shook her head and said, "It's too much for me sometimes. One is born to negotiate with suffering, my father says. It's our lot in life, he says. The war taught him stoicism, he says."

"I know, I know," said Howie. "You've been a real trooper. Everyone really appreciates the job you're doing. We all know how hard you work to keep things running smooth. We know you have our best interests at heart. Everybody thanks their lucky stars that you're the Chair. We call you the go-to girl."

"The go-to girl?" Judy Turner's mind was filled with bliss and optimism.

"The one you go-to when you need things done."

"I try to be worthy."

"You are! You are!"

Judy Turner lowered her eyes modestly. Yes, it was a thankless job full of worries, but it had its perks. "Someone has to take the bull by the horns," she said. Immediately she regretted the metaphor and wished she had come up with something more original. "One is born to negotiate with suffering," she repeated. And added, "Not to be happy but to tolerate unhappiness and do some worthwhile work, that's what my father always says."

"How is he?"

"Ornery as ever. You wouldn't know he had a heart attack."

"Feisty."

"Yes."

"And your mother?"

"Oh, you know, disaster is just around the corner."

Howie nodded. He reached out and straightened the nameplate on the desk, squaring it with the opposite wall. "You know, Raleigh is back from sabbatical."

"Who? Oh, him. Is he going to the meeting?"

"I hope not."

"Me too."

"So damn sarcastic," said Howie. "He never agrees with anything. He's . . . he's so combative. Mister Tough Guy. He wants everything run his way."

Judy Turner's eyes narrowed. "We'll see about that," she said, angling the nameplate towards the door once more. She leaned back in her chair, feeling the creamy warmth of the walls, her lips smiling warmly at Howie, and Howie smiling warmly at her beneath the mantra—

ONLY THE JEREMIAHS OF THE FEMINIST CRITIQUE CAN LEAD US OUT OF—

When Director of English Judy Turner went to the meeting there he was with his long hair and goat beard and smirky mouth. Kicking back in his blue jeans and sloppy shirt with its wrinkled pocket flaps and frayed collar, he had one foot on a vacant chair—an absurd wannabe hippie left over from the sixties. Judy Turner wanted to tell him to sit up straight. She wanted to tell him to at least *try* to look professional. But instead she said, "So look who's back! How was the sabbatical, Raleigh? I heard you got a lot of work done."

"Hey, Judy Q, yeah, I worked my ass off, baby. The book is finished and my agent is reading it."

Judy Turner inwardly cringed at him calling her baby and using the letter Q as if they had some sort of special relationship. But she kept smiling. The fact that Raleigh had written another book made her want to throw something at him. "That's great," she said. "Just great!"

"Thanks," he said. "I really enjoyed myself. Getting out of this sorry-ass joint for a year was just what the doctor ordered. I was overdosing on students and administrators. I was choking on bureaucracy and bullshit."

"Aren't we all!" said Judy Turner. "Things are much tougher now, you know. We've gone from teaching ninety a semester to teaching one twenty-five minimum. It's exhausting. They've cut our budget to the bone and beyond."

The others around the table nodded. They all looked glum, worn out, their skin gray beneath the fluorescent lights. No one had given her any trouble since she had assigned classes and announced the new numbers. There had been a huge bitch session and she had bitched with the best of them, but in the end they had all bowed their heads to the inevitable. They were putty. They even looked like putty. Judy Turner would have hated to look like her sunless colleagues, their reddish nostrils, pale cheeks. Mournful eyes.

"So why did you go along?" asked Raleigh, his hand making a general sweep of the table. "Just say no."

Sue Jordan laughed and said, "My hero." She winked at Raleigh.

Judy Turner noted the wink. Built like a fireplug, her voice a gruff, no-nonsense drawl, Sue Jordan was another one of those part-timers who had sneaked past the two-year barrier and thought she was entitled.

No one else at the table commented. Judy Turner reminded herself that Raleigh was the same fool he had always been, the same mouthy, anachronistic hippie out of touch with the times. He reminded her of her ex-husband always putting his foot in his mouth. Cold day in hell before she ever married another American male, unless he was a clone of her father. She could handle Raleigh Mailer. When she reached into her pocket to turn on the tape recorder, she coughed loudly into her fist.

"I mean, what would happen to you if you didn't go along?" continued Raleigh. "What if you just said no? What if I don't make my one twenty-five quota, what will they do to me?"

Jim Stauffer offered mildly, "They got a little room where they take you."

"Fascists bastards. Let em try," said Raleigh, smiling, chuckling. His thick shoulders rolled and his fist shot upward. He had been a boxer at one time in the Army, a middleweight. Or was it a lightweight? Judy Turner decided on lightweight. But there he was, same old unprofessional jackass, a square peg jammed into a round hole, a duck out of water, a man without a country. Well, he had a country, but he didn't appreciate it. No one was more unpatriotic as far as she was concerned. She wondered if he was really a veteran like her father. She wondered how she might find out if he was telling the truth. So many phonies in the world, tons of them. She looked around the table and saw that all her colleagues were wearing masks. Sue Jordan's iron jaw gave away the contempt she felt for just about everyone. Jim Stauffer trying to look agreeable, his mouth small and inoffensive, his face saying *all I want to do is slide by*. And there was mousy Albert Chi-Chi who wouldn't hurt a fly. And the godawful grinning Andrea Salter, so perpetually bubbly and saccharin sweet she made Judy want to puke. And finally Howie Planter's fawning frogeyes, his Adam's apple panting like the breast of a nervous bird. Judy Turner wouldn't trust him any farther than she could throw him. He was maneuvering to be the next Chair. Judy Turner would be under him one day calling him boss. Not an eff'n chance in the world!

But Raleigh was the one Judy Turner needed to deal with now. Raleigh was dangerous. He was volatile and he had killed men in combat (or so the rumors said) and he was admired on campus because of the novels he had written about war and because he had an international reputation and he always got respectful reviews. He thought he was above everyone. He thought his reputation would protect him and he could say anything he wanted. He thought he could chastise his colleagues and call them cowards and sneer at them and keep that arrogant smile on his arrogant face and roll his arrogant eyes and— Oh, he was too much! How did such a one ever get on the faculty at all? And tenured too! Ridiculous.

"What a weenie world we live in," he was saying. "They would never have gotten away with it when Dan McLeod was director."

Judy Turner swallowed a gasp. There it was; he was slamming her! She wasn't as good as Dan McLeod. She couldn't handle the administrators.

"He took care of his troops," said Raleigh.

At that moment she decided the bastard had to go. He was a male Martha Mason, a thorn in the department's collective side, an embarrassment with his nothing M.A. With him around, the department would never grow. Never realize its full potential.

"Well, it's ten minutes past the hour, everyone," she said. "I guess we better get busy. Let's look at the agenda."

Obediently, her colleagues grabbed the agenda and looked at it. All except Raleigh, who sat staring at her and stroking his bearded chin. Who did he think he was with that little beard, Robin Hood? But that was all right. The clock was ticking for the Raleigh Mailers of this world.

§

Judy Turner woke with a sense that her lungs were collapsing. She sat up panting. What was it he had said? *What the fuck you doin, lady? You're picking creative writing over Shakespeare?*

So close in her face she could smell his smoky breath and she had almost choked and she was glad again that she was half-Asian, thankful for her ancestors, their ability to switch off their nerves when unpleasant people were hassling them. After a few tense seconds, she had felt Buddha entering her soul. She knew she was smiling. She knew her eyes were inscrutable. She knew she had already won and that it was just a matter of time before her nemesis would be out in the cold.

She reached over to the nightstand, turned on the tape recorder and listened to him almost literally hanging himself:

"That decision," he said, "is on a par with the hiring committee's decree to hire a PE instructor over a poet. We need a poet, damn it! An artist! We need some *heart* in here. We need some *humanity*, some *soul*." But then he had lowered his head in what Judy Turner knew was an unconscious gesture of defeat. She had done the right thing in dropping his Shakespeare course from the spring schedule.

"Actually we didn't want a poet, not really," he told her, his voice smarmy with sarcasm, "we wanted a generalist, but no one would come out and say it. We wanted someone who would slip into any slot the dean wants and not whine about it and keep the conveyor belt going, keep boxing up the products we call students and shipping them into the commercial world, where they can lick the asses of this nation's rulers waiting to chew them up and spit them out."

"You think this is a reactionary college?" she heard herself asking.

Raleigh growled, "Damn right I do. Fascists are running this fucking survival-of-the-fittest goddamn country, and this un-universal university is feeding them more fodder for the corporate world. What's the difference between us and China? Nothing. We're both slaves to a system. Call it communism or capitalism, it amounts to the same thing. Step out of line and you're toast."

"Freedom—"

"Freedom your ass. Talk to the street people or the dying middle class about freedom. Freedom to work yourself into an early grave. Freedom to beg. Freedom to starve." Raleigh made a strangling noise and said, "Don't get me started."

There was a pause on the recorder. This was the part where he was waiting for her to comment, so he could yell at her some more. But she hadn't complied. There had been two people in her office, but only one babbling fool.

"In any case, Judy Q," he said, his voice softening, "the verbal contract I had with the former dean and director assured me that I would not have to teach two creative writing courses in any one semester. Teaching those courses drains me of every creative spark I might have. When I teach them, I give it my all and I'm drained to the core and can't write. It's an absurd phenomenon and an irony of fate that a fiction writer can't stand to teach fiction. But there it is, Judy Q. It kills me to teach fiction. It's the ninth rung of Dante's hell. I'm asking you to be sensitive to that. Give some consideration for my years in the trenches."

Again he waited. Again she was silent. She had had her legs crossed and was kicking her leg, making a covering noise for the slight slur of the tape in the drawer.

"Okay," he said, his voice no longer mild, "listen up, lady. The old dean and director in those days used creative writing as a pretext to hire me. The slot opened up and they asked me to fill it and I said I would if I didn't have to teach more than one creative writing course a semester. They agreed to that, they promised me—"

Judy Turner heard herself saying kindly, "Do you have that in writing, Raleigh? Because if you have it in writing—"

"You know damn well I don't have it in writing. Yeah, like I'm going to say to my good friend Dan, 'I don't trust you. Put it in writing, Dan.' C'mon, get real."

"Well then—"

"You calling me a liar, lady? Are you saying I'm lying about it?"

"No, no, Mr. Mailer. I believe you, but I can't go to the dean and give her that story. She wants you to teach two creative writing courses and drop Shakespeare for now. It's going to take something really solid to change her mind. She's adamant."

"You're hiding behind the dean," Judy Turner heard him saying. "You're pulling the strings. I'm no fool. You can't fool me. You're doing to me what you did to Martha Mason. Taking away any incentives to stay here."

"What happened to Martha Mason was done by Martha Mason."

Judy Turner could hear the barely repressed rage in her voice. She hoped Raleigh couldn't hear it. She was thankful when he topped her words with, "Bullshit! You are so full of shit, lady it's no wonder you waddle when you walk. I got your number long ago when you told me you would play the race card if they didn't give you tenure. Do you remember saying that? I knew who the fuck you were then. Everybody knew. Race card, you fucking phony. You're father's a white man, a WASP! You make me sick, Turner. If you were a man I'd—"

Again she heard the swish of her pantyhose as her leg swung

142

harder, her foot bouncing-bouncing. She could hear him standing up, the chair chirruping on the tile. "You should have fought harder for me, Judy Q," he said, his voice now surprisingly grieved and docile. "I would have fought my ass off for you had our positions been reversed."

"The dean—" she started to say.

Gently, almost whispering, he cut her off with, "Fuck the dean and fuck you."

She heard him leaving the room, the door not slamming like she thought it would, but softly closing, the lock clicking into place.

Judy Turner turned the recorder off and called her mother in Pierre and the two of them chatted for an hour. She told her mother all about Raleigh Mailer and what a burden the directorship was and how the college was working her half to death. Her mother's voice soothed Judy Turner. "I wish you live closer," her mother said for perhaps the five-hundredth time. "You still our girl, you know. We don't like you been seven hour away. Why you don't go work for college in Mitchell or Sioux Falls, honey?"

"Mom, how many times do I have to tell you, they didn't have any openings? I'm good here. I'm the big cheese. I'm the director of my department."

"We proud of you."

"How's Daddy?"

"You know you father. We born to suffer. But not in silence. Some days, I switch off my hearing aid." Her mother laughed. Then added, "When people lose everthing is when you know who they are. That when you know who you are too."

"Poor Daddy. He's had a rough life."

"He patriot join Army and get shot, get a medal. And then get me and get disability. I just a kid when I marry you father. Neither of us know what we doing. But we come here and it come right. Work hard. No complain. At least he still alive."

"Daddy's too tough to die."

"When you come visit?"

"Soon, Mommy. Soon."

Judy Turner hung up feeling sad but also secure in the knowledge that there were two people on earth who gave her unqualified love and understood her and would support her no matter what.

She took a shower, stayed a long time, soaping herself, washing her hair, standing quietly satisfied while the water drummed on her like a thousand fingers massaging her. She dried her hair and fixed her face and got dressed and drove to work. She tried to listen to the classical station, but it was full of static.

"Life is full of static," she said and she thought of Raleigh Mailer. She had overheard him talking to someone in his office and threatening to resign. He had said that everyone was blithely dismissing the promises made to him and he wasn't going to stand for it. She heard him touting his Shakespeare course as the most popular course on campus. Which it was, of course, but what did that matter? Experienced as he was he hadn't learned what really mattered about life—the ability to go along to get along. Judy Turner had known that little fact since grade school. Why bang your head against a wall? Give power what it wants, make it believe you are a team player, and someday it will give you what you want. It was just that simple. Judy Turner wanted to be dean of the college of arts and sciences. A dean and then vice-president of something. Someday in the not too distant future, she would be one of the few female college presidents in the country, guiding her university and winning respect and the rights of women. *OUT OF THE EGYPT OF FEMALE SERVITUDE TO THE PROMISED LAND OF THE FEMINIST VISION.* She had every confidence in herself. She knew she was special. She knew she had what it takes.

Judy Turner parked her car in the faculty parking lot and pulled her briefcase from the passenger seat. When she closed the door, she noticed two men staring at her. No, they were looking at the back of her car. One man said something to the other and jerked his thumb her way. She almost said, "May I help you?" But caught herself in time. She knew what they would do. Men always hit on her. They always said things like she was hot or she was cool or she was a major fox. "I'd like to turn you upside down and eat you like an ice cream cone," a man had told her once.

Judy Turner shuddered at the memory. She walked to the back of her car and saw what the two men were staring at. Someone had put a bumper sticker there that covered the width of the lid, just above the BMW insignia. In bold letters the caption read: BITCH ON BOARD.

Instantly she knew who did it. It was just what he would do, the underhanded, vicious backstabbing—

She clawed at the sticker, clawing at a corner, trying to peel it back, but maddeningly it stuck, maddening little pieces peeling off. It would take her forever. She had a class to go to and then a meeting of directors. She whirled facing the men.

"What're you looking at!" she said.

"Whoa, baby," said one.

"Cool it, baby," said the other.

"Don't you dare *baby* me!"

They walked away, sliding between the cars as they headed toward the commons, their snickers filling the air.

Judy Turner took out her lipstick and ran bright red smears across the caption. It didn't work. In fact it made things worse, made the black letters shine as if they had been varnished. She looked at her watch.

"I'm late. I'm never late," she said. Her throat tightened. Tears started in her eyes. "No, you will not cry, Judy Turner," she said. "Tears are no fair! No whining!"

She stomped off toward the Arts Building where her critical-thinking class was waiting. The hell with it, she told herself. Bitch on Board, she would show him Bitch on Board!

§

He came into the dean's office and sat down, sprawling and untidy as usual. "Judy Q," he said smiling crookedly. He looked at the dean. "What's this all about?" he asked.

"Someone put a bumper sticker on Dr. Turner's car."

"No shit? What does it say?"

"I know you did it," said Judy Turner.

"It says I KNOW YOU DID IT? What did you do, Judy Q?"

"Quit calling me that!"

Raleigh's eyebrows shot up. "What's going on, girls?"

145

"You know."

"Like hell I do." He looked genuinely puzzled, but he wasn't fooling her.

"It says BITCH ON BOARD," said the dean.

Raleigh pressed his lips together struggling to contain himself. Then he threw his head back and laughed. And said, "Wow, have you been driving around with that? Think of it, every car behind you reading BITCH ON BOARD. Oh man, that kills."

Judy Turner's throat was so tight she couldn't speak. She tried to clear her mind. A disturbing heat seared her face and she wondered if she looked flustered. *Don't frown, don't frown*, she cautioned.

"Okay," said Raleigh, clearing his throat. "I get it now. You're saying I did it. You're saying I put that sticker on your bumper."

"It's on my trunk, actually."

"Oh?" he said. "You know that could be tough on the paint. But look, I didn't do it, Judy Q. It's not the sort of thing I would think of. No, I might disable your car, maybe. Maybe slash your tires or steal your distributor wire." He sat up, leaning forward, elbows on knees. "Let me tell you a story. When I was a kid I worked in a bowling alley setting pins. Yeah, that was definitely a long time ago. It was in this old joint that didn't have automatic pinsetters. But I was so fast I could service two alleys at a time. There was no wage. We made our money on tips." He paused, his eyes seeming to see something in another dimension. "So anyway, there was this boss man and he didn't like me. I don't know why exactly, but you know how it is. Personalities clash. So he fired me one night when I came in. I didn't ask him why. People do what they do and who gives a fuck why. Lots of sonsabitches in this pissed off world." He arched an eyebrow at the dean and at Judy Turner. "I learned that little truth by the time I was six or seven," he said. "Sonsabitches and bitches everywhere. So what the hell, I left the bowling alley. And then about a week later a cop shows up at my house and this cop says I have to go with him to the station. He wouldn't tell me the reason. When we got there he led me inside and there sits this oily-haired, fat-lipped dago bastard from the bowling alley. I ask him what's up. And he says to me, 'I know you did it.'" Raleigh paused. "Sort of just like you, Judy Q. You see, somebody had slashed his tires, all four of them. He had a Cadillac and somebody had put it on its knees. What kind of car do you have, Judy Q?"

"You know."

"No I don't."

"I'm not telling."

"Okay, whatever. My point is: that fat bastard accused me without any proof. The cops got rough with me, but fuck them, I wasn't going to confess to something I hadn't done. They kept me in jail overnight, but the next day they had to let me go. Guess what happened to the new set of tires that bastard bought. And the set after that. Until the game got old, he had to buy an awful lot of tires."

"He's threatening me," said Judy Turner.

The dean leaned forward and looked at Raleigh over the rim of her glasses. "I better not hear of anymore stickers on Dr. Turner's car."

He nodded. "Whatever you say, Vita. But you better find the right guy to say it to. Judy Turner here has more enemies than she can imagine. So do you, Vita. You and Judy Turner and Howie the bug-eyed barracuda. My, my I would be very nervous if I were you, if I had all the enemies you and Howie have made round this damn joint."

The dean's mouth was open in astonishment. Judy Turner felt herself blinking in disbelief. Had he actually said that? "How dare you! I've sacrificed everything for this department! I've—"

"You've taken a bad situation and made it worse. You and Vita and the rest of these ass-licking administrators have demoralized an entire college. Open your eyes, take a look. It's you, Judy and it's you, Vita."

Before anyone could reply he was out of his chair and out the door.

Judy Turner looked at the dean. "Now do you see what I've had to endure?"

"He's dangerous," said the dean.

"He's the most dangerous person in our department," said Judy Turner.

§

A week went by and nothing happened. Then one morning Judy Turner came in and saw BITCH ON BOARD stuck to Howie Planter's office door. Her first reaction was relief that Raleigh hadn't gone after her again. But relief changed to outrage when she came to her office and there was a BITCH ON BOARD for her too. "Oh, this is . . . this is . . . this is so unfair!" she cried. She marched right down to his office and entered without knocking.

"Well, just come on in," he said.

"How dare you!"

"Now what?"

"Oh, you bas—"

"Now, now, Judy Q. Careful."

"Are you going to keep doing it?"

"Got another sticker on your car?"

"You know damn well where it is." She looked towards the hall.

"Let me see," he said.

He hurried to her office and saw the BITCH ON BOARD and saw the one on Howie's door. "Geez," he said, "Somebody really don't like you guys. This is kind of crazy. I mean, only someone half off his rocker would do a thing like this."

"You!"

"No, you got that wrong, lady. You don't need to be afraid of me. No, whoever is doing this is sending you warning signals. I'd call these posters *shots* across your bow. I'd watch my step if I were you. Maybe get a bodyguard, I'm serious. Someone is stalking you. Someone wants revenge, Judy Q. Be careful, okay? I wouldn't want anything happening to you."

He went back to his office and Judy Turner stood awhile feeling waves of rage and fear running through her and thinking: *He's stalking me. He wants revenge. What's he going to do?* She didn't know any bodyguards. She wondered how people hired them. How much did they cost?

His threat preyed on her mind all day. She mumbled through her classes and a committee meeting and couldn't get her heart to settle down, couldn't get the cottony fear out of her mouth. Everywhere she turned she saw Raleigh Mailer watching her. He would peek from behind pillars, watch her from a second story window. He was on the roof. In a tree. In the bell tower. At the top of the stairs and then at the bottom of the stairs. By the time the day was over, Judy Turner was sick to her stomach and dizzy. She went into the bathroom and stuck her finger down her throat and vomited.

She wanted to talk to Howie, but he wasn't in his office, so Judy Turner went home. She called and left a message for Howie, told him to watch out for crazy Mailer. Then she called her mother and asked if she could come visit for a few days. Of course her mother was thrilled. Judy Turner said she would be there in about seven hours. She would stay for four days at least. She didn't have to be back until Tuesday. She hung up and hurriedly packed some things. When she put the suitcase in her trunk, she could see the slightly faded spot where the sticker had been. She had scrubbed it off with water and 409. A long, thin banner shape, like the ghostly shadow of a two by four, was still there. She slammed the trunk and headed for highway 14 north of Mankato.

§

Once on the road, she finally relaxed. She called her mother on the cell phone and told her she was on the way. She listened to classical music and when the station faded past New Ulm, she switched to CDs, *Bach, Mozart, Brahms*. The music put her in a nice place, a sweet zone, and she found that for the first time all day she was hungry.

In Brookings, South Dakota she stopped at McDonald's for a hamburger and Coke. She was feeling better and better. So good in fact, that she thought she might just turn around and go back. But then she thought of Raleigh Mailer waiting to strike, so she decided to keep going. She would definitely do something about him. Her father would know what to do. Nobody messed with her father. Heart attack or no heart attack he would follow her around with a shotgun if he had to. Four days with her father and everything would be fixed.

It was late-afternoon when Judy Turner passed Huron. Fifty-two miles later she was rounding a long, slow curve and saw a fat stick in the road and her reflexes took over. She swerved and lost control for a moment and went off the edge of the pavement, hit some rocks and blew out a tire. The car slid to a stop. She sat behind the wheel trembling.

"Boy, that was close," she whispered. "Boy oh boy."

After a minute she regained her composure and got out of the car, the door softly clicking behind her. She looked at the stick and saw it moving, curling itself into what looked like a . . . like a huge beret? Yes, or a fat Frisbee. Or a basket lid. Pleased with the similes, she whispered, "Rattlesnake. Rattler, gross city. Should've run over it." When it didn't move towards her, she went around to the other side of the car and inspected the damage. The tire had a huge gap in the side as if it had been slashed.

"Raleigh Mailer," she said. And she saw him working on the tire, slicing it cord by cord, almost through but not quite, leaving it weakened and ready to blow. "God forgive you, Raleigh," she said. "What a low-down, mean bastard you are." She could see him gloating, his smile hovering. She was living in a dangerous world, a world full of monsters, a world full of victims, especially random female victims. Rotating round and round, her eyes took in the dry late summer landscape dotted here and there with trees and brush. And black hills far to the north. The odors of desiccation and dusty fields stung her nostrils. She knew bodies were buried out there, off the apron of the road, in shallow graves, in ditches, bones numberless, dumped by serial killers and scattered by animals. People just disappeared. Vanished. And not one trustworthy man to help a stranded young lady change a tire. Raleigh would have the strength to use the wrench thing and get those chrome nuts off. Yes, and it wouldn't surprise her one wit if he had been following her and was out there, a watcher waiting to see what she did next. Waiting and sniggering, hoping the snake would chase her, hoping to hear her scream or cry or beg for mercy.

She would show him a thing or two.

Judy Turner marched to the trunk and then realized she didn't have her key, and she wasn't really sure where the jack went anyway, or how it worked. She decided there was no need to exert herself so much. She would just call a tow truck and wait in the car.

She went to the driver's side and pulled the latch, but the door wouldn't open. She blinked and the thought ran through her mind that what was happening couldn't be real. She pulled and pulled on the door.

How could it be locked? It couldn't be!

"No! No!" she wailed.

Had she locked it when she got out? Very likely she had. It was such a habit from living in the stolen car capital of Minnesota that she even locked her car when she parked it in the garage. Yes, she must have absentmindedly hit the button as she was getting out. She stared through the window, at the comfortable leather seats, the lacquered cedar-grained console in the middle. She could see her cell phone in its holder, green eye glowing.

"Oh, you fool, how could you? Oh, this is so stupid." She stomped around for a second in anger. But the snake, which was twenty or so yards away, started rattling its tail. The air around the snake glowed bluish, a bluish halo. An uninspired cricket sang a temperate note in some brush close by. Slow wind scattered a few spears of straw and grains of dust over the highway.

Judy Turner took a calming breath and said, "Get a hold of yourself, Go-To-Girl. Break the window. What does it matter? Insurance will pay for it."

She struggled with a rock she found in the ditch beside the car. She managed to get the rock chest high and slam it against the passenger-side window. The glass cracked into a spider web pattern but didn't break. She hit the glass again. And again. No matter how many times she hit it, the glass wouldn't give.

"What kind of window is this?" she asked. Then she remembered the salesman saying something about the windows being shatterproof. "It would take a two-hundred pound man with a sledgehammer to get into this car," he had said.

Judy Turner's bowels went watery. Her anus puckered and itched. She stared at the harvested fields, thousands of brittle stalks of something sticking out of the earth like spears surrounding her on both sides of the highway. The snake had stopped rattling. But she could see his stiffened tail six inches high and she knew he was watching her. What was it doing here this time of the year? Didn't snakes hibernate when nights started getting cold? Had it come for the warmth of the pavement?

"All right buck up," she said, "I'm still in charge, the hell with

151

this." She knew she was closer to the town of Highmore than Ree Heights, ten miles maybe. She would just walk it, that's all, and if a car came along she would see its lights from far off and she would hide. No use taking any chances on perverts. When she got to Highmore she would get a tow truck. Things like this happened to people all the time. She could handle it. She straightened her shoulders and started walking and felt comforted by the warm pavement seeping through the thin soles of her shoes.

"March, march, march," she ordered. "He'll see. He'll see what I can do."

Cadaverous Howie Planter with his popping eyes, flaring nostrils and triumphant smile came to mind. He winked obscenely from behind her desk and reached over and squared her nameplate. Only it was his nameplate, not hers. And she saw how easily things had changed. It was as if there had never been a go-to girl.

She looked over her shoulder and saw her car glinting in the dimming light. She could hear its motor idling. There was comfort inside. The rattler had disappeared. She walked faster, her eyes searching. Was he following her? Was that a rattle she just heard?

§

Six miles later Judy Turner had walked out of her shoes (they were killing her) and now her feet were blistered and bleeding and cold. She was horribly cold all over and utterly exhausted. *Do people die like this?* she wondered. And she knew that people did. Of exposure.

What they did would do them in.

"No, I won't die," she decided. "I refuse to let him win me." Or was *him* a *her*? For some reason, Martha Mason entered Judy Turner's thoughts. *Director, my ass! You've been nothing but a disruptive force since you got the Chair. You and that pirate Planter!*

Enemies everywhere. You just try to do your job as best you can and all you do is make enemies. Why? Why? Jealous that's why. It wasn't fair. Nothing was fair.

"I'm so tired of . . . of this . . . this." She racked her brain for a metaphor, but nothing happened. "To hell with Aristotle!" she screeched.

A few yards from the road, Judy Turner saw a scraggly tree with a stunted log lying in front of it. The little log had a chair-like depression in its center. She went to it and sat down. She was shivering so hard her teeth rattled and she thought of the rattlesnake. How his blood would be so cold now he wouldn't be able to move. And she would be able to walk right up and drop a rock on his head. And there would be nothing he could do about it! She wished she knew where he was. She would definitely fix him.

Judy Turner crossed her arms and hugged herself. Six miles of hiking and scurrying off the road to hide from cars going by full of murderers and it felt like she had done it all for nothing, like she was trapped inside a surreal box full of dead stalks and brush that never changed. Where was that town, that Highmore? Where was her car? The snake? And, God oh God, the temperature was freezing. Everywhere were the same shadows and vague ribbons of blue-black air and silhouette after silhouette of phallic fence posts on all sides now. Where were the farm houses? Where were the yard lights? She imagined herself inside a freezing meat locker full of carcasses. All her world post-to-post barbed wire. Nowhere to go.

After a while the shivering stopped.

Stopped also was the churning in her bowels. And she could no longer feel the lacerations in her feet. All she needed to do was close her eyes and sleep through it. This vile dream. "This Egyptian female servitude of a desert hell," she said aloud. And she paused and repeated it in her mind—*Egyptian female servitude of a desert hell.* "There's a metaphor that works! Ha! Take that, Aristotle, you bald bastard." She stomped her freezing feet, felt them stinging. Take that! And that!

Yes, and the metaphor was a good omen. It meant everything would change tomorrow. The sun would come up and warm her blood and she would walk to Highmore and get help. Just a short sleep away and then Judy Turner would wake from this stupid life and put things in order, lined up precisely at their proper angles again. For a while longer she would have to negotiate with a private war of suffering that had come upon her unearned. But then her suffering would end and she would be back in her office, safe in her captain's chair. Director of English Judy

Turner finding some worthwhile work to do.

Her feet had quickened to a rhythmic shivering that was out of her control. She wanted to get some sleep, but—

The feet could not stop . . . They could not listen.

Annette's Work in Progress

Minnesota State University, Mankato (MNSU): Creative writing, emphasis poetry. Wrote my first paper on Endymion. A thing of beauty is a joy forever. (Pretty sentiment, but so not true.) College freed me. Made me bold. Made me believe I could become someone new. An exciting Annette, yes! No mother hovering, riding herd. I went wild. Dated a boy (half Swede, half Afro-Am) named Hamlin. Hamlin made me feel liberal. A free thinker. Charitable.

Gave him my virginity.

Glad to get rid of it.

Two months of orgies until a pregnancy test turned blue. The news made me so frightened I couldn't focus. Missed all my classes. Broke with Hamlin. He didn't understand. I didn't tell him why.

Days later, sitting on the toilet cramping, this Annette miscarried. A blob the size of a marble floating beneath her. Flushed it away. Took a shower. Padded with Kotex this Annette packed her clothes.

And ran.

Caught a Greyhound.

Independence behind her, she wanted Mommy.

The secret is a thorn inside. The one that really started it all. That made me finally record it. Expose myself.

Scandalous exposé: a therapy? So *they* say.

Save as Document: Annette Annaba Walker

§

Minneapolis: This Annette moved back to her parents. Mommy worked at a dentist's office a few doors away from a general practitioner. When he told her he needed a receptionist, she offered her daughter.

Love at first sight. Married him four months later. I was twenty. He was twenty-nine. His mother had named him Danny Beau. Danny Beau Walker.

In the early days of our marriage, we were insatiable. Obsessed? Yes. At least I was. He was SO scrumptious. This Annette was always wondering what new eroticism he would invent to entertain her. He told her anything goes. As long as we both consent, nothing is perverted. If it feels good, it is good. I believed him. I also believed that if I were always faithful, keeping myself exclusively for his pleasure (Madonna and whore), then everything would be well with our marriage. Mommy had told me I would have to endure a lot from a man, but if I kept our squabbles out of the bedroom, the rest would sort itself out.

She said: Remember, Annette, marriage is a work in progress. Even after twenty-five years your father and I have to work at it.

What I didn't know was that my willingness to *progress* beyond what might be called *normal* erotic boundaries eventually made my husband suspicious. Distrustful. Tie me up. Tie me down. Sit on my face. Oh yes! So willing. So easy to train. As the years passed, my eager passion became … dangerous. Is there anything you won't do, he once asked me.

Save as Document: Annette Annaba Walker

§

Warnings everywhere. If you can read the signs: A cat slithering over the fence. Gone before I could throw a rock at it. Lovebird Tootie inside the aviary fluttering and frantic. Panting. Beak open. Tongue needling. Calmly I cooed, You miss Tommy, Tootie? Me too. Poor little thing. Poor tiny Tommy. Stepping inside the aviary I closed the door. Filled the feeder with seed. The birdbath where I found Tommy dead was bubbling with innocence. Filtered water circulating. No scum in the bowl. The pump humming happily. Water wriggling. I like the word *wriggling*. *Wriggling*.

My movements made Tootie fly to the top of the cage. Clinging upside down. Tiny claws wire-meshed. Head ticking like a metronome timing my movements. To calm her I sat on the bench and sang those sad words about finding a blue bird *(because my heart's been broken)*. The bench surrounded by a nest of flowers needing eggs to secure a future. Not gonna happen with Tommy gone.

156

Tootie bending a wary eye. I can see that tiny bright bead as if it were me looking in a mirror. Instead of once upon a time years ago when Annette's identity was wife and mother. So many riptides inside. Ambiance: unreal. Also thinking: *much … too … long.*

Save as Document: Annette Annaba Walker

§

Emily Dickinson: Yes I tried to write like her. Knowing I'm not worthy to touch the hem of her dress. I'd kiss her foot if I could. Call me queer if you want to. Worshipfully I named my children after two of my top ten. Son Keats. Daughter Emily. Emily had my olive complexion, Moroccan eyes, dark wavy hair. Keats, slim like his father, has reddish hair. No one on either side of the family has reddish hair. Keats' father was dishwater blond when I met him. The first time he saw his son mummy-wrapped in the infant ward, he said there was no resemblance. Nothing. None. Who is this flat-faced gnome? He looks like someone's nub-nosed-ruddy-cheeked grandpa.

Keeping my voice light I said, All infants look like that, silly.

As Keats grew his father claimed he still couldn't see anything of himself in the child. I tried not to take offense. Tried to see it as his humor hassling me. Oh, stop it, Danny Beau, I told him. You're two beans from the same pod.

He said, One a lima, the other a kidney. His eyebrow arching seriously, sort of.

Save as Document: Annette Annaba Walker.

§

July Fourth ten years into the marriage: Jerry and April Fields came over for barbecue, First thing Danny Beau said was, Look at my son's ears. Don't they look like Jerry's moth wings? And what about that hair? Pointing at Jerry's red hair, Danny Beau narrowed his eyes. But then laughed and said, Come on, only joking.

Jerry Fields laughing, Heh, heh—no heart, no mirth in it.

The mailman has red hair, said April the bottle blond bitch.

But Jerry has easier access, Danny Beau told her. Hop over the fence and he's in there! His hips thrusting in my direction. We all laughed. Only a joke. Danny Beau rarely told jokes. He went back to the steaks. Flipping them. Fat sizzling.

Also thinking: some memories are molten.

Save as Document: Annette Annaba Walker.

§

Daniel Beau Walker: Moody broody. Not easy to get along with. Drank too much and when he drank he often picked at me. Said I was overweight and because we had been married a decade I felt secure enough to let myself go. Dumpy Annette metamorphosing into her hippo horse mother. She wants to be a poet. She's no poet. Wannabe isn't enough. She's lazy. She isn't bright. She has no work ethic. Blah blah. *Bash!* Best to agree with him. Best to agree with every putdown meanness can muster. I hate to argue. If I didn't defend myself he would talk his nasty self out.

But! Not always a browbeater, our Danny Beau. Not always insufferable. Not always a bully. No, Danny Beau could be sweet and thoughtful. He erected the aviary in the backyard and bought me those two lovebirds for Valentine's Day. Poor Tommy at the bottom of the bowl didn't last long. Maybe a heart attack? Maybe a stroke? Do birds have heart attacks? Do birds have strokes? I buried him in the rose-garden. Danny Beau had planted it for me. Red roses. Deep royal red. Like overripe cherries. Danny Beau had gentle hands. Doctor hands. He knew how to use those hands. He knew how to do plumbing and electrical repairs and take care of the cars. Things he learned growing up on a Minnesota farm. The house never had a drippy faucet for more than a day or two. It never had tricky light switches.

Save as Document: Annette Annaba Walker.

§

Marriage unraveling: It was the night the Walkers and the Fields

158

watched porn together. An old movie called *Blue You*. We laughed at the bad acting, the absurd camera angles, the overdubbed sounds, the characters flooded in fluids. Juicy, juicy, Danny Beau kept saying. (Wickedly.)

As Jerry and April were leaving, we couples hugged at the door and Danny Beau saw Jerry pass his hand over my ass. Just a touch. Jerry's palm drifting. I was boozy and smiling submissively. Feeling … tamely serene. Ready for what the rest of the night would bring after Danny Beau took me to bed.

As soon as the door closed, my husband said, Playing with my wife's ass.

Still smiling I said, What's that, honey?

Jerry couldn't keep his hands off your ass.

He couldn't? (Still smiling.)

Come on, woman, don't tell me you didn't feel it.

(Not smiling now.) Feel what? I didn't feel anything. (Little white lie.)

Danny Beau shook his head. You broads, he said. (Eyebrows: arching apostrophes.) Caught in the act and still denying it.

What act? What's the matter with you? A voice told me not to question him. Laugh it off, get him in bed and everything would be all right. But booze had made me slow-witted. Aggressive.

Then he said, If I walked in on the two of you balling your brains out, you'd probably say I was hallucinating. Don't give me that offended look. Women aren't really offended by anything. You can't offend them, they wrote the book.

You're talking about your foul-mouthed mother, I shot back.

Yeah, her too, he agreed. I just wish you could be honest. That's all we ask is some fucking honesty.

I didn't *feel* Jerry! If I had felt him, I'd say so.

Right. He went to the bar, poured another drink.

Please don't drink anymore, I begged.

Shut up, Annette. Shut your fucking mouth *now*.

This was not how the night was supposed to end. Usually when we watched the sexy movies it was like an hour of foreplay and we would fly to bed and make fierce love after. I had expected him to pounce on me as soon as the door closed. I had been so ready for that! But now I was angry.

I've never done anything to make you not trust me, I said.

His eyes were cruel. Haven't you? Haven't you, really?

Like what? I asked. Heart hammering. He suspects me of some terrible treachery!

You tell me, he said.

I defended myself: There's nothing to tell! Will you please stop? (I thought about Hamlin getting me pregnant. The miscarriage. Flushing the evidence away while blood ran down my legs. There was no way he could know about that! No one knew, not even the fetus's father.)

You've always been a bit of a slut, Danny Beau said. None of you is off-limits to anything. You'd do all the things the whores do in those movies, wouldn't you. You'd like that. I know you, Annette. I know a gangbang would be right up your many alleys.

I was flabbergasted! Speechless. What the … what the … Also thinking: would I? Also thinking: hell no!

Keats and Emily hiked down the hall. Stepped between us. Why you guys yelling? Emily asked. You woked us up.

Danny Beau took Keats by the hair—Ow, Daddy!—shaking him and saying, So what about this little fellow? Whose little trout have I caught?

I gasped. My head whirling. Where am I? I whispered. Also thinking: has he gone crazy? Is he insane?

Let him go, Daddy, said Emily. She grabbed her brother's hand and told him to come to bed.

Sick to my stomach, I tried to talk but words failed me.

Look at your face. I finally caught you without your mask on, said Danny Beau. Tone bitter, voice vinegar. Did you really think you could keep it from me forever?

Keats staring at his father resisted the tugging of Emily's hand. Mommy? he squeaked.

Mommy's been bad, said Emily. Come to bed.

Danny Beau let go of my boy's hair, bent down, gripping him by his collar. Pulling him close and saying, Here's a lesson for you, Keats. Take it from Danny Beau Walker, never trust a woman. Are you listening?

Do you understand? Never trust a goddamn broad.

Okay, Daddy.

Inches away, eye to eye, they looked at each other and I saw the likeness. Keats already getting his father's arching eyebrows, dimpled chin. The trim body growing toward the same dimensions—six feet three inches, same strong hands and wrists one day.

Recovering my voice, I said, Will you look at him, Danny?

I have, he answered. I've watched this redhead becoming Jerry Fields.

Oh my God! My hands covered my ears. I'm having a nightmare!

He ordered Keats to go with his sister.

On wobbly legs, I stumbled to the couch. I expected him to tell me all his suspicions, but he didn't.

He said, Stew in it.

A moment later I heard the bedroom door close. Booze talking, I murmured. It's the booze.

Also thinking: maybe this isn't happening. Maybe he comes back smiling and saying Gotcha! C'mere, you gullible goose! Maybe we are about to take our showers, brush our teeth, climb nude into bed. Make love.

Maybe.

Hmm, maybe not.

Save as Document: Annette Annaba Walker.

§

Days passed and we did not talk. At night Keats and Emily watched their favorite shows as usual, Emily on Daddy's lap, Keats on the floor. I often fell asleep in front of the TV. Nervous exhaustion. I woke uncomfortable and cold in the morning, my hands shaking, my eyes always verging on tears. Feeling the chill around my heart.

A heart that was breaking.

After dressing and feeding the kids, I drove them to school. When I returned my husband was always gone. I cleaned house. Did laundry. Game shows and soaps on TV keeping me company. Counseled myself to get a job. Get out of the house. Get a life that doesn't revolve around *him*.

Also thinking I had a life. Or thought I had a life.

Save as Document: Annette Annaba Walker.

§

Memories: fiercely alive. Memories made of sulfur. Memories igniting. Creating a light that only old-age senility will snuff out.

I started smoking again. Trying to calm my nerves. Trying to lose weight. It baffled me that something as trivial as an accidental caress had driven such a wedge between us. How could this be? It was … it was ludicrous. Had he not trusted me all these years? Had he always suspected me? Had I ever lied to him? *Had* I ever done anything to make him not trust me?

Also thinking: Yes. But nothing he knew about. It had all happened before he met you, Annette. The past doesn't count.

When he learned I wasn't a virgin, I lied to him. Said I had broken my hymen when I fell on the crossbar of a boy's bicycle. Feet slipping on the pedals. This had actually happened to a girl I once knew. So maybe he hadn't believed that story? Thought I was whoring through high school and college? Doubts brewing inside him all those years? And Jerry's hand on my butt had been a confirmation of my husband's fears. Times of promiscuity. Liberated women acting like men. VD and AIDS waiting to take advantage. How could I convince him that I had always been faithful?

Also thinking: sure, I had looked at Jerry and wondered. But that was as far as it went. A swift little fantasy, like something in a movie. Passionate bodies, get-it-on music. Afternoon delight. Jerry and Annette doing the pretzel. Oh my!

Save as Document: Annette Annaba Walker.

§

More days passing: Danny Beau and I talking to each other:

Where's my pants?

In the laundry.

162

Where's the *TV Guide*?

In the rack under the coffee table.

While you're at it, will you make me a drink too?

Sure.

Came a night we got drunk and ended up in bed together. This Annette cried afterwards, thinking the torture was over. But the next day he was distant again. I thought of offering to take Keats for a blood match. But then the very idea outraged me. Anger settling in: a pool of hot lead in my head. I stayed remote. To hell with him. Also thinking: this is how marriages end—with distance distrust jealousy egos insults.

Weeks went by. We made love occasionally, but it wasn't the same. Wham-bam. No cuddling after. I put on more weight. New lines appeared on my forehead. Wrinkles bordering my lips. Fine hairs flourishing between my brows. I plucked them with tweezers. Only 32 years old and yet and yet. Also thinking: this Annette has become an aging crow.

Danny Beau told me he had always known I was stupid, but now too much booze had made me imbecilic.

Why did he hate me so? What did I do?

Liquor stealing my brain cells?

Also thinking he speaks truth: Annette = imbecile.

Gazing from a mirror was the stupidest woman imaginable. But I didn't know what to do about it. I'll join a gym. Do aerobics? Maybe go back to school? Study something? Nursing? Teaching? Too dumb for either? In any case, who would watch the kids? Danny Beau told me that pretty soon no man would want me if I didn't slim down. He said no self-respecting man would look at me with my ass fat as a Hottentot's. I imagined myself on a diet, exercising hard, getting my figure back. Then would he want me? Would a streamlined body bring him to his senses? In a man's world the body is everything. Well, nearly everything. Ninety-five percent I'm thinking.

Save as Document: Annette Annaba Walker.

§

The revelation: April and Jerry came over. Coaxed us into getting a babysitter. Going out on the town. April helped me with my hair. Picked out my silky black dress to enhance my eyes. A string of white pearls for contrast. Let's have fun, she told me.

Are you sure this dress isn't too tight? I asked. I didn't want to look like a call girl.

Honey, you're a knockout tonight.

We went to dinner.

In the course of the evening my husband danced—with me.

A slow dance sweet romantic:

Unforgettable, that's what you are . . .

The air tinted indigo blue. He looked young again. The handsome young doctor I worked for a decade ago. I recalled the night he first asked this Annette to dinner. How we drove to the beach after. And made love on the front seat of his car. The passenger door open. I was nervous and dry. The sex was abrasive. Until he climaxed and slid me into a slicker gear, an *easy* rhythm I could follow. Hamlin invading my mind: The college dorm. His succulent mouth. The way he used it and everything else. But Danny Beau didn't continue long enough to complete me. When he stopped I was … regretful, I guess. Mournful, maybe.

Later, he told me he had thought he would find me a virgin. And he said, No reason why you should be, of course, but that was how I imagined you. Weren't you taught to save yourself for someone special? He wanted to know how many boys I had slept with. You're the first ever, I answered.

(Look, Danny Beau was right about what he had said—all women are liars; it's how we survive the journey through the labyrinth of male expectations.)

After the lie flew out of my mouth, the bicycle crossbar became a piece of my history. I added also that my parents were Catholic and had taught me that my body was a temple, but I hadn't been able to stop myself with him. I've been in love with you from the first day I met you, I said. God knows I couldn't deny you anything. Romeo and Juliet: *Prodigious birth of love it is to me.*

Right answer.

He said he thought he loved me too. But he wasn't sure because he didn't really know what love was. He told me about being raised on a farm near Elk River. How distant and stoic his parents were. How his mother ran off with a hay-bucker who later dumped her. How his father took her back, but from then on they slept in separate rooms. She dressed in farmeralls and transformed into something that looked mannish and sour. Danny watched her hair go gray in a year. Her face aging along with her hair, she looked like her own mother, grumpy Grandma. Cussing the animals. Cursing the world. There was never any affection. Nothing but exhausting work and smelly cows and crazy chickens and filthy pigs. Not once had he ever heard the word love when he lived there. When he was seventeen he went into the Navy to get away from it all. Served as a medic. After he got out, he went to college on the GI Bill and became a general practitioner. He admitted that he had no bedside manner and probably shouldn't have become a doctor. He knew people inside out, he said. He wanted to love them, but couldn't find anything to love. He wondered if I could teach him. I said I could show him what real love was. Also thinking: this is my reason for being, this is my religion now.

Dancing with him that night, ambience dreamy, the old feelings returned. Of course I loved him and my love would overcome all obstacles. Things were going to go back to the way they used to be. It was his past, you see? Especially that backbreaking farm and mean mother that made him so callused and vicious from time to time. I would have to work harder to overcome those acrimonious years. Be more patient and understanding. He didn't really believe Keats wasn't his son (absurd) or that Jerry and I …

No, he was just testing me, like the husband who tested Patient Griselda, waiting for her to prove him wrong. Raising my lips, I kissed his cheek. Put my hand on the back of his neck, whispering, Isn't this nice?

He stiffened. His voice entering my ear like an ice pick when he said, It might be if I were with someone else.

Scarcely able to breathe, I let him lead me back to the table. Jerry stood up, took my hand. Automatically I followed him.

I danced with Jerry. April danced with my husband.

So what's with you two? said Jerry.

Shaking my head, I told him it was nothing. I apologized for being a drag.

He told me I wasn't being a drag. He added that I looked very fetching in my silky dress and high heels. I love your pearls, he said. We danced a second time, while April and Danny sat in the booth watching. Underneath the table, I saw their legs touching. I saw April's hand groping.

As soon as we got home and the babysitter was gone, Danny Beau asked me if I enjoyed exhibiting myself with my lover. I refused to answer. Turning on the television I channel-surfed.

Answer me! he commanded.

I never know what you're talking about, I told him.

The world is full of cunts, he said.

You should know, I said. What about you and April? What was that about?

What the hell are you saying, you stupid bitch!

Turning the volume up on an old war movie I muttered, I know what I saw.

You must think I'm a moron! he yelled. You must think I'll swallow anything. Is that what you think? Don't answer. You'll only lie. I've had enough of women's lies in my life. Your face is an open book. I see right through you. You're a *chameleon*, Annette. Look at me! Tell me something! Hey!

What was the right answer? What did he want to hear? What would get me out of trouble? On the screen a man was charging a tank. He leaped on the tank, opened the hatch, threw in a grenade. Don't those hatches lock from the inside?

I've never thought you were a moron, I said. You're a smart man. Everybody knows how smart you are. You're a doctor, after all. Doctors can't be dumb.

You think sarcasm will work? he asked, his eyebrow the shape of a scythe. He was good at that. Good at arching that eyebrow.

I was stammering: I didn't . . . I wasn't . . . I didn't say . . .

Shut up! I'll tell you what you said!

Unwanted tears filled my eyes. I can't stand it, I told him.

He gazed back mournfully. Oh, woman. Oh, woman! There was a catch in his voice, almost a sob. And I wondered what's going on. Is it April? Is it more? Is he having a nervous breakdown? Am I?

Emily padded into the room, fingers twisting her hair. She stood next to her father and frowned at her mother. Mom's bad, she said. Vicious little voice. The voice of a gremlin. Oh, I hated her then!

Go to bed, her father ordered.

Down the hall stood Keats picking his nose and looking baffled.

What you listening to, moth ears? his father asked him

Mommy's bad? said Keats. He inched back to the bedroom, repeating over and over the question is Mommy bad? Jesus Christ what a night!

Save as Document: Annette Annaba Walker.

§

Keats' birthday: I threw him a party, inviting all his friends. I baked a chocolate cake, with chocolate frosting. I poked nine red candles into the cake. I put candies into paper cups. I made a bowl of fruit punch. The living room was decorated with balloons and streamers and a sign that said HAPPY BIRTHDAY KEATS!

Danny Beau told me he couldn't stay for the party. He had to go to the office to catch up on paperwork. After he left, Jerry came over with a Charlie Chaplin movie called *The Gold Rush*. He said that April had gone out shopping, so he thought he would give the children some laughs. I knew the truth: I knew where April really was. But I no longer fretted about such things. I made myself not care. What did it matter? Time flying. Also thinking: what matters is surviving until I can get the hell out of this house.

We watched comedy together. Jerry sitting next to me on the couch, the children on the floor close to the TV laughing at silly Charlie turning into a chicken and being chased by a man with an ax. As the movie continued, Jerry asked in a whisper what was wrong. I looked so sad all the time, he told me. He wished there was something he could do. His arm was stretched behind me. His fingers combing my hair.

I'm getting so fat, I whispered.

You look fine, he said. Really, you needed some extra weight. You've got a nice hourglass figure now.

Flattery will get you everywhere, I told him, rubbing my finger across my lips to stop them from trembling. I told him I was going to do aerobics. I'll go there in the evenings and work this fat fanny off. Maybe I'll get all my frustrations out. Maybe I could get a job teaching aerobics. Why not?

It would be good for you, said Jerry. Exercise keeps a body sane.

Yes, that's true, I agreed. You're right. God, sometimes I feel like I'm going to explode, spontaneously combust. Boom, where did this Annette go? I waved my hands emphatically and added, Itty-bitty atoms. It happens, you know.

I wonder, said Jerry. Spontaneous combustion. Aerobics, huh?

I'm thinking about it. Get my old body back, the petite thing Danny Beau fell in love with. All I ever wanted was for him to love me. He doesn't love me anymore.

Of course he loves you, Jerry countered. Don't be silly, Annette.

This Annette = silly. This Annette = imbecilic.

Not the way he used to, I answered. He used to really be hot for me.

Jerry bent over and kissed my cheek and said, Lucky Danny.

His moist peck ran like electricity to the true cause. Also thinking: *vera causa*. It had been so long since anyone—

I offered my mouth to him, but he was already watching the screen again. I crossed my legs, squeezed my thighs. Wanted him to kiss me hard—harder! I wanted him to love me. Sweet Jerry. Sweet understanding Jerry. Such sympathetic eyes. Images of myself and Jerry, kisses flashing through my mind. That's how far I had fallen. That's what life was doing to me. Making my brain as fat as my ass. I'm going on a diet, I said. Also thinking: at least I can do that!

When the movie was over, Keats opened his presents. The one from me was a baby duck in a yellow box wrapped with a silky black ribbon. The children went nuts over the duck, all of them grabbing for it. Trying to hold it. Trying to pet-it-kiss-it. I had to rescue the tiny thing and warn the children to be careful. For it was a delicate life they must not abuse. Keats knotted the black ribbon around the duck's fragile neck. Pulling the duck along, Keats said, Look, it walks like Charlie Chaplin.

That's its name! It's Charlie Chaplin! Don't touch him, he's mine! My duck!

The children ran to the back yard to watch Keats parade the duck up and down.

Peep, peep, peep, it peeped, sounding like a baby chicken.

Charlie Chaplin! Charlie Chaplin! chanted the boys and girls.

Jerry and I stood at the slider watching them watching the duck. I was very aware of how close he was. Timidly I glanced over my shoulder and said, It's been a lovely day, Jerry.

Also thinking: his smile is egging me on.

Pivoting and impulsively rising on my toes, I put my palm on his cheek and offered myself. He leaned forward, his lips brushing my forehead. I caught him. Forced our mouths together. But felt him recoiling. His hands, instead of pulling me in, grabbed my waist to push me away. In desperation I kissed him harder, lips and tongue churning. My belly searching for the telltale sign, feeling it happening leaning into it, rising to meet it.

No, he nearly shouted, backing away. Geez, Annette.

His eyes were blinking, his face flushed with confusion. What's this? What're you doing? he said. Then he laughed (an effeminate titter) and said, Hey, don't get dangerous on me, I'm only human. He patted me on the back like a pal. Whoa, would Danny Beau be shocked, huh?

I said, Nothing shocks Danny Beau. Also thinking: or your slut wife.

He looked away, looked out the window at the kids and said he couldn't do that to April. I love her, he said. I love you too, but not that way. Maybe if things were different I might, you know. But Danny Beau and April, golly, I couldn't betray them, Annette.

His words made me see a terrible truth: my husband had known all along I was a chameleon. Had Jerry wanted me, I would have done anything, opened every orifice like one of those whores in the porns. Jerry's gestures were gestures of kindness. Sympathy. Pity probably. But nothing to do with the lust I felt. At that moment my husband seemed as insightful as God. Danny Beau looked into souls. He saw me for real. Also thinking: what an awful woman am I!

I went to the bar. Mixed a martini. Lit a cigarette. And for a while I made small talk with Jerry. Something about Minnesota needing rain. Always cloudy but never any damn rain. The children were shouting outside. The plaintive peep of the duck could be heard.

Jerry went sheepishly home.

At least to me he looked sheepish.

Eventually the children went away as well.

Two martinis later, I found myself giggling at what I had done. What he must think of me! I shocked the poor boy! I remembered my tongue in his mouth, his tongue pushing back, ejecting mine. I wanted something moist. I wanted chocolate. I stuffed myself with leftover frosting. Who cared if I got fat as a pig? No one cared. I sucked pieces of hard candy, my cheeks bulging. I drank punch, spiking it with vodka. Stumbling to the slider I tumbled outside to see what my son and daughter were up to. Emily was kneeling by the roses petting April's cat. Keats was running round the lawn towing the duck.

Spitting out the candy I screamed at him: Keats! Keats! Look what you've done!

He stopped and looked at the duck.

Pointing to it I cried, Charlie Chaplin is dead, Keats! You killed him!

My duck! said the little brat, stamping his foot. My duck!

Sorrowfully I picked it up. Untied the ribbon and glared at my stupid son and was consumed with a smothering hatred. You little bastard, I said. You stupid little bastard! You and your red hair! Everything is your fault!

Astonished, Keats backed away. He and his sister scurried to the slider, slamming it behind them. I heard the lock click. A moment later, I saw their faces pressing against the glass.

Mommy's bad, I said.

(Everything dying in me. Everything crushed.)

A flash of something dark moved past my peripheral vision. I saw April's cat slinking toward the aviary. I saw the bird in the fichus flickering. I kicked off my shoes, threw them at the cat. He ran to the wooden fence, leaped on top, pausing, glaring. Eyes saying, Fuck you, bitch.

I might not be able to fix much else, I told him, but I can fix you!

Opening the cage I stepped inside waving my hands, telling her to run. Run, Tootie, run! The bird darted out the doorway. Climbed toward a hole in the sky. Became a dot … a work in progress fading.

Vanishing.

And the world turned. And nothing was ever the same. I climbed out of myself. Became this Annette. This Other.

Save As Document: Annette Annaba Walker.

A Mate for the Soul

Norman Ten Boom's eighth book of poetry, a collection called *Ecstasy: Love Poems for Lovers*, was a thin thing containing seventy short poems exploring themes of violence and love, May/December romance, morality and sin, war and peace, health and illness, time and death. Its cover depicted a cloudy border surrounding a blue, impressionistic flower opening its mouth as if to swallow the reader. Ray read the dedication inside to Norman's new love: *"For Annette my loving muse."*

"She completes me," Norman told Ray. They were sitting in the university cafeteria, Norman quoting his own poetry when he said: *"We are the same blood, breath and heart."* His chest swelling with ardor, ample chins quivering, he repeated, *"Breath and heart, breath and heart."*

"Yes, I remember that poem's spare simplicity," Ray told him.

"Every word a gem, a nugget," claimed Norman.

He played with his coffee cup, turning it in circles, staring into its opaque pit as he said, "Well, who knows if my collection will be appreciated? But I don't care because it brought me *her*. You see what I'm saying? I'm saying that without Annette, *Ecstasy* would never have been written. Nothing else matters." He laid a hand on Ray's forearm, squeezing it. "I'm saying that at sixty I have finally found my soul-mate."

Soul-mate.

Mate for the soul. One of those.

When *Ecstasy* debuted Ray had blurbed:

Norman Ten Boom confirms his place as one of the most distinctive poetic voices of his generation, a man musing on love as a value system that makes its own laws, its own occasionally mystical world of morality, where we would (if we could) embroider the one we love into the very valves of our heart.

Not very inspired, but it was the best Ray could do given his limited opinion of the book. Not that it mattered anyway. To Ray's relief, Norman declined to use the blurb. More prestigious names marked the back cover, all of them more or less putting Norman's name in the company of Pablo Neruda and Garcia Lorca.

"You're coming to my reading," said Norman, pointing a stern finger at Ray.

"Absolutely. Wouldn't miss it."

"You're in for a treat, my friend. You're in for a ride. I always put on a good show."

"Do you?"

"Let me tell you something, Ray. This is the voice of experience, so you better listen to me. At least ninety-eight percent of the audience will be women. Every one of them will believe herself a poet. They'll coo and swoon over what I read them. You watch, Ray, you'll see. I know these things." He was wagging his finger. "I'll have them creaming their pants. Watch how they cross their legs and jiggle their foot. You know what that means when a woman crosses her legs and jiggles her foot?"

"She's nervous."

"She's masturbating, Ray. She's masturbating. She's squeezing her vulva. She's milking it. It happens all the time. I've seen it for years, Ray, for years. This is what my poems do to women, the love poems and the violent poems. Love and violence gets them off. You believe me?"

"Whatever you say, Norman."

"Got to go teach my class, but let me leave you with this proverb: *Sour, sweet, bitter, pungent—all must be tasted.*" He wiggled his tongue as if licking a lollypop. Rising, he pulled a stack of flyers from his briefcase. "Here," he said, "pass these copies out to your classes."

The flyers announced:

ACCLAIMED POET NORMAN TEN BOOM WILL BE LAUNCHING HIS 8TH BOOK OF POETRY TUESDAY, MARCH 10 AT 10 P.M.
THE POET'S GROOVE,
BLUE NILE RESTAURANT
2027 E. FRANKLIN, MINNEAPOLIS

Even though Bobbi was having one of her bad days, she and Ray went to Norman's reading arranged by a local writers' group, consisting of a number of poets who got together monthly to critique each other's work and give advice.

The audience sat at dining tables in the restaurant. Inspirational Norman stood on stage, his white hair haloed, the key light intensity shimmering around him like a cape.

Accompanying his recital was a clatter of dinnerware, the soft prattling of the staff, double doors shuffling as waiters came and went. At the table closest to the stage sat luscious Annette Walker basking in Norman's glory. She kept stealing glances at Ray. He made sure he didn't meet her gaze, even though he wanted to gawk at her, trim as she was, her dark hair cascading, her crescent eyes magnetically bright—everything about her the opposite of Ray's overweight and unwell wife.

In spite of the setting and disturbances, Norman read beautifully—arm waving, lion's head jerking side-to-side, mane flourishing, his silky baritone rising and falling in full command of his language.

The lines he read were mostly *romantic*, but romance injected with something clinging like syrup to the syntax, words seeking to pierce the heart, devastate the soul, disconnect the rational powers and go with the emotional flow; yet, like the rabbit racing the tortoise, never quite getting where they wanted to go—the elevation of love as something spiritual, a higher calling. Ray's impression was that a love-struck, talented teenager might have written many of Norman's lines.

He had been right about women being ninety-eight percent of the audience, many of them cooing over each rendition, their oohs and aahs exhaling rapture, audibly longing for a love as sweet and true as the love expressed in Norman's lustrous tones. The applause at the end of each poem seemed on the verge of ovation, passionately urging Norman to give more vis-à-vis—Love *deep as the ocean, wide as the sky*. Ray watched them crossing and uncrossing their legs. Feet jiggledee-jiggling.

A number of his poems may have been as brilliant as Norman claimed they were. The ones exploring jazz, political chicanery, the treachery of warmongers, the lamented death of innocence at the hands of evil men, the blamelessness of children caught in the midst of unjustifiable wars—Ray thought those poems were insightful and a

175

pleasure to hear (though doubtfully linked with the theme of *Love Poems for Lovers*). Ray believed that Norman would have been more impressive if he had stuck to currently crucial topics, rather than mingle the reading with mushy matters: the soul in emotional throes, romantic revelations arriving in the form of a muse named Annette Walker:

> *I need these ethereal transports that set the nymph of*
> *uncontrollable cravings throbbing towards the beacon of*
> *beauty's passionate promises.*

Ladies all around Ray and Bobbi nodded their heads knowingly. So did some of the men. Annette sat starry-eyed and trembling over *a love like this seemed out of reach/ lost as I was in the slough of despond that aging brings.* Falling in love had restored Norman's youth and made him believe that soul-mates truly existed, for he had found such a mate—

> *in the form of an angel*
> *who treads so lightly upon the earth*
> *she never leaves a trace except in the softest sands of a summer beach*
> *where waves wash in greedily caressing the slender signs*
> *of immortal beauty passing by.*

After the reading, Norman and Annette drove over to the Poe's house for a late dinner. It was a cozy celebration to honor the new book, and also to make Norman feel that Ray and Bobbi believed he was as important a poet as he said he was—"Contemporary poets rank me as one of America's finest. Many say I am simply the best of my time."

(At the university library Ray had looked for critical opinions and studies that might verify Norman's statements, but couldn't find any. All eight books of his poetry had been published by small, independent presses, most of which had come and gone, except for Purity Press based in Berkeley, California, which still advertised that they published "where no publisher has gone before.")

The dinner started with champagne toasts to Norman's new book and to the new love of his life, lovely Annette Annaba Walker.

"*Slainte!*"

Ray lifted his glass and quoted Omar Khayyam. "*Drink! for you know not whence you came nor why. Drink! For you know not why you go, nor where.*"

"*In vino veritas!* boomed Norman.

Bobbi touched the wine to her lips. She didn't dare drink any of it. Under a daily bombardment of prescription drugs her liver had become a liability. Medical problems hadn't weakened her cooking skills, however. She served deep-fried shrimp and calamari hors d'oeuvres, followed by sole with lemon and caper sauce, tossed salad, saffron rice sprinkled with ground walnuts and fresh parsley, toasted sourdough dipped in olive oil. Wine and more wine. Three bottles by midnight. Ray knew he was drinking faster than usual, but he didn't care. He loved the warmth of the wine. Loved the background music, Antonio Vivaldi's *Four Seasons*, filling his ears, mixing with and partially muting the monologue flowing from Norman, whether his mouth was empty or full.

After the four of them retired to the living room, the guest of honor sat cross-legged like a pasha on one of the great cushions near the fireplace, Annette by his side. He told them he was going to get her first collection of poetry published. He was going to write the forward and arrange some readings. The book would be out in seven months, at which time Ray and Bobbi could give a dinner in Annette's honor.

"Yes, of course," they both agreed.

Annette's smiling eyes sparkled with gratitude. She stared at Ray and childlike stated, "You would do that for me?" He noticed a slight cast in her left eye and found it curiously alluring.

"I'd love to read some of your verse, Annette."

"Oh no, not yet, Ray," she demurred. "I'm still working on it."

"She doesn't need to work on it, it's perfect," said Norman, Annette looking down timidly, Norman stroking her cheek. "She writes like an angel I tell you. Don't you think she's beautiful? Have you ever seen such delicate cheekbones? Look at her eyes. How they always seem to be smiling. She could have been a model. No, no, I'm serious. Let me tell you something—I know these things! She and I met in another life where she was the model for Iphigenia in my *Cymon and Iphigenia*, 1848. No, I'm serious. Take a look at it sometime. It's her! Annette Walker to the core. Just hers is a darker complexion. She's Moroccan, you know. Aren't you, Annette?"

"Moroccan and French," she replied.

"*Your* Iphigenia?" quizzed Bobbi.

He raised an arm, pointing godward and declaring, "I was the Pre-Raphaelite John Millias in one of my other lives. Do you know how I know this?"

No one could say. Ray heard Annette whispering, "Reincarnation."

"Transmigration of the heart the instant I saw a Millias' painting," insisted Norman. "It was *Christ in the House of His Parents*. I recognized every detail. The carpenter's shop, the open door looking out on the sheep in the field, the figures of Mary and Christ that I had drawn. The very wood shavings on the floor were intimately familiar. That was just a year after I met the 1848 Annette and had her pose as Iphigenia. Later I used her in my *Ophelia*. Different hair, but the same face. Didn't I tell you that you and I were old souls, my darling?"

"That's what he said," she said.

"And I took her straight to the painting in *Nineteenth Century Paintings*. Didn't I, my darling? Didn't I just stick my finger in and flip the book open to the exact page?"

"It was uncanny."

"Preordained," said Norman. "And there you were. Wasn't it you?"

"If you say so."

"But the point is we are eternal lovers. Remember when we turned over the Tarot cards and we both got the Sun as the last card? We did! It's true! These are phenomenon we can't ignore. A higher power. It's spiritual! What else could it be?"

Bobbi's stare shrieking at Ray: *This man is woo-woo!*

(Ray, a mite tipsy, was thinking: *But how do we know these things? Maybe there are special beings that can see into the occult, see the Beyond where our many lives litter the scene like beads of dew waiting for sunrise. Hmm, maybe I should write that down.*)

He looked above Bobbi's head at the print hanging on the wall:

The White Calico Flower. Beneath the snowy flowers was an epigraph: *If winter comes can spring be far behind?* Ray had written the epigraph to remind himself of Percy Shelley's indomitable spirit. Whatever life threw at him, he took it and went on with his work. That's how Ray wanted to be, a doer, a survivor, and a believer in the mission of art and artists.

"Shelley believed that artists were the higher power," Ray offered.

"The unacknowledged legislators of the world!" said Norman, his finger a rigid wand. "The artist mirrors the future. He's often not conscious of what he is doing, he's a medium. *I'm* a medium, a clairvoyant who expresses the beauty of the earth by what I create. My words on paper outlast pyramids. Even if you bury my words they will rise again and conquer. You see what I'm saying? My words are immortal. Oh, my friends listen to me, listen to Norman Ten Boom saying yes to the universe, yes to life, yes to his desires, yes to the adrenalin rush of being in love. Yes to withering and rebirth."

"Yes to the risen Jesus," said Bobbi beatifically. "We die to be born in the bosom of the Lord."

There was an awkward pause.

Then:

"Listen to me," Norman continued. "The desire to live or die moves in cycles. If over time the cycle to go on living doesn't return to possess your heart, you are done for. You'll die and that will be it. Snuffed out completely. Your soul floating nowhere. That is why you must never commit suicide, you see? It's an irrevocable denial of life. It sweeps you out of the cycle forever. Annette and I, in our many lives, have always said yes to life. Yes, yes, even as we were dying. Isn't that right, Annette? We say yes we will, *yes!*"

Annette agreed.

When she glanced at Ray he fancied the cast in her eye was signaling a cross-eyed apology. Were his own eyes rolling? *Be serious*, he counseled himself. *Nothing is pure humbug. Truth as evanescent as snowflakes. Truth variable. Truth dependent on the true cause, vera causa. Today's fiction: tomorrow's truth. And who was it that said there is no science so hard as to know how to live this life well? Maybe Norman knows best. Say yes to withering and rebirth.*

"We read each other's thoughts all the time," insisted Norman.

"We finish each other's sentences. We are so in tune that if I have a panic attack from missing her so badly, she will always call me and say, 'What's wrong?' And one way or another she'll get out of the house and come over. Isn't that right, Annette?"

"Sometimes it's hard. My kids and my husband don't approve, of course. My kids call me bad Mommy. Mommy's bad ..." She grimaced. Looked away. "Well, never mind about that."

"They'll grow out of it," said Norman. "Right now they're behaving like selfish brats. They want their mother to stay with their father, but the man is a brute. Isn't that right, Annette? He has no respect for you as a persona, my darling."

"He has no respect for me as a persona," she echoed.

"He cheats on her. He's a doctor and he cheats on her with his patients. He uses her like his personal slave. She's everyone's personal slave. Those two kids clinging to her apron strings. Isn't that right, Annette? They want to own her body and soul. They don't want her to have an identity of her own. Isn't that right, Annette?"

"To them I'm only a wife and mother," she said, voice hollow, the thin line of her smile expressing martyrdom.

"I want to give her *freedom*!" cried Norman. "I want her to live with me and let me make her into a great poet. I'm her truest lover, friend, and mentor. Isn't that right, Annette?"

"He's helping me realize my potential," she said.

After a clumsy moment Norman added, "You know, I wake in the night and feel like I'm having a stroke. And I have to call her. But one night she didn't answer the phone." His eyes accused her.

"I switched my phone off by accident. It's an old habit," she explained.

"Tell them about your heart monitor."

"I had to wear a heart monitor," she said. "I was having pains in my left arm. My blood pressure is dangerously high and so is my cholesterol."

"See what I'm saying?" said Norman. "It's stress. She needs to get out of there before they kill her. They're killing you, my darling. That husband! You should hear some of the things he says to her. I won't repeat it, but if he ever said those things in my presence I'd break him in half!"

His eyes narrowing dangerously, "I can be dangerous," he said.

Ray believed him. Corpulent bearish Norman could probably do it, snap that husband like a piece of kindling. But another part of Ray was saying beware of a bragger, beware of braggadocio. As Norman stared at Annette, his eyes swimming with hunger hope uncertainty, something else was revealed—hatred? fear? a mixture? And what for? Because she wouldn't leave her family and move in with him? He was terribly lonely he had told Ray. He hated the silence at night in his apartment. Lying in bed, the silence. Waking at three. Staring at the ceiling in silence.

"All I want is what is best for her," he told them, stroking her hand, gripping it, kissing it. "It's not for myself that I do what I do. I do it all for her. I wrote *Ecstasy* for her. I didn't know it at the time, not until I hired her to edit it for me. The instant I saw her, I fell in love and the poetry started pouring out of me. Didn't it, Annette? Don't tell me about Romeo and Juliet or Ferdinand and Miranda. Did we not exchange eyes that first day, Annette? We looked at each other and I knew I had found her once more in the halls of time. But I didn't say anything. Not right away. I'll tell you this from my heart: a voice inside me kept saying, 'Your eternal lover has returned.' But I didn't act on it because I was married. Right, Annette?"

"He changed the title and completely rewrote the book. All these love poems were pouring out, and as I'm editing them I'm thinking how lucky his wife is."

"It wasn't until weeks later I showed her Millias' *Ophelia*," said Norman, "and beautiful bare breasted Iphigenia." He laughed hugely, his chins quivering. "The hairs on Annette's arms rioted as if those paintings were static electricity. Or maybe it was my standing over her. I saw my breath playing with her hair. I'll never forget it. She looked at me like I had popped out of a bottle. *Poof*, I was her genie." Norman threw his head back and roared. Then he pointed his finger and said, "Ah, but I knew. I *knew!*"

"What about you, Annette?" asked Bobbi. "Did you feel like he had popped out of a bottle?"

Annette massaged her lips with her index finger. Her eyes searching Bobbi's eyes. "I can't say exactly how I felt. Except I was confused. I remember thinking, did he really say that? Had he told me he painted the *Ophelia* when he was John Millias? We were sitting there flipping through the book, and Norman is pointing out painting after painting he had done. I think one was a Titian?"

"*Venus of Urbino!*" bellowed Norman. "I defy anyone to look at it and my *Ophelia* & *Iphigenia* and tell me they are not the same woman."

"You were Titian?" said Bobbi.

Norman's eyes protruded. Shiny as stainless steel. "Of course you don't believe me. But there is more in heaven and earth than found in your suffering *Jesus*, Bobbi."

"No, no, I don't mean to doubt you," Bobbi protested.

"Eternal lovers know nothing of time. Annette and I have had countless lives together, and that's all that counts. Right, Annette?"

Annette flexed her fist. "My hand keeps going asleep." She shook the hand. Norman grabbed it, rubbed it between his palms.

"So cold," he said, "for someone so beautiful and young. Hold it in front of the fire. It's those BP pills she takes. They make her hands and feet cold all the time. She's only thirty-five. This shouldn't be happening to her. It's the stress of her home environment this past three years, no doubt about that. She's been married fourteen years to that monster. This is what it's done to her. Broken her heart. It's criminal. Criminal! A philandering husband who accuses *her* of having a fling with the neighbor next door. He even said he wasn't sure their son is his! That's how twisted the bastard is. She's so cold, Ray. Build the fire, will you?"

The room was already overheated, but Ray put another log on and stirred the flames with the poker.

"It's really *hard*," whispered Annette, her voice almost choking. "My children have turned totally against me. They don't understand I fell out of love with their father when I was thirty-two and caught him having an affair. I stay in the marriage because I don't want them to be products of a broken home. I don't care what feminists say, children need both parents. Fathers are as important in their own way as mothers. I stay for my babies. I want so much to create a—"

"All he does is take advantage of her," blurted Norman.

"—secure home."

"He never helps around the house. She cooks and cleans and buys the groceries. She does everything. All he does is sit on his fat ass giving orders."

"Actually, his ass is slim. He's slim all over."

"The kids are the same way. A pair of parasites still sucking Mommy's titties."

"Norman!"

"Well, it's true, isn't it? Metaphorically speaking."

"They're young, they don't know anything yet."

Norman's eyes shifted as if looking for enemies. His round face was flushed, his jaws grinding. His heavy lips petulant and wet. His white hair falling forward from the sides like a curtain closing.

Flipping his hair back, he said in sympathetic tones that Annette was absolutely right. "And I will do everything in my power to help those two make their way in life. I can snap my fingers and get them into any number of first-rate universities. I know famous political and literary figures all over the world, and they will know you and your children because you'll be connected to me. A letter or phone call will open any number of doors, my darling. I'll take care of them just as lovingly as I'll take care of you. But the thing you've got to do is make your decision to *live*, not just *exist*. Pack your bags and come to me. Everything else will fall in place. I know these things! You've got to believe me. Do you believe in me, Annette?"

"This is the hardest decision I've ever had to make in my life."

"It will kill you to stay there. It will kill both of us. I'll die."

"Oh, Norman."

"No, I mean it! I don't want to live without you. I can't!" Norman grabbed his left arm, rubbed it. "You see?" he said. "Sympathetic pains! You see?" He dug in his shirt pocket. Pulled out a bottle of pills. "Some water!" he ordered.

Bobbi rose painfully. Waddled to the kitchen.

"Bring me an aspirin too," he said.

"What are you taking?" said Ray.

Norman was taking a blood pressure pill and Prozac. Bobbi brought him the aspirin. Annette hovering, her lips pinching with worry.

"I had a mild stroke," he said almost blissfully. "When my marriage was breaking up I was going cuckoo. I was dizzy all the time. I couldn't walk straight. I was walking into walls. I didn't know what was wrong with me. I'm telling my wife that maybe I'm having a stroke and she's telling me to get out of her house. The look on her face said she wanted me dead. You never know, you understand what I'm saying? *You never know who you can count on!* I mean I hadn't done anything wrong. Sure, I might have been attracted to Annette, but we hadn't done anything, had we, Annette?"

"I was editing his manuscript," she said. "We were together a lot."

"Well, we had to be! But the wife got jealous and started accusing me of having an affair. She said she wanted me out of her life. She said I had driven her crazy for five years. And here I am having a stroke and she won't lift a finger. I had to get the guy next door to drive me to the hospital. Have you ever heard of such a thing? A hard woman. A cold-hearted woman. Cold as January let me tell you."

"She's throwing you out and you're having a stroke?" said Ray.

"Lucky for me it was very mild. They fixed me right up. I've been exercising like mad ever since. Don't you think I've lost weight?"

"I can see that."

"Except for these poetic chins. I'll need surgery to get rid of them."

"He has such a sense of humor," said Annette. "My husband is just the opposite. No humor at all. He was raised on a farm. Farms are *dour*."

"I love life!" shouted Norman. "God, I love living. I want to live forever. Every day I wake up wondering what wonderful thing is going to happen to me. Yes, yes, and one wonderful day it was *wunderbar!*" He pointed at Annette.

"I had no idea what answering his advertisement would mean," she said. "I just wanted to get out of that miserable house and do something. And look how it has changed my life. Everything used to be so ... so predictable. Now it's like I'm riding a whirlwind."

"*Their life a storm whereon they ride,*" Norman quoted. "But what I was saying is ... when are you moving out, Annette? I'm getting old. We don't have time to waste."

Annette's finger was stroking her mouth as if zipping it. "It's so hard," she murmured. "So hard it seems impossible. I wish you wouldn't pressure me, Norman."

"But what can you expect, my darling? I'm a poet. Every fiber of my being throbs with love of you. I'm like an over-wound violin, an E string ready to break. I feel it right this moment getting tighter and tighter. Can't you hear my soul shrieking?"

"No."

"I can. It's driving me cuckoo. Listen, my darling, all I want is to protect you and nurture your talent. If it were possible I would take you to some island and keep you there writing poetry, while I waited on you hand and foot. I'd be your sex slave."

"Norman, now—"

"No! I mean it! I wouldn't hesitate a moment, not a second." He looked at Ray, his eyes imploring. "Do you see *now* how I love her? Do you *see*?"

"No ordinary love," Ray admitted.

"Shattering," Norman replied.

Annette closed her eyes. The fingers of her left hand kept flexing.

"Don't worry, I'll get you out of that house," said Norman. "If it's the last thing I do."

"What can I say to this wild man?"

"Between us there is no need for you to speak," he said. "It's always been obvious that you understand everything I say. I *see* things! And I know far more than what I see. All that matters is that we love each other. The rest can go to hell."

"I can't wish that for my kids, Norman. Don't ever ask me."

"Annette, listen to me. This will never come again. There is only now and the two of us. He who hesitates is lost!"

"Oh, can't we talk of something else? We're monopolizing everything." She looked at Ray, her eyes apologizing. "Poor you and Bobbi having to listen to this."

"No problem. What are friends for?"

"We make good sounding boards," said Bobbi.

Norman's finger was in front of Annette's face, admonishing.

185

"Life breeds excuses," he told her. "Rationalizations. And we miss our chances and they never come again. A hundred years from now no one will remember anything about us except the art we've left behind. With me you'll become an artist. Without me your family will pull you back into slavery. You'll be dying an inch at a time and as you're dying you will know that you've never really lived at all." He paused.

Words hanging. Fire crackling.

Annette stared at Ray again and said, "I suppose he's right." She glanced at the books lining the shelf behind the couch. "I've read your books," she told him, "all three of them. They're amazing. *So Much Heroism*. I think that's my favorite. The one about your father. The war and that stuff."

Norman said, "Ray had to be selfish to write them. He didn't let anyone get in his way. Isn't that right, Ray?"

"I guess so."

"A writer who doesn't live for his art is no artist."

"Is that how you feel, Ray?" said Annette.

Ray looked at his novels and wondered if they were products of selfishness. He decided they were.

"He's selfish," said Bobbi. Adding quickly, "But he has to be. Art comes first. Then his teaching. I'm somewhere down the line, God knows." She chuckled, her fat cheeks wiggling, her mildly warped fingers covering her mouth, her eyes sad slits nesting within orbs of what appeared to be aching flesh.

"That's all I have to say," said Norman. "Let's talk about something else. The reading went well, don't you think? I had them in the palm of my hand." He gazed at his palm serenely.

Annette was leaning forward, rubbing her belly round and round. Her other hand covering her mouth as she brought forth a burp. "Oh, excuse me!"

"As good an opinion as any," said Ray, chuckling.

"Take a Tums," said Norman. "You got any Tums, Bobbi?"

"Do I have Tums!" Bobbi reached in her pocket and pulled out a roll. "Keep it, honey, I've got plenty." Smiling wistfully Bobbi looked at Ray.

He knew what she was thinking. She was wishing he would say to her what Norman said to Annette. *All that matters is that we love each other. The rest can go to hell.* Ray loved dear Bobbi. But not the way Norman apparently loved Annette. Norman's way of expressing his feelings was far beyond Ray's unreliable heart. At times he wished he were different, wished he could let himself go the way Norman and Annette were letting themselves go, letting themselves have this passionate affair that didn't take their ages or marital status into account. But it wasn't possible for Ray. He was who he was. They were who they were: Norman and his poetry—his ego its own universe; Annette and her abusive husband, her ambitions bleeding outside the boundaries of a house that had become a prison; Bobbi and the numerous ailments that her cruel god refused to cure; and himself trying to find a *raison d'être* in the life of the mind, in the life of art. No one can be other than what he is. Everyone plagued by separation, everyone groping blindly, never making anything other than dreamy connections. Stay warm. Bless your reveries. Be humorous. Be cynical. Be decent. Be kind while you can. Keep babbling.

Babbling gets us through, thought Ray, inclining towards Norman, waiting for him to pick up where he had left off. His volubility faltering, making him instantly old now, chins hanging, lips hanging, cheeks hanging, hair hanging. Old man vulnerable-vulnerable. Ray nudged him, coaxing him gently while saying, "You had them in the palm of your hand."

Breakdown

One evening the phone rang and Bobbi answered it. Even though Ray was sitting in his easy chair on the opposite wall of the room, he could hear Norman Ten Boom's voice spewing panic. Annette wasn't answering his calls. He had called her six times in the last hour. "It's her husband!" he bellowed. "I bet he's taken her phone away. Maybe I should go over there and confront him."

Bobbi told him to calm down, give Annette time to get in touch. Certainly there was some reasonable explanation. She widened her eyes at Ray. He knew she didn't know what to tell Norman. Why had he involved them anyway? No business of theirs. *Cuckoo bastard.*

For at least forty minutes, the Dutchman circled the same territory: Annette loves him drastically and he loves Annette, but her family is doing everything they can to control her. The husband never stops berating her, *that motherfucker!* The daughter has said she can't talk to her because she is too disgusting at her age acting so juvenile. So thirteen-year-old daughter is giving mother the silent treatment now. Parents, mothers, uncles, cousins are all against the new Annette: Annette the poet; Annette the capricious; selfish Annette; ambitious Annette; Annette who cares about no one's feelings but her own. And so on and so forth ad infinitum, until he finally asked Bobbi to give Annette a call and see if she would answer. "Call me right back!" he commanded. He gave her the number and hung up.

Bobbi turned to Ray and said, "He kept cussing horribly. I couldn't believe it. He kept calling Annette's husband a motherfucker. What makes him think he can use those words to me, talk to me like that? Oh, I've got such a headache!"

Ray said, "I don't think he knows what he's saying. I mean, what if you couldn't get in touch with me? What if I didn't answer my phone when you called?"

"I wouldn't go crazy and foam at the mouth," said Bobbi. "I'd leave a message. I'd know that something had come up and you would get back to me as soon as you could."

"But we've been together for twenty-two years. Norman and Annette have six months in the saddle."

Bobbi looked dubious. "His tone was so disrespectful! I tried to be sympathetic, but really I felt like slamming the phone in his ear. He's awful. What should I do? Lord, all my joints are aching. I feel like I have the flu. Oh, my poor head. This arthritis! He thinks he has troubles, he should try being me for a day."

Ray told her she had made a promise to call Annette and she needed to keep her word. So she did. She called and they talked briefly. Annette said she had packed a bag and left her family. She was staying with her girlfriend Irene. She needed time to sort things out. There were so many voices in her brain she felt like she was exploding. Norman needed to leave her alone. Give her some space.

Bobbi understood completely.

When she hung up, she said, "Poor Annette. She sounds terrible. Her voice was squeaky, hysterical. Oh, I hate pain and suffering! Why can't everyone just behave?"

"Do you want me to call Norman and tell him?" Ray asked. Yes, she certainly did. So Ray called him and listened as Norman went berserk, yelling into the phone and cussing and saying he was going to kill that husband, that sonofabitch! Norman thought he might bring the daughter around. Maybe the son. They were both so young. But the husband was beyond reason and had more control over Annette than God Almighty, the selfish prick. Selfish motherfucker! On and on, words spewing from Norman's mouth, a more or less constant repetition of Annette's situation and what he, Norman, was going to do about it.

Ray took it for twenty minutes, but he was not a phone person and Norman's tirade was hard on the nerves. Ray's brain shut down along with his patience. He whispered to Bobbi, "This man is a piece of work best taken in small doses."

"All right, Norman," Ray interrupted. "It's getting late. I have papers to grade for tomorrow. We'll talk later, okay?"

"I don't mean to keep you," Norman said. And then he went on for another ten minutes. Ray wasn't listening. He held the phone away from his ear and rolled his eyes at Bobbi, who looked apprehensive.

"Got to go, Norman!" Ray shouted.

"Just one more point," Norman said. "That Irene woman Annette is with—I know her! I know what she's up to! She's a Lesbo living alone. She's for getting Annette to move in with her and cut me out of the action. That's what she's up to. A Lesbian! I know these things! Jesus, what a world we're living in! I'm too sensitive for this world. That's what being a poetic genius does to you. Makes you neurotic!"

Then he was off on a rant about Irene scheming to take over Annette's life. Five more minutes, Ray insisting, "Calm down. Take your Prosac. Get some sleep. I'm hanging up now."

"You're such good friends," Norman said abruptly, his voice fawning. "Friends like you are how I survive in this dog-eat-dog world. Your support means everything to this tender-hearted versifier named Norman Ten Boom. God bless you and Bobbi. I'll try to get hold of Irene. If only Annette would answer her phone! Just a little hug of assurance that's all I'm asking! If you love someone wouldn't you want to at least give them a hug? Doesn't she realize what she's losing in me? If the system wasn't rigged, Ray, I'd be called America's greatest living poet. She's losing America's greatest poet! Does she know that? Tell her, Ray. Get in touch with her and tell her, for God's sake! If she sticks with me, she'll be famous. I know these things. Mark my words, Ray, it'll happen. The critics will be forced to recognize me, you'll see. Everyone will see. Everyone who has ignored me will be goddamn sorry motherfuckers!"

When Ray finally hung up, he told Bobbi not to answer the phone if it rang again. Which it did five minutes later. The answering machine saying to leave a message and Norman saying, "Pick up, pick up, I know you're there! I called her and she refused to talk to me! Why aren't you answering? You can't be in bed already. I can feel you there, Ray. I can feel you listening to what I'm saying. You don't want to talk to me either, but for your own good you should, Ray. You should talk, Ray. Talk! I need it! Listen, Ray. Those who turn their back on me, bad things happen to them. No, it's true. No, no. Yes! Bad things. This spiritual force within me goes forth and there's nothing I can do about it! Remember this, Ray, I'm the Dutchman! I'm the Dutchman who is part bear! It's my fate. It's my destiny! I can't help it!"

"He's having a breakdown," whispered Bobbi.

Ray said, "You know what he's got? There's a medical term for it. It's called logorrhea. Diarrhea of the vocal cords. Obsessive chatter. I'm not picking up that phone. If I keep talking to him *I'm* the one who will be having the breakdown."

Norman went on until the machine ran out of recording space, his words clipped in the middle of "She had her chance to—"

To what?

To take charge of her life? To become the Dutchman's disciple? To have a grand love? To be famous? To tell the world to go fuck itself? To seize the day? To—

A week passed with no more calls from Norman. Ray did his best to avoid him, but one afternoon he was caught in the hall outside his office. Norman asking him to have coffee. They went to the cafeteria. At the center table beneath the overhead dome (sunrays falling like manna on their creatively coiffed heads) were four secretaries from the College of Arts and Sciences. Norman stared at them longingly as he said, "I wouldn't kick any of them out of bed, would you? Look at that: they're all wearing halos."

"So how are things with Annette?" Ray asked.

Norman shrugged. "To hell with her. She's gone over to the dark side. Let her have her puny little life. She's back with her husband. I knew she would. I *knew*. Never date a woman who has children, Ray. Listen to me. A woman with children will always put them first. She'll always choose them over you. You understand what I'm saying? But don't worry about me." His finger wagging sternly. "I'm a survivor. Nothing can kill me. Men like me are immortal. You knock us down, but we keep coming back again and again. We are the artists on the horizon beckoning, showing you the way to enlarge the meaning and purpose of your life. If you don't want to listen to us, that's *your* tragedy. Others will listen. In every incarnation we make a difference. Look at Chaucer. Look at Shakespeare or John Donne or Milton. Look at Da Vinci or Michelangelo. Titian. All of them ahead of their time just like me. All of them prototypes for posterity, for the art that follows after. Listen to me: what great artist is appreciated in his time?

I mean *really* appreciated? No one. None. Not really. They call us nut-jobs. Then later they berate themselves for ignoring us. Annette will wake up one morning and realize what she's done. She'll hate herself. She'll die wishing she had had the courage to leave him and come to me. What a lousy, two-bit future she has now."

"All those years with him," Ray said. "And raising her son and daughter. And her extended family going back to when she was born. It would be superhuman to break that off, to leave it all behind for what might not be possible. I mean seriously, Norman, is she great material? Great artists are forgiven, but no one else is. Is she really a poet? I mean *really?*"

Glancing at the table, the women basking, the women chatting, Norman sniggered and shook his head no. "Not a chance," he said. "Her poetry at best is mediocre. She could have been better if she had listened to me, but now it's too late. Nah, Ray, Annette will never amount to anything. She doesn't have that special touch poets need to be top notch. I have more talent in my little finger than she has in her entire body."

Again he stared at the women, their voices bubbling. "Women," he continued. "Let me tell you something. I once fucked three women in one day, one in the morning who I met for breakfast, another in the afternoon who stopped by my office and ended up bending over my desk, and the third one that night straddled me in her car. On the wall in the women's toilet on the fourth floor right here at this university some cunt once wrote: Norman Ten Boom is the best fuck! My fifth wife saw it and flipped out. 'What the hell you doing?' she said and I had to explain that I had no idea who could have written it or why. She didn't believe me. I wouldn't have believed me either, Ray. She packed up and moved out. She went all the way to South Carolina to work at Clemson. "You know why she went so far away, Ray?"

"She needed the job?"

"No, Ray. Because she knew if she stayed here I'd be too much of a temptation. I can have any woman I want, Ray. No, no, don't smile! It's true. Every semester I look over the new crop and pick one out and by the time the semester is over I'll have laid her. I've fucked at least fifty of my students, man. Once I start working on them their willpower wilts and they can't help themselves. It's mystical. It's charisma. They sense the spiritual power, the manhood, and they know I'm for real." He tapped his chest. "Me," he said, "I'm not tall and handsome. I'm fat and my hair is white and no woman should want to look at me. But what I've got going is my voice and my talent. I talk to them. I write them poetry. And I get them. They look into my eyes and it's a hypnotic experience." (His eyes *were* rather riveting, Ray thought. Pablo Picasso had eyes like that.) "They lose themselves in my eyes and voice and my Dutchman power, the bear in me. It's happened so many times I can't count. How many times you been married?"

"Just the one," Ray told him.

"Just Bobbi? That's it? I've been married many times," he said. "I was even a bigamist for a while. Every marriage was heaven until it became hell. Every wife was a muse that inspired me to write poetry. I look on every woman as a potential muse. She might be a gift from God. You believe in the spiritual world, in God, don't you?"

Ray shrugged.

"But you must!"

"Bobbi does. Bobbi is born-again."

Norman shook his head. Face expressing disgust. Then he said, "Let me tell you something. I once had twin sisters at the same time. You know what I did with them?" He closed his eyes a moment, his fleshy lips tightening into a sensual smile before saying, "I don't have to tell you."

"No problem," said Ray.

Again the finger pointed at Ray's face. "But I know you know. And I know you wish you had that kind of daring, that kind of stallion energy. When all is said and done I'll have lived ten lives to your one when this round is over. Remember what I'm saying. If love beckons, don't be timid, don't be shy. Take it, Ray, go with the flow. When the last page is written, you'll have that memory and you won't be sorry. I'm not sorry for anything. Fuck em! Fuck em all."

"She would have to be someone incredibly special," said Ray, "for me to cheat on dear Bobbi."

"Piffle," said Norman, waving his hand. "You're wasting your life, Ray. Minutes of your life ticking away never to return. Not me. Whatever time is left I'm using it." He stared at the nymphs bathed in the light of the dome and added, "Later, Ray."

Chair chafing, Norman stood and strode towards his prey, their eyes luminous watching him coming for them. Expectant. His arms opening as if to gather all four unto him. "Dear ladies," he intoned, "what radiance, what pulchritude you secrete, what loveliness shining in the midst of darkness—this dark, cacophonous world." Light glittered around their beaming faces—light emanating from the Dutchman, the clarity of the air.

Obsession

When I get home that night, Ray's kisses still on my lips, I take my clothes off and go to bed, not bothering to shower, not bothering to remove my makeup, or brush my teeth. I want to wallow in my organs. I want to review the kisses over and over, the vodka-mouth, the sucking lips, tongue touching. Musk of Ray Poe.

I keep the lamp on and stare at his portrait. I read the titles on the spines of his books. I wonder for the umpteenth time what it would be like to be married to a man so gifted and handsome, so intelligent and obviously wise, obviously kind. Everything dull and drab would vanish, would be transformed into something new and vibrant with Ray in my life. It doesn't matter that he is eighteen years older. Norman was twenty-five years older and that hadn't mattered.

Also thinking age: only a number.

But before anything more can happen, Ray will have to get rid of that wife, that Bobbi. And I will have to get rid of Buddy Kerr, my current boyfriend and employee. I wonder if I will miss his beautiful body. Possibly, but not his narcissistic prancing in front of the mirror, his lying back on the bed and wanting me to suck him. At first it had been wild and exciting, like making love to a movie star. But now it's boring and I can hardly work myself into a passion when he wants me. Ho-hum, I'd rather sleep. Everything about him: too familiar. His conversation running the gauntlet from me to me. Look at my trophies. Look at my six-pack belly, how narrow my waist is, I'm a perfect V from waist to shoulders, have you ever had a man last as long as I do? I have to admit I haven't. But more often than not as he pounds away at me, I will be thinking of my first love sweet sybaritic Hamlin. Oh, to be that young again, everything fresh, everything new and on fire. Also thinking: Jesus, get it over with, Buddy! Also thinking: With Ray Poe it will be different. It's his mind not just his body I want. But I do look forward to that insatiable honeymoon period I've had with all my other lovers. I wonder how long on average couples sustain those wild, uncontainable cravings?

Danny was fun and inventive. He had satisfied me for the first ten years of our marriage. Until he started accusing me of sleeping with next-door Jerry. And all the while Danny is sleeping with Jerry's wife April! What a time that had been! The experience cracking something in me, that innocence about men lost forever. Losing it? Like losing your virginity, no more *virgo beata*. Men are not to be totally trusted. Always keep something in reserve in case the relationship sours. Learn to shut down quickly, stifle emotion, cast a cold eye on what had once been fiery—thrillingly so. Also thrillingly *nasty*.

The marriage became a grinding agony. Near the end I couldn't even stand to look at Danny's face. A face I had once thought handsome. How could I have ever sucked those sarcastic lips, his arrogant prick? The sound of his voice abused my eardrums. His eyes mocked me, belittled me. So why did I stay as long as I did? Who remembers? Who knows the why of anything? For the kids. For the sake of the kids. How many women spend their lives living a lie for the sake of their children? How many men? What a muddle we make of it.

And yet, here I am preparing to make even more of a muddle. A married man is not to be trifled with. Breaking up a family is dishonorable, in some cases criminal. Maybe evil. But whatever it is, I am determined to have Ray Poe.

Also thinking: Wife Bobbi be damned.

My thoughts stay on Bobbi and the time we met after Norman Ten Boom's poetry reading. I had felt incredulous that such a tub could be Ray's longtime wife. She was pretty enough, but what a lugubrious body! A body not good enough to please him was my opinion. Not good enough to hold his attention for five seconds. Bobbi didn't deserve him! A woman who won't take care of herself any better than that is just asking for it. I don't buy the excuses. Arthritis. Acute anxiety. Slow metabolism. Etcetera. Bobbi might be sick, but she shouldn't have let herself go so utterly.

Also thinking: Frankly she's repulsive.

"I love eating, but I refuse to get fat," I tell Ray's portrait, his smile the smile of a kind man mellow. A man with a good heart. I can see it in the radiance of his eyes, in the brilliance of his entire countenance. The soul of an artist. Which is what I have also.

Leaving my husband's control taught me that there is more to Annette Annaba Walker than just a pretty face and a nubile body. (Is thirty-eight still young enough to be nubile?) My love of reading has filled up a spiritual well that is overflowing into brilliant verses. I write at least one poem a week. I don't show them to anyone. I will show them to Ray when he becomes my lover.

Also thinking: He will edit them and tell me where to get published.

Norman the Dutchman had told me there was no doubt about my talent. All I needed was "time in the saddle." His time in the saddle with me had been unexpectedly fulfilling. For a man of sixty he had been surprisingly vigorous. I remember him pumping away for all he was worth, trying to make me climax, which I did occasionally, though I also faked it when I was ready to stop. I might have been able to love him if he hadn't talked so much. He would never stop talking! Drove me crazy! I had wanted to tell him to let some silence into the room once in a while! The barrage of words had driven every nascent thought straight out of my head. I hadn't been able to write a single poem when I was having my affair with him. Everything he read of mine had been a product of the early years with Danny: Dan you are the man holding my hand/The only love of my life/ As we walk along the sand/ And absorb the roar of the ocean/ And the waves pounding the land like a potion.

Dan never liked anything I wrote. I know now that Norman had faked his admiration, telling me what I wanted to hear.

Also thinking: Those years with Danny had given me a tin ear.

Part of my lack of invention during the affair with Norman had been the by-product of guilt, the sneaking around, the painful lying. The stress on my nerves had given me heart palpitations and high blood pressure. My doctor couldn't understand what was happening. "You've always been so healthy," he told me. "What's going on in your life, Annette?" "I wish I knew," was what I had answered.

After I broke off with Norman and stayed with Irene for a while, the poetic impulse came back little by little. The palpitations, the blood pressure problems faded. But they returned when I went back to my husband and children.

Again the writing stopped. I started drinking and taking Xanax in order to sleep at night.

My leaving home had been a wakeup call for Danny. He had never believed I would actually leave him. I returned to a subdued husband. I felt as if I had broken his spirit, and, truth be told, I didn't give a damn, didn't care that he was inordinately kind, didn't yell anymore or try to make me feel inadequate, hopelessly defective. He no longer accused me of having affairs. He bought little gifts, gave me candy and flowers. Even wrote me some clumsy poems. He tried very hard to become a new man, a man who could win my love back. But by then none of it mattered. Repulsive kisses. When he made love to me the feel of him inside, the smell rising between us was nauseating. The marriage was irrevocably shattered, but I hung on for another year before leaving and filing for divorce.

Living with Irene again, I explored a side of myself I had vaguely known existed whenever I watched women making love in the porns. Irene was a good listener and undemanding. Many nights we went to sleep in each other's arms. When we made love, I was the aggressor. Irene lying back passively receiving. Poems poured out of me, all of them sub-textually Lesbo:

My tongue swims
Out to taste
The wick of your soul
Your scent lingering

On my lips
Becomes the bouquet
Of dawn
Every blessed morning
Lying here hand in hand
The aroma of light
Growing in my heart
An intimate reverence
Savored.

I was writing stories as well, even planning a memoir based on my life with Danny Walker—how naïve I had been, how immature, how easily fooled. A simpleton for nearly sixteen years, fawning on a husband unfaithful to me, while also nurturing and spoiling two little vipers who ultimately broke my heart. Children, who needs them? Not this Annette.

Danny had phoned my mother and played the aggrieved husband. She took his side, as did everyone, agreeing that I had lost my wits, was mentally unbalanced, needed professional help. "Go home to your family," Mommy kept telling me. "You're going to lose those children, Annette!" And all I could think at the time was *so what?* The little monsters had been against me for years. They were tools of their father who had used them to make my life miserable. I was sure they were happier without me. And if not? Tough-tittie.

"You won't have Annette to kick around anymore," I hear myself murmuring, thinking of a quote I had read in a Richard M. Nixon biography, Nixon saying he was getting out of politics. And then he went on years later to become President, one of the most reviled in memory, second only to that son of a Bush the country had to deal with, the war monger warrior wannabe who left a shattered nation behind when his term was over. Wrecked everything, that imbecile! That fool! Can't think about him without wanting to vomit.

Turn the page, Annette. What happened next?

The divorce settlement had given me every other weekend with Keats and

Emily. The judge told me it would have been more if I hadn't so obviously abandoned them. He called me selfish and unnatural. Two adjectives that stuck to my continuing story. Whenever I talk to my mother on the phone or go over to her house for dinner or meet her at a restaurant, the judge's words will find their way into the conversation. Selfish and unnatural. Only a selfish, unnatural mother wouldn't be torn to pieces inside over the loss of her children. "You've always been willful, Annette. You've always made sure you got your way, no matter who pays for it."

Mommy still thinks Danny is a prince. "What a devoted father. What a loss to any woman, but especially to my daughter. If he was as malicious and unkind as you say, Annette, I know you, and my guess is you drove him to it. I've never seen him be anything other than a perfect gentleman."

"And you wonder why I hardly ever call or come over," I told her, she who is always there in my mind, a dominate force whose reason for being seems always to find fault with her only daughter. I believe my father's death at 59 was at least partially self-willed. Death being the only way of getting away from his wife *forever.*

What is right? What is bad? Who is wrong? No one is wrong. Feelings cannot recognize wrong when it comes to loving or hating. The feelings tell you that you're alive and need to make the most of every opportunity that might enhance your life. You might die in your sleep tonight. Yes, maybe a sudden sleep-death is already programmed into you. The Damocles Sword of genetics hanging over you every second. Maybe you are doomed to die early.

Also thinking: *No time to waste!*

I climb out of bed. Put my clothes on. Grab a pen and a yellow sticky and write a short note to Ray: *His kiss, his kiss — impossible!*

I get in my car and drive to his house. I stick the note to his windshield.

Staring at the house, I wonder in what room he is sleeping. Is he still awake, maybe lying in the dark thinking of me, thinking of the drinks and the kiss in the bar tonight? I tiptoe up to one of the bedroom windows. I remember the dinner to celebrate the launch of Norman's book, the conversation that he dominated, the growing coldness towards him I had felt that night. The egomaniac! The growing interest I had felt for Ray Poe, the distaste for bloated Bobbi. I recall that both Ray and Bobbi have offices in their home. Do they sleep together? I can't imagine them sleeping together. Having sex? Not impossible, but definitely improbable. How can a man rise to the occasion lying next to such a whale? Touching the cool glass, I tap it with my fingernail. I am breathing hard (actually panting), my heart hammering. Mouth so cottony I can't swallow. What if he comes to the window? What if he opens it and I crawl in, crawl into his bed into his arms? What if?

What are you doing, Annette? What are you doing, girl? This is beyond crazy. This is cockeyed, this is sick. This is what some love-struck teenager would do. Get away before someone spots you and calls the police! I scurry to the idling car. Put it in gear, drive away. A plan forming in my mind, a way to attract his attention, a way to get what I want. I know I can do it. I know he wants me. His kiss told me he wants me. Also thinking this is my rendezvous with destiny and anyone in my way doesn't stand a chance. Whatever I have to wreck I'll wreck. Come what may that man is mine! Also thinking: *fait accompli!*

    Save As Document: Annette Annaba Walker.

Bodies in Motion

In bed with her, watching her sleeping, Ray focused on her loose mouth while recalling the note she had stuck to his windshield: *His kiss, his kiss—impossible!* His first thought had been that she was a *stalker*. Now here she was, so it must have been true. The sun rising, light filtering into the room. Exposing her body, which for some strange reason made him think of *Rhapsody in Blue*. Ray wondering what to do, wondering if she expected him to go on seeing her, or had this been a one-night stand? He was pretty sure she got laid a lot. He recalled her telling him about Buddy Kerr, the two of them running the fitness center in Minneapolis. Two beautifully-tuned bodies. Sure they have.

Ray slipped out from under the sheet and stood at the window peeking through the curtains at the early morning street, the houses arranged like steppingstones all the way to the bottom of the hill. He had another day before he needed to be in Bellingham. He would spend the time with her, why not? What his wife didn't know couldn't hurt her.

An odor of stale sex issued from Annette's mouth. The sight of her lying on her side gave him conflicted feelings. Tenderness. Lust. He wished he had the talent to paint her, the curving hip, the tapering legs and feet, the glossy toenails. My God, had she really given all this to him last night? Passionately again and again. She had told him she was open to anything. He revisited kissing her, lingering a long time between her legs. And then sliding up and in. And thinking, That's me inside her! Inside a woman named Annette Annaba Walker. My mouth full of her.

He touched himself and wondered: How can this be at my age?

When he kissed the side of her neck she rolled onto her back.

"I can't believe it," he whispered. "I don't know what's come over me."

"The same thing that's come over me," she said. "I love you, Ray. I've loved you for ages and I knew it would be this way and I knew we would fit and I knew when I read your books that I had found the love of my life, my soul-mate."

"Soul-mate," he repeated, remembering what the Dutchman had told him about Annette being *his* soul-mate. Ray wanted to believe that soul-mates really existed. And if you have found your soul-mate, you are destined to make love to her. It had to happen because if you have found your soul-mate, making love to her is not the betrayal it might be for others. If you didn't make love to your soul-mate, well, *not* making love to her would be a crime against nature.

"Therein lies the sin."

"What?"

"Impediments," he said. "Inhibitions."

Light from the window glancing off her forehead. Her eyes full of desire.

Later that day, hunger drove them to shower and dress and walk down the hill to Winslow. They ate Mexican soup at a place called *Isla Bonita*. Afterwards they went past Eagle Books, where she had been waiting for him last night. Like a panther ready to pounce.

"Ambushed."

"What did you say?"

"I'll never forget this bookstore," he said.

"Are you saying I ambushed you? Is that what you mean?"

"I mean it in a nice way," he told her.

"I *meant* it in a nice way too."

"You had an agenda."

"Yes, that's true."

"*Veni, vidi, vici.*"

"Does that make you angry?"

"Not at all."

"But you're saying I conquered you, seduced you."

"Didn't you?"

She stared at him as if trying to read his mind. "Are you mad at me?"

"No."

"Do you want me to leave?"

Did he want her to leave? Hmm. Yes and no.

"Am I making your life too difficult?"

He didn't know what to say. Difficult? Yes! But at the same time sort of spicy. Difficult but lively. Ray was full of adrenaline. He wanted her in his arms again. They had less than twenty-four hours before he would take her to the airport and himself to Bellingham.

"Tomorrow I've got to be in Bellingham to continue the tour," he said.

"You didn't answer my question, Ray."

"What can I say?"

"Are you regretting me now?"

"Am I regretting you? Yes … and no. I regret I've betrayed my wife. Never done that before. Not in twenty-five years of marriage. But I also regret I'm not free and can't be open and not feel guilty and not hate myself for being what I am. For being a cliché, you know, a man."

Annette was pouting. She folded her arms. Walked away. He put his hands in his pockets and followed. They left downtown and entered a street close to the shore line. The street was full of houses that looked Scandinavian. There were lots of evergreens and hardwoods. The sun was shining. The cold air smelling of seaweed, salty ocean. Out there far away was Asia, Japan, China. Exotic lands. Anonymity. A new life. Annette had her tennis shoes on, her woolly white socks, her black jeans so tight they look painted on. Her leather jacket was buttoned up all the way to her chin. Dark hair shifting in the wind like a restless mammal. A ferret.

"I don't want this to be the end," she said, finger rubbing her mouth thoughtfully. "I can't let it be over." Soft words, hard undertones. The cast in her left eye gave her a dreamily cross-eyed appearance. Strangely attractive. The bimbo allure.

He wanted to get away from her. He wanted his old life back intact. He wanted to get the tour over and return to his boring routine at the university. Prolonging things would only make it harder to break up later. For surely there was no way he could continue having an affair with her. A quick, clean break right now, that's the best thing, he told himself.

"Annette—"

"I feel like crying," she said. "I feel like I've said something wrong. Look at your hands in your pockets. You don't want to touch me. You

207

won't hold my hand."

He took her hand. "You haven't said anything wrong, Annette. No, no, I was just … preoccupied." He looked around helplessly. Wondering what else to tell her. Through a gap in the houses he saw the choppy, white-capped water. Water once known only by coastal Indians. Water that had been slapping the island's shores for millions of years. And now he and she were watching it and soon both of them would be gone forever and something *other* would be gazing upon this little bay of the Pacific. What did their tiny lives matter?

"These steep-roofed houses make me think of home," he told her. "They belong near a nice, deep Minnesota lake like Big Winnie or Lake of the Woods. I'd like to have one, wouldn't you?"

She gave him a teary smile and said, "I'd like to live in that one," pointing at one of the houses, white with yellow trim, fir trees hovering like guardians. "I'm sick of Minneapolis. I want to stay here."

"I'd stay if I could," he told her. Did he really mean it? Did wavering Ray want to open a new door? Be younger? Start anew? Go with the flow wherever it took him?

With this woman?

Well …

Working their way back to the motel, they went to the room. When they lay down for a nap, she clutched his hand in hers and fell asleep. Later, Ray woke surprised to find that she was still holding his hand. Sunlight fading. Curtains gray. Traffic noise negligible. A foghorn moaning as if in pain.

Where should I be? he asked himself. Yes—far away from this immoral behavior.

The next morning he drove her to Sea-Tac Airport to catch her plane. He parked the rented car. Walked her inside. Waited while she checked in at the counter. *Almost over* he kept telling himself.

"All set," she said.

"They won't let me through security without a ticket," he said.

"I know." She had his hand again, impulsively kneading it. "Will you call me?"

"Sure I will."

"Tonight?"

"Tonight? Sure. What time?"

"I close the center at ten. Home by ten-fifteen."

"Ten-thirty then."

"Will you really call me?"

"Yes."

"Honest?"

"I said I would, Annette."

She pulled him aside near the stairs and stood against the wall. She hugged him and whispered, "I'm not a whore, you know. I've never done this before."

Yeah right.

"I've loved you a long time, Ray Poe. You just didn't know it until you gave that reading in St. Paul. When I saw you were going to be there, I took it as a sign and I said it's now or never. And you were every bit as wonderful as I knew you'd be. God, if you could have felt how fast my heart was beating when we went for drinks afterwards and I kissed you. I swear I almost fainted."

"You were looking like someone needing a kiss."

"Not just any kiss. Yours. Only yours."

How long ago was that? Just a few weeks? Was it October? So actually *he* initiated things, not her. Taking her for a drink because? Because she had asked him. Because he had wanted her to. And so Annette flying to Seattle was his fault. He had an impulse to run, to hide. To get rid of her. To be the marvelous, brilliant man she mistook him for. To take her back to Bainbridge Island and fuck her until they both churned into butter.

Her breath caressed his ear as she said, "I've been waiting for you all my life. All these decades, I've been feeling this horrid void and praying you would come along one day and fill it. And now that you have I can't lose you. I don't care about your wife. I don't care what anyone does or says or anything. No one on earth can love you the way I do. When you've fallen in love with a dream and then that dream comes true, you are no longer accountable. There's no morality greater than love. Love rules without rules."

The term *soul-mate* flew through his mind again. He heard Norman Ten Boom the Dutchman saying: "I have finally found my soul-mate, Ray."

Soul-mate.

Mate for the soul. One of those.

And soon after finding his soul-mate she broke up with him. Broke Norman's sixty-year-old heart. Gave him a nervous breakdown. You don't want that, Ray. She's fickle.

She kissed him, wetting his face with her tears. Her mouth pushed into his neck as she said, "You believe me. I know you do. You know that I honestly love you and because I honestly love you what I'm doing is not evil. In my wildest dreams I never saw myself as a home wrecker. But if I am. Well, then I am."

"Shh," said Ray, "Shh."

"I should never have married Danny, you shouldn't have married Bobbi. We both wanted something deeper in our lives. More fulfilling. You fell into your marriage, I fell into mine and from there we just went along with things. When my marriage fell apart, I saw what a mistake it had been. He never really loved me. Maybe I never really loved him, not the way I love you, not with a love I couldn't control. Forgive me for hurting Bobbi. Forgive me for hurting you. I can't help myself. Do you know how *much* I love you!"

He looked into her eyes and saw fear and wonder and pleading. Ray had no words. He held her tight for an instant. Then got out of there. What kind of ghastly emotion was this? His heart throbbing in his throat. The glass doors swishing open. He ran across the street towards the parking lot. A horn blaring.

"Watch it!" someone yelled. "You wanna get killed?"

In Bellingham he stayed at a Holiday Inn. In his room he turned on his laptop. Sat there staring at a cratered moon on the screen, a dry dead scene that filled him with awe and wonder. Why did astronauts stop going there? We should have been on Mars by now.

He put his fingers on the keyboard. He wanted to write about Annette, but didn't dare. What if he died of a heart attack? Bobbi would be given the computer. She would search through his journal for his final words.

Oh, my God, Ray! Was this one of your stories or did it really happen?

So sorry, Bobbi.

She would never get over it. Ray didn't want to be remembered as a cheater, a liar. A man who couldn't control his appetites.

He started typing:

I'm better than that.

No, you're not, Ray.

Yes, I am. I was ambushed. I lost my bearings.

Listen to him. Get real, Ray. You're not the first, and you won't be the last. You're one of millions. Of billions.

I think about her all the time. It's like I'm caught in a whirlpool. I want to swim out, but I can't.

You are so screwed.

Maybe I should go hide in Canada. Maybe there I could learn to write again. My mind feels like particleboard. I blame it on stress. This month will go down as one of the least productive I've ever had. I'm so stupid. Old and stupid. A stereotype. She'll kill me, you know.

You're not old. You're only fifty-five! Fifty-five is the new forty-five!

I feel sixty-five.

Ray, listen, the future is smoke and mirrors. Live while you can, Ray.

The word love feels dark, touching dark spots in my heart, a night journey. It's not a word offering goodness and joy. Love is joy's opposite.

Ray, it won't come again like this. You pass it by, you've passed it forever.

Who am I, anyway?

You're Ray Poe and you're on a roll.

She is lovely, isn't she?

The fact that beauty exists is proof of the soul.

This is really going to cost me.

Come on, Ray, she's worth it!

Oh, leave me alone.

Pressing Delete, Ray shut down the computer and picked up the phone and called his wife.

"It's you," she chirped. "How are you, honey?"

"Tip-top. How about you?"

"It's been the week from hell. Rain every damn day. All the leaves are gone and my arthritis is killing me."

As Ray listened to the litany of her ailments, his heart shuddered. His mood became more and more dour. Gloom and despair trickling through his frayed nerves. "Jesus, Bobbi."

"Yeah, I'm falling apart, honey." Incredibly, she laughed. And then said, "I wish you were home, honey. I miss you so."

"Yes," answered Ray dully. "I miss you too."

"So this reading tonight is your last?"

"This is my last."

"So, you'll fly back tomorrow?"

"Hmm."

"I'll be so glad to have you home!"

"Yeah."

"You okay, honey?"

"Sure I am." Then to change the subject he said, "So what was the column you wrote today?"

"Want me to read it to you?'

"Read it to me, yeah."

There was a short pause and then she said: "This letter is from a woman who suspects her husband is having an affair. He goes into the backyard and paces while talking to someone on his cell phone. He comes home late from work and says he's swamped and is trying to catch up. She calls his office and gets the answering machine. He tells her he unplugs the phone so he won't be disturbed. She found an empty blister pack of Viagra when she emptied the trash. When she asked him about it he said he had been embarrassed to tell her he had been using it for months."

"He's toast," said Ray.

"Something else," said Bobbi. "Five years ago she found a phone number in his coat pocket and the name Pam written above it. She called Pam and everything was exposed. And now this! And what do you do at her age with half-grown kids and bills to pay? Should she confront him again? Or should she keep her mouth shut and see if he comes to his senses? Maybe it's just a fling? A middle-aged crisis thing. P.S. Last week he bought a Porsche."

Ray chuckled. And said, "So what advice did you give her?"

"Dear Downhearted in Bloomington: Your husband, a convicted adulterer, bought a Porsche, got a prescription for Viagra, stays late at the office and paces the backyard while talking on his cell phone to you don't know who. Pour all those acts into a fish bowl and stir. Then hold the bowl up to the light and what will you see? You will see something fishy. You should buy a net and catch that guppy before things get more out of hand. Don't pretend an affair isn't happening. You know it is and you know you've got to deal with him, or what he is doing will destroy your family and may even destroy your faith in God. If your faith is destroyed, all you'll have left is a one-way ticket to hell. Jesus loves you and will give you the strength to do what you need to do. First thing to do is open your Bible to Matthew 26, paying particular attention to verse 39: My Father, if it be possible, let this cup pass from me; and verse 41: The spirit indeed is willing, but the flesh is weak. Reading the entire chapter will remind you of how our Lord suffered but did not break. And now say after me: I believe once again, not mindlessly as a child but with a woman's knowledge that a man's weakness is at home in his flesh. Next, you must go to your pastor and the two of you must interface with your husband. Tell him you know he's being unfaithful. Tell him that if he wants to keep you he must start going to a Christian therapist specializing in sex addiction. Enlist your church community in helping your husband stay on the true path. In time his good behavior will become a habit. I am sending you the name of a therapist who has worked miracles with wayward husbands and wives. Faithfully yours, Bobbi Poe."

He heard her wheezy breathing and thought of her sister battling emphysema. Health issues always plaguing those girls. His own health deteriorating too. A heart valve leaking fluid into his lungs when he was sleeping. A problem that would only get worse if he didn't have an operation.

"Poor bastard," he said.

"Poor *her*, Ray."

"Yes, yes, of course."

"Is my advice good?"

"You bet. Just what she needs to hear, I'm sure."

"I love doing this, honey. I know I'm doing God's work."

"Yes, you found your calling, Bobbi."

"Jesus and Ecstasy are one."

"Gotta go, Bobbi. Time to read to the multitudes."

"I love you, Ray."

"Love you too."

"Don't forget to come home to me, honey. Don't forget."

"Won't be long now. Goodnight, Bobbi."

"Call me tomorrow before you leave?"

"Sure thing."

At Village Books, Sandy, the store manager, a sweet smiling doll with dimples and wire-rimmed glasses, introduced Ray by reading a review of *Bodies in Motion* in the *Bellingham Herald* done by Ara Taylor. Taylor called the novel "the latest great effort by Minnesota author Ray Poe." She made parallels between the bodybuilder in the novel and the former governor of Minnesota, Jesse Ventura, and said that in Ray Poe ran a "current of eccentricity that smacks of comic insanity." She closed by saying: "Graphic lewdness aside this is one gorgeous tale full of wickedness and fun."

Sandy gestured toward Ray and said, "Please help me welcome a brilliant comic novelist, Ray Poe."

Ray stood at the lectern, opened his book and read a fictionalized section based on his mother's decline into senility. About halfway through he realized that he was supposed to be a comic novelist and there was nothing funny about what he was reading. Twelve pairs of eyes were gazing at him, all of them elderly except for dimpled, smiling Sandy. Ray suspected the old ones were bused over from a retirement home he saw just as he turned off the freeway: LUXURY RETIREMENT LIVING. They were listening politely, looking intense or puzzled at times, as if they were trying hard to understand what he was saying about the old woman named Olivia who was fading into the pages of a paperback western she was reading. When Ray described her hopping on a horse and riding toward the sunset, one of the old ladies in the audience said, "What's so funny about that?"

"It's not meant to be funny," answered a man sitting in the back row.

"She said he was gonna read comedy!"

"Sorry," said Ray. "There are parts that are funny. I should have read one of those."

"I don't wanna hear about no old fart hopping on a horse and riding off. It don't make sense! Can you see me or her or him hopping on a horse at our age?"

"It's all in her imagination," said Ray, forcing a smile. "She is separating herself from reality by becoming a cowgirl in the western she's reading. It's her escape, you see. We all try to escape don't we when things go bad?"

Ray's vision blurred. He stared at the words on the page but saw only fragments.

The old man in the back row spoke up again. "The mind is its own place and can make a hell of heaven, a heaven of hell."

"Yes!" said Ray. "That's it exactly. Thank you, sir. Thank you."

"I used to teach Milton," the old man said. He ran his palm over his hairless pate. "It's all still here, but you get to a certain age nobody gives a damn what you know. If you can hop on a horse and ride off like your ole gal in that book, well, more power to you. Go on, finish what you started." He bent his eyes on the woman who said the words made no sense. "And Melissa, just keep quiet if you don't understand. Let the man tell his story."

"All I said was—"

"Melissa!"

"All right, all right."

Ray heard someone grumbling that Melissa always had to be the center of attention. He cleared his throat, coughed. Finished the passage:

The land rolled peacefully in front of her as she and Old Paint moved slowly toward the rusty horizon. And the song from Dr. Zhivago sang somewhere my love inside her head and her jingling spurs kept time with the tune and the rhythm of the horse's hooves plodding over the sage-laden prairie leaving all her sins forever behind her.

"Thank you for coming," Ray said, closing the book as the people applauded. He stepped away from the lectern quickly, so no one could ask him a question. The dimpled manager caught up with him at the door.

"Beautiful," she said, holding onto his arm. "I want you to know that *Bodies in Motion* is one of my favorite books ever. Listen, can I buy you a drink or maybe a sandwich or something? There's a nice little café just down the street. I'd like to talk about having you back. We can get a bigger crowd than this."

Ray rubbed the side of his neck. Everything feeling stiff and sore as if he had been in a wrestling match. "Sandy," he said, "I think I might be coming down with something. I've got such a bad headache and all. I wish I could take you up on your offer, but all I want right now is to take a hot bath and climb into bed."

"Oh, you poor thing," she said. "Go on then. Get a good night's rest. Will you come tomorrow if you're up to it and sign stock?"

"I promise I will, yeah. If I'm not sick. My flight doesn't leave until noon."

Back in his room Ray opened a bottle of vodka he had been saving to celebrate the end of the tour. He got a bucket of ice and made a drink. He turned on the computer to check emails. There was one from *her*:

Dearest Raymond James Poe,

I left Buddy to lock up the center at ten and came home early. I have been so nervous about your call I couldn't stand to be at the gym another second. I sit here wondering if you will pick up the phone and dial my number. Will you really do it? Or at least send me a e-mail? Give me some kind of sign, I guess that is what I am asking you to do in the name of . . . I was going to say God, but what I really mean is in the name of LOVE. I wonder if you can possibly know what it means to be me these past few days since meeting you on terms that have evolved into such close intimacies. Oh, Ray, Ray, I have never felt like this, believe me! I know in my heart, in my soul, that you and I are meant for each other. After all we are both Pisces and artists. You are everything my spirit has been longing for. There is nothing I don't love about you. I love the whole package! You are my destiny. I am yours. I sound silly, don't I? An hysterical woman begging you to love her. Of course you can't love me just because I want you to! But I am betting that if you look deep in your heart you will find me there. There has always been a chamber set aside for me. You just didn't know it until now. Maybe I'm being tiresome. Maybe I'm turning you off. I'll quit for now. I'll sit here by the phone and wait to see if you call. Ten thirty can't come soon enough. I can't wait! Don't forget me, Ray! Don't forget me! Don't forget this Annette who ADORES you so!

Ray groaned. He closed his eyes and muttered, "A chamber set aside for you? How about a fucked up heart valve?" He grabbed more ice. Poured another drink. Glared at the phone. Gritted his teeth.

On the keyboard he typed:

Your mind is full of scorpions, Ray!

She torments me. I want her. I don't want her. If I go on with this it will change my life forever. Nothing will be the same again. Goodbye honesty. Hello lies and deceptions. Hello sneaking around. For what? For a piece of ass? This is maddening. This is mad!

For your soul-mate, Ray!

Tell Norman that! Soul-mate, bah!

Ray, honestly, what makes life worth living if it isn't the mad times we have? Listen, nothing ever goes the way you think it will. Forget about making plans. You know the old saying, you want to make God laugh, make plans. Don't construct scenarios, pal. They never happen the way you want them to. Mostly, they don't happen.

I never anticipated any of this! I don't want it! I won't call her! Forget it! I refuse to wound Bobbi this way.

She'll never know! And look, Ray, we are all wounded. We are all dodging the truth about how wounded and weak we are. Embrace the fantasy. Live a little.

He thought of the old Milton scholar at the reading. Heaven of Hell; Hell of Heaven. Ray could have quoted him what he often quoted to his students, the observation from Santayana ... *he has no true idea either of the path to happiness or of its real conditions. His notion of nature is an inverted*

217

image of the moral world, cast like a gigantic shadow upon the sky. It is a MIRAGE.

It's a mirage, Ray. She's a mirage.
Yes, goddammit, I know she is!

Ray stood up. Moved carefully from one wall to another, back and forth, back and forth, one foot in front of the other as if he were walking a tightrope. He imagined a sailor between two shores. A new port or the old one? Which one to choose? One more drink might yield the answer. He wondered if it was possible to live a dual life. Could a man survive sailing port to port over and over? Take care of Bobbi and still have Annette? Was such a thing doable? Or would it ultimately kill him? A mistress at his age!

Might give him a stroke.

Cancer.

Norman's nervous breakdown.

Ray had no idea.

He sat on the edge of the bed.

Was there some purpose in keeping him alive? None that he knew of. The digital clock said 10:29. He entwined his fingers, held hands with himself, his conscience warning—you are courting *disaster.*

He muttered, he said, "Moronic bullshit. Ridiculous."

He glared at the phone with hatred in his heart.

The instructions on the receiver said:

DIAL 9 FOR OUTSIDE.

Stupid Cunt

The Beckers were headed home after leaving the Fourth of July backyard barbecue, hot dogs, hamburgers, potato salad, baked beans, beer, sodas, grilled corn on the cob. The chatter of too many voices, grating laughter, shrieking grandchildren, a yapping poodle named Fifi. The Minnesota weather was witheringly hot under a heavy overcast adding its weight to the humid air. The air-conditioner's effort was not enough to keep the sweat from pooling in the pit of Tina's back, inner thighs, crotch, armpits. The arthritis in her knees, fingers, elbows and shoulders was about as bad as it had ever been. Her feet and ankles were swollen from all the standing she had done, all the beer she had drunk, all the food she had eaten. Pains in her joints came and went for no apparent reason. A jab here, a pinch there. She had been wrecking her health for two decades. Overeating, piling on the pounds, her body protesting, her conscience nagging her: go on a diet! Join a gym! Exercise, you stupid cunt!

Right now all she wanted was to get home and take a shower, put on her nightgown and plop in front of the TV. Watch whatever. Something silly, something funny. She wanted to smile. She needed to laugh. She wanted her cats, Jerry and Jazzy, lying next to her purring. She wanted Bob upstairs in bed watching the Playboy channel, his sleep-inducing soporific. It never failed to hypnotize him, visions of nubile sluts dancing in his head. Seventy-one years old and still a pervert.

She glanced at the speedometer and wished she were driving. Everyone was passing them, highway 169 stuffed to the gills with worn out revelers just wanting to get the trip over, get away from this big Lincoln SUV plugging along like a lumbering old bear sniffing the road as if it had all the time in the world. Tina knew better than to say anything. One word of complaint about his slow, uneven, jerky driving and he would call her nasty names and tell her to shut up.

Forty-five years of marriage. How had that happened? Why had she stayed with him so long? She had known within the first two years of their marriage she had made a mistake. She had stolen him from his wife, broke up his family, a terrible thing to do. Unforgivable. Paying for it ever since. It's what happens if the sin is severe enough to rouse God's hatred. No thunderbolts. Nothing overtly obvious. Two miscarriages. A stillborn boy. A lumpectomy and five years of taxol. And a daily dose of melancholy caused by the man sitting next to her whose name should have been Rain in the Face. Or something equally gloomy.

The cancer could have been worse, lots worse. Could have had a mastectomy. The oncologist had wanted to do surgery, but she knew Bob would never have touched her again. He had told her dozens of times how much he loved her boobs. They were her finest feature, he had said.

Better than Venus.

Back then. Long, long ago.

Look at them now.

No don't.

None of it mattered these days. He had stopped making love to her when she was in her late fifties. Hard to get used to a life without sex when there had been so much of it from her sixteenth to her fifty-eighth year. Forty-two years of balling. And now seven years of drought, her body ballooning. Bob no longer leering lustfully at her. Looking at the Playmates instead.

Well, she was 65 and couldn't care less what he did.

"You used to look like her," he had told her not long before they stopped screwing each other. They had been lying in bed watching TV, a naked beauty gyrating in front of a mirror. "I couldn't get enough of you, remember? Nature made men so goddamn visual, that's the thing. Men are too damn dependent on their eyes. When a woman's body goes, everything goes."

She had wanted to tell him that he wasn't exactly eye candy either, but she didn't dare. It was his radar eyes that had first attracted her. He came into her parlor to get a tattoo of the word *MOM* wreathed in red roses on his arm. A six foot hunk of Vietnam Vet standing there pointing to his left biceps and saying, "A tattoo for my mom."

A horn startled her. A car flew by, the driver giving Bob the finger. "Look at that idiot," Bob said. "What's his fucking hurry? Why is everybody always in such a goddamn hurry? Won't be long and that

220

bastard is dead. Think of that, Tina. Everyone in every car you're seeing right this second will be dead soon enough. The doomed to die will be burying the already dead. Another cycle. Another step up to the plate for the next generation. What I'd like to know is what's the point? What's the goddamn point of it all?"

Tina shook her head. Shrugged her shoulders. In one way or another over their many years together, Bob had asked that same question a thousand times. She used to answer that God was the point. Leave it in God's hands and stop worrying. But then one night in a drunken tirade, Bob shouted, "God my ass, you stupid cunt! I used to believe in that shit, but the life I've had tells me there ain't no goddamn God. That's Santa Claus bullshit for feeble-minded morons like you and your father and mother, your whole righteous family. Adults our age should know better. Grow up, Tina! We live alone. We die alone. Here and now is all we got. Don't give me no more God crap!"

So she didn't. She went to Mass by herself, took Communion and prayed for God to give her absolution and courage and understanding. She put on the pounds. She stopped spreading her legs or opening her mouth. She cultivated a life of the mind. She read a novel a week, mostly fantasy and science fiction that took her to worlds far more interesting than her own. She went to doctors, but none of them could cure her arthritis or headaches. The arthritis had forced her to sell the tattoo parlor. She made a lot of money from the sale, but she missed the parlor, missed meeting new people, drawing artful designs on their bodies. Arthritis had no mercy. She took 800 milligrams of Ibuprofen three times a day to mitigate the pain. She cooked and she cleaned and did her best not to agitate her husband, not give him any excuse to berate her and call her names. She daydreamed about his death and inheriting the money he had inherited from his mother's estate. All the traveling she would do! Europe. England, Germany, France, Italy, Greece. She wanted to visit Bora-Bora and Tahiti. New Zealand too. Live on a South Sea island. Go native.

"Your old man is headed for senility," Bob said, interrupting her thoughts. "He's told that same story the last six times I've seen him."

"What story?"

"That fuckin fish jumping into the boat. The walleye. Dinner jumping into his lap just when he had given up and was headed for shore. Jesus Christ, Tina."

"What's wrong with that story?" she said. "It's funny. C'mon, old people always repeat themselves. You repeat yourself. We all repeat ourselves. He's eighty-five. Give him a break."

"Stupid story. What the hell—does he forget he's already told it a million times?"

"Just trying to make you laugh, Bob. You never laugh anymore. Do you know that?"

"What's to laugh about, Tina? Look at the state of the world. This country ain't the America I fought for, not by a long shot. Twenty-five and all man." He jabbed his thumb in his chest. "Fought for my country and what does it get me? A nation full of bubblehead politicians and whining Americans. I'm telling you this ain't the country I fought for, not no more."

"You know who you remind me of, Bob? You remind me of Dilbert."

"Dilbert?"

"The cartoon character. The cloud of doom hanging over his head. He knows when something or someone is doomed. You're just like him. You're Dilbert." She chuckled while repeating "Dilbert, Dilbert ..."

Bob growled at her, "I don't know no Dilbert, but it doesn't take a genius to know we're all doomed. Everything is doomed, Tina. You're doomed."

"Gloom and doom Dilbert, that's you."

"Not gloom and doom, Tina. *Realistic.* I see life more clearly than you or anyone I know. It's made me depressed for at least fifty of my seventy-one years on this fucked up planet."

"I know."

"I need to drink to dull the pain of living."

"Yes, you've told me."

"I've probably got at least ten more years of observing this revolting world before I die in some nasty fucking way."

"Yes."

"My mother died choking on a piece of bread."

"I know."

"What a ridiculous way to go. How she must have hated it. Destined to die with a wad of bread stuck in your throat? How goddamn absurd is that?"

"Very."

"I chew each bite of food at least thirty times. Sometimes fifty. Depending on what it is."

"You've told me this a million times, Bob. You're *repeating* yourself." She giggled.

"You eat too fast," he said.

"I know."

"How boring your old man is, Tina. Why don't you just say, 'I've heard that story a million times, Pappy'? And that's another thing. Why does everyone call him Pappy? Call him Dad. Or Papa. Pappy makes him sound like he's a hick from the Ozarks."

Tina looked out the side window at another Minnesota lake going by. The wrinkling water grayish. Narrow piers jutting from the shoreline like runways for fashion models. Houses peering out from landscapes teeming with trees. When Bob died she would buy a cozy little home on a lake. That would be the thing to do. Sit on the porch and watch water skiers going by laughing, having fun. Watch the fish jump. Watch birds glide and dive. The wind in the trees the only music she would need.

Glancing at her husband, she took in his dour expression, mouth turned down in an old man's stereotypical frown. Bags under his eyes. Stray wisps of hair still clinging to his head. Who is this guy? Did she really marry him? Once upon a time she had thought he was ruggedly handsome, dangerous and sexy. A war vet with undress-you eyes. His insatiable cravings. They had that in common back then. Do whatever you want, her body always said. They would get drunk and plow the bed for hours in various states of sexual delirium.

She'd feel slutty after. Slutty but satisfied. After the first two years of marriage the only time he ever showed she meant anything to him was when they fucked each other. No holding hands going for strolls as they had before they took their vows. No spontaneous hugs or kisses. They would go out for dinner three or four times a week. It's what he liked. A steak, a few drinks. Home to bed. The Playboy channel.

They had all the money she could spend back then, money from the tattoo parlor and the sale of the estate. But for Tina the money soon lost its luster. She had a house full of clothes and crap she never used. She gave lots of stuff to his daughter now that she had grown up and her martyred mother had passed on. Cancer eating her ovaries. How that poor woman suffered!

Soon after she was gone, the daughter switched from men to women. Tina blamed Bob for that, his macho-man example turning the daughter off. Stingy with his money these days because he lost upwards of a million in the stock market. Only two million left. *Only.* She chuckled into her hand.

"Where did it all go?" she murmured.

"What?"

"We never hear from Jenny."

"She knows where we live. That's what thanks I get for giving that Lesbo everything she ever asked for. Her mother was raped, you know. What the hell, my heart went out to her. I wasn't even sure whose kid it was, but I married that woman anyway. It was pity. That's how damn dumb I was back in those days."

"I know."

"Can you imagine that, what a sucker I was?"

"It was a kind thing to do, Bob. You had a kind and loving heart. Really, you used to be sweet."

"Rape is a natural instinct for men, you know."

"Rape? Is it? Is it really?"

"Programmed into our genes. Look at history. It's crammed full of rape and murder and pillage. What a species."

She had heard the same words many times before.

She let her mind drift to her youth. Meeting him by accident at Medicine Lake sitting on a bench with a bag of popcorn in his hands. He was feeding the ducks, throwing popcorn one puff at a time into the water, watching the ducks race each other for it. She had swam in from the raft and was walking to her towel when he called to her, his finger pointing at a mulberry tree near the road as he said, "Oriole." She looked at the tree and saw a Baltimore oriel pecking at the mulberries. She told him she hadn't seen an oriel in years. "Me neither," he said. "It doesn't look real. I saw a cardinal yesterday in almost the very same spot. They come for the mulberries. This is a good place to rest and watch."

What a kind and gentle man he is, she told herself. A birdwatcher.

"Do you remember me?" he asked.

"Of course I do. I tattooed roses and the word mom on your arm," she answered.

"I bet you think I'm a mama's boy."

"Not a bit. More boys should love their mothers that much."

"She's given me everything. My father died young and I became the center of her life. She lives right over there." He pointed at a mini-mansion on the other side of the lake."

"Beautiful house," Tina told him.

"Too big," he said. "I like little houses. Cozy cottages."

She had picked up her towel and was drying her hair, glancing at him now and then. And wondering: *Is he married?*

A quiet minute passed before he said, "Oriels have nothing on you."

And that's how things started. He came in his outboard at noon day after day, a bag of popcorn or birdseed in hand. She found herself sitting beside him feeding the birds and telling him about her life, about living with her parents in Crystal, about going to college and taking art lessons, about opening the tattoo parlor and how much she loved it. She learned that he was one of the original Beckers who had settled Golden Valley back in the nineteenth century.

He started showing up at closing time. The first time they made love was in his car in a parking lot at Powderhorn Park. Oh, those contortions! She was agile then. She had to admit she loved those whorish meetings, the infidelity. She thought she loved him. She thought she had never been so happy, so fulfilled. Cars became motel rooms. Motel rooms became lovers' nests. She was his mistress for three years before his wife found out and divorced him.

The tires thumpety-thumped over the tar strips patching the concrete highway beneath her. Cars storming by. The landscape blurring. Sweat staining her pants, the armpits of her shirt. She hoped she didn't get a rash.

225

Were we happy? she wondered. Was feeding the birds the best time of our life together? The stolen moments in the car. The motel rendezvous.

Happy? If happiness is feeling excited, feeling passionate. Passion and excitement equal love don't they?

Love has to be more than that, Tina, she told herself. Does it exist really, really?

"I've got a killer headache," he said. "It's getting dark and my night vision is shot. My eye is throbbing. I hate this long drive, Tina. It exhausts me. Makes me nervous as hell. I wish we didn't have to do it. Next time you go up there alone. Tell them I'm sick or something. Why did they have to move so damn far north?"

The Lincoln rocked side to side, slowed for a second before bucking forward faster than ever. He had aged into a terrible driver. She thought it was mostly because his eyesight was failing.

Maybe they would crash. Maybe they would die together. It wouldn't be a tragedy. Fitting justice for what they had done to the martyred one.

The sky was sailing towards a darker shade of gray. The hidden sun was a pale glow beyond the rim of the world.

"I wish it would rain," she said.

"Don't wish for rain!" he said. "What's the matter with you? Rain! Jesus Christ I'm having a bad enough time as it is."

"You want me to drive?"

"No, goddamn it. We're almost home goddamn it all."

They arrived the moment the streetlights flickered on. He parked in the driveway and sat a moment collecting himself. His hands were trembling on the wheel. She pitied him. She hated him too. He had never made her happy. Not truly. Not even when they were younger and feeding the birds. And certainly never ever in bed. Satisfied yes. But never happy. She supposed it was not really his fault.   Happiness is what you have to do for yourself. No one can do it for you. A fleeting moment now and then, but that was it. That was all. She kept staring at her husband, waiting for him to move. He had curvature of the spine now. Osteoporosis had shrunk him down to five foot ten.

226

She wasn't getting any younger herself. I'll leave him, she thought for the thousandth time. I'll take Jerry and Jazzy and move north and stay with my parents till I can figure it out.

Now or never, Tina. Now while you still have your legs under you.

He wiped a palm over his head back and forth. His collar was wet with sweat. She could smell him—smell his rotting body, his sour breath.

"Let's get you into the house," she said. "I'll make you a ham and cheese sandwich with lettuce and tomato. How does that sound? We can have some chardonnay. How does that sound, honey?"

"Anything. Anything at all, Tina."

"It'll calm you down. You can take a relaxing bath and go to bed. Watch your girls and fall asleep with sugar plum fairies dancing in your dreams. C'mon, old man, it's been a long, tiresome day, a tiresome day."

"You have no idea," he said. He lingered. Then he said, "You know what I think? I think I'm close to the end of my life and haven't really lived at all. Hell of a thing, Tina."

"Nonsense. Don't talk like that. Are you hungry, honey?"

"I need a whiskey."

"Not on an empty stomach," she said. "Remember your ulcer, honey."

"Yeah, yeah, I'll eat first. Don't nag me."

She got out, went around to his side, opened the door, took his elbow and helped slide him off the seat. He was very shaky. *Doddering old man* is what came to mind. She locked her arm in his arm and walked him carefully into the house.

As she steered him towards the kitchen, the cats came running and began sinuously circling their ankles.

"Fuckers gonna trip me," he said, kicking at them feebly.

While he sat at the table, his face in his tremulous hands, she opened the fridge and brought out leftover ham and made him a sandwich thick enough to choke him. She wondered if choking was a trait he had inherited from his mother.

Jealousy & Doubt

It was another one of those evil days wherein Ray doubted everyone, even those closest to him. All liars and betrayers. All of them living sordid lives. Not just them, but all humanity. The whole world. Dishonest. Disgusting. He hated them and he hated that he hated them and hated that he had such hateful thoughts about them. His mother had always told him not to hate others because hatred destroys the hater. But he couldn't help it. He trusted no one and believed in nothing. Especially not himself. Two years since his wife died. Two years of pessimism. Two years of guilt and self-loathing.

"God, I'm in a mood," he said, exhaling putrid molecules. "And it's all her fault, the little bitch. Look at the time. Where is she? Why doesn't she call? Should I go looking for her? I could go to Buddy Kerr's house and see if she's there."

No, Ray, no you don't. That would be demeaning. Desperate. It would be pitiful.

"If she's there, I'll kill her."

Often it comforted him to remember that we all die tomorrow and all desire and pain dies with us. All striving caring loving hoping will end one day in a minuscule evaporation of a minuscule thought. Poof. That 5,000-year-old frozen corpse found in the Italian Alps had once been a living, breathing man. Just as greedy for pleasure as anyone alive today. But what did it matter? Embedded in a granite niche as the centuries ticked by and no one noticing. Maybe he had a family. No doubt they had wondered what happened to him. They cared for a while—where is Ugha? He went up the mountain and didn't come back. They searched for him. They called out Uuughaaa! Uuughaaa! But all that returned were echoes. The moon changed shapes, rose and fell and life was for the living. Must go hunt and gather. Got to stay alive somehow. Ugha's disappearance remained a mystery to his relatives and friends. The memory of his voice faded as the months went by. The years. Eventually, they forgot what he looked like. And his wife and children went on until one by one they wore out and died too. As did his grandchildren and his great-grandchildren, generation following generation, so on and so forth. All Ugha's descendents departing. Bodies in ice clutches. Flesh and blood evolving into tusks.

"Life is short," Ray snarled, clenching his teeth, wishing he could bite someone. Bite Annette especially. "Better to acknowledge the brevity and the insentient state to which we sink, all of us great or small. Better not be fooled by an afterlife no one's seen. From whose bourn no traveler returns. Shrug it away. Be philosophical. It's coming. So who cares? It may not be today or tomorrow. But it will come. The readiness is all. Said Hamlet. Or was that Lear? No, Lear says ripeness is all. Actually no, it is Edgar saying it to Gloucester. And Gloucester says that's true too. Because everything is true. And then he died. Hamlet died. Gloucester died. Lear died. Uhga in the Alps died. My wife Bobbi died. I killed her. With kindness. Morphine is kindness. Need to take death with a grain of salt. The only way to handle such an outrage. The trick is to know when to go. Give me the hemlock; it's time. Give me the morphine."

Ray waited a moment to see if being philosophical made him feel better.

It didn't.

Where was she? Why wasn't she answering the phone? Instinct told him it was for sinister reasons. She was with someone. Maybe she was at Kerr's house now, she and he thrashing on that Persian rug. Or was it Turkish? Yes, Turkish she had said. "I wish I had Buddy Kerr's Turkish rug. It's gorgeous. I wonder if he would sell it?" She was always wanting to buy things. "I want, I want," she was always saying. Ray saw her naked on the rug, her head thrown back, her mouth open, her hands gripping her lover's arms. What did he look like? Ray could see him. Bulky and dark. Smelling musky like the dark ones do. He had seen how she looked at men. Always younger men. Older women were hot for young studs. An article in the paper this morning told of an older woman arrested for sexually abusing two teenage boys, fifteen and sixteen. The charges included oral sex and sodomy. She got two years. What perversion of the mind made those boys tell? Ray knew if such a thing had happened to him at that age, he never would have told. He would have made a sacrifice to Aphrodite. Given a golden apple offering.

He went into the kitchen, grabbed the vodka, splashed some in a tumbler and added three ice cubes. Swirled. Waited for the drink to cool. Squabbled with himself: Why shouldn't she go for some younger guy? No reason not to, not when you're impotent half the time, old fart. Not when your face looks like a cluster of grapes hanging over her in bed. She never wants to make love with the light on anymore. It's been ten years and your sixty-six-year-old body no longer turns her on. Wrinkly neck. A wattle beneath your chin. Rusty skin on the V of your chest where the sun used to tan you. Age spots surfacing like seaweed on your forehead. That tiny lesion on your nose is probably a basal cell. Not your fault. You tried to warn her. You told her she was too young for you, but would she listen? She said your age meant nothing. That you didn't look nearly twenty years her senior. Maybe ten years at most. That's when you were working out, lifting weights, jogging a mile every morning. And you had more hair. And you used an acid that sloughed the dead skin off your face. Left your cheeks shiny and smooth. You had looked good for a man in his mid-fifties. Don't look in the mirror now, Ray.

He took a sip. Swished it like mouthwash over his teeth. Held still for a moment breathing through his nose, feeling the vodka bite. After he swallowed, his tongue felt antiseptic. She claimed he hardly ever had bad breath. He told her it was because alcohol, plus Listerine kept his palate squeaky-clean. And that was why he never got sore throats or rarely caught colds. Germs can't multiply in an environment pickled in alcohol. She laughed at that. She loved to drink one or two and laugh at his jokes and have fun.

God, he loved her!

He loved that she had such control. Not him, not Ray. Once he started he couldn't stop. How many drinks had there been over the years, especially after Bobbi died? Gallons of vodka, whiskey, wine to alter his moods. To tuck away truth. Seek oblivion. They had walled their love in a bubble for a few days every week, before he had to go home to his wife. Did it for five years! Such a shitty way to live. Ray the adulterer.

Annette's willful behavior, the need to have her way at all costs, had taken a large toll on him. Knowing that if she would get rid of her husband and go after a married man and persuade him to betray his wife— she was capable of anything. She would betray him finally. And why not?

He was a burned out old bag. Heartburn, indigestion and bowel troubles. Arthritis in his knees. Constant guilt about Bobbi. Was it the extra pill that killed her? Take three, Bobbi. Take four. Four will make you sleep and dream those stories you want to write. I'll help you write them, baby. Create a Bobbi Poe legacy. Ray is here. Ray will never leave you.

He had wanted her suffering to be over. She must have known it. Like Uhga, 5,000 years will mean nothing to her now. Soon enough it will mean nothing to Ray Poe either. For the past year the man has been impossible, a pain in the ass. A drunk haunted by dreams. Bad dreams. Dreams about Bobbi. The enduring grief in recalling her final breath exhaling: the sound of overwhelming exhaustion. And how does one go on living when living means continual rewind and playback? No wonder Annette had that look on her face when she looked at him now. The look that said what am I doing here with this loser?

She used to say, "Sex is how I express my love for you. Sex is the closest we can physically be. You inside me is spiritual. I never knew I could love this way."

Stuff like that. Stuff she didn't say anymore. Like: You are my soul-mate, Ray. She hadn't said that in ages.

Soul-mate.

Cynic that he was, he used to sneer at such drivel. Before he met her. As the weeks became months became years, he began to wonder if a mate for the soul might be true. Now he knew he was right in the first place. He was a sentimental dupe. He was a grieving widower, a romantic old douche bag.

"That's me," he said. And then he said, "When I die there will be no one to give the folded flag to. Annette will bug out, I know she will. If a man does not keep pace with his companions—"

She was all that was left in his life, no one else to turn to.

He paced the floor. Went into the study. Frowned at the bookshelves, the rows of British literature. Shakespeare and his ilk and all things Donne—the metaphysicals. All the lovely words he used to quote to his students. His mind overflowing endlessly able.

Things are not truly, but in equivocal shapes.

"Thomas Browne," said Ray, satisfied that he still had a good memory.

And next to Browne on the shelf, incongruously (or maybe congruously?) was *Alice in Wonderland*. Down the rabbit hole. That's where he was. Has been. Will be ever and ever now.

Ray put forth a trembling finger, touched *Alice* and said—

Speak roughly to your little boy
And beat him when he sneezes!

A coughing laughter following. He blew his nose. Wiped his eyes. Laughed heh heh. A mad scientist.

"Thou shouldst not have been old til thou hadst been wise! So where is she? Whose arms, whose hands, whose—Jesus, the thought is unbearable! I'll kill her. I'll kill myself." Eyes closed he whispered, *"Let me not go mad. Oh, Fool, I shall go mad!"*

He pictured the gun in the nightstand. Inevitably we die anyway, so why not get it over with? Reset time to zero. You will *not* wake wondering. You will *not* feel guilt, you the man who broke your wife's heart. You the man who fed her an overdose. You the man who wished she would to die. Let her die! Yeah, but you knew it would end this way. Bobbi's cancer had only one way to go. The same way Annette's passion for you has died. You knew Annette's passion would fade as you aged and the ills of aging started plaguing you just as her mother had warned you that day in your office: "You're too old for her. Have you ever thought about how she'll cope when time has its way with you and you start looking the way you feel?"

That bitch was right. Time has stamped your stupid face and corroded your organs. Those gall stones that won't let you digest fats. That burping routine after every meal. Disgusting. Even more disgusting is the IBS that comes and goes. And also your swollen prostate, the itching, burning in there that has made you short-tempered. Doctors can't help you. Forget those bastards, those pompous frauds, those phony fakes. It's a benign hypertrophy. It will be with you always. Nothing to be done. Don't drink alcohol. Alcohol is hell on stomachs and prostates. And stay away from spicy foods. Some day we may have to operate if the gland becomes cancerous. But surgery is the last resort. They shoved pills at him for his indigestion. Tylenol for the arthritis in his shoulders and fingers.

What a joke that junk was. Might as well drink snake oil. His ailments overwhelmed every elixir, his courage especially. But, oddly, not his love for her. Why did he love her? No reason. Something wrong with your brain, Ray. She's a mental disease.

He wondered why, with so much wrong with him, he continued to drink so hard.

Not true.

He didn't wonder.

No, he knew.

Every night at least five or six drinks. Or as many as it took to calm him down. Make him not care about anything. Stop caring! When you care that's when it hurts: that was what Buddha had said. In his cups Ray tells himself that he most certainly has a death wish now. Several times he has taken the gun out and put the barrel in his mouth and pressed the trigger and thought—*All I'd have to do is flick the safety off and this world will know me no more. Would you like that, Bobbi? Would that avenge you?* And then Annette coming in and finding him with the back of his head blown off. She would freak. He can hear her screaming. He sees that funny eye of hers—that cast—if it wasn't a bad omen Ray's not an adulterous fornicator.

But would she really care? She wouldn't care a fig. She had told him recently that his black depression was destroying her. She had given an ultimatum: See a psychiatrist and get some help or it's over. You're drowning and I'm drowning too. You've got me halfway down the road to crazy, Ray! She hasn't a clue how the outcome is killing him: feeding Bobbi the morphine, watching her drift into permanence. Rest in peace, my poor unlucky baby. He should walk away now. Give up Annette. Go live in a monastery and pray daily for Bobbi's soul. But he has no will to give Annette up. She is his addiction. His obsession. A reason for living.

Let it be, let it be.

Basically it is for Annette that he hasn't killed himself. Maybe he should kill her first. And then: COUPLE DIE IN SUICIDE PACT.

Returning to the kitchen, he lifted the bottle. One or two more drinks and it would be empty. Should he go to the store now? Or should he finish the bottle first?

Finish the bottle. Then kill yourself, Ray.

What would she do if he were dead? What did Ugha's wife do when she realized he was never coming back? Ray can see Annette crying. He hears her asking why. She knows why, but pretends not to. He sees her running to her children and mother for comfort. Her friends would be there for her. She has lots of friends. Friendly, popular, always hanging on the phone. A social butterfly. He hates it every time the phone rings. Sometimes it's for him. But mostly it's some friend of hers. But would she miss him? Sure she would miss him. Then she would move on. She loves life. She loves her pleasures. She would find someone else. Someone closer to her own age. People have got to get on after a loved one dies. And besides, women have a life force that men don't have. Men die easily. Most women go kicking and screaming. But they die anyway and 5,000 years later everything and nothing has changed.

Looking out the window, he watched the wind tickling the trees. Ah yes, Nature. He used to care about the environment. Leaving it livable for the next generation and all the poor, dumb animals. But that was no concern of his now. Who gives a damn? Not Ray Poe.

Go now or wait for her? Where is she? She didn't used to be so evasive. Always kept her cell phone on. Always prompt. Phone calls always on time. If she said she would call at five, she always did. Give or take a minute or two. The past year or so she had spent lots of extra time at the office, the housing slump. She's an optimist. She thinks soon she'll be raking in the dough again. She had asked him several times to invest, take a chance. But he took early retirement and lives on a fixed income. He has some savings for a rainy day, but that's it. Nothing left to gamble with. No risk left in a man sixty-six. And besides, he didn't really want anything more than what he had. The condo was comfortable. He owned all his furniture and his car. He didn't need more clothes. Except some new skivvies. The waistbands in the old ones were wavy. Maybe she started pulling back after he retired and she realized he would never amount to anything more than what he was—a lazy-semi-functional-alcoholic-wannabe-writer who couldn't sell his work.

He could have taught school longer. He could have hung in there and piled up five or six more years on his 401K and the bonds and Social Security and his State Retirement fund. He had thought retirement was what he needed. Give him time at last to work on his books. Write every day. Zone-in. Focus. Create something brilliant—a brilliant work of art that would outlive him. Time to read all those novels he had piled on the nightstand over the years. He hadn't realized that when you're no longer in the thick of things, the writing and reading don't mean very much. There is only you and the words. You and someone else's words. Only you and the gesture unshared. On the page where no one cared to see it. She was far too busy to read his scribbling and encourage him. He belonged to no writing clubs. He didn't do readings in bookstores anymore. Because they filled him with anxiety. No one buys literature, anyway. People wanted thrillers, mysteries, westerns. Scandals that exposed the seamy sides of celebrated lives. Biographies that cut their subjects down to size. Literary novels? Forget it. And he was guilty too. He hadn't made a dent in the stack he had been saving. He lacked the energy to read or write or eat out or go to movies or— How in the world had he become so boring? A man like him who used to strip nude and dance like a pagan for her. Stevie Ray Vaughan, John Lee Hooker blasting away. Those were the early days of their affair, days when he had had energy to burn. No more. The backs of his hands, his corky arms tell him he is too old to be living. He should have died at forty, like Jack London. Or like Byron at thirty-six. Instead of this living on and on to no purpose. And becoming what he used to dread.

He finished the first drink and poured another, whirling the vodka, the ice cubes clicking. He went into the bedroom, opened the drawer. Took out the gun. Put the barrel in his mouth. He slipped the tip of his tongue round the rim of the muzzle tasting tangy metal. He backed up to the wall. She would find his brains and hair on the wall. He wanted that. He wanted an image that would haunt her forever. *You did this!* That was what Bobbi had told him when she was dying: *You gave me cancer!*

He watched the secondhand sweeping a circle round the face of the clock on the dresser. Another minute gone forever. Just do it, he told himself. Flick the safety off and end time. You're going to die before long anyway. Get it over with, you coward!

Taking the gun out of his mouth he shouted, "Where is she, goddamn her!"

He put the gun in his waistband and phoned her again. Nothing happened. No ringing. No voicemail saying, *Please leave a message after the beep*. He slammed the receiver down and swore. He said, "Fuck shit motherfucker whore." He poured himself the last of the bottle and said, "Ray, we got to make a booze run, my boy." He bolted the drink and felt dimly genial. He felt borderline fine.

"Ray's cool," he said. "Everything's cool, Ray."

He reminded himself to be philosophical. Let her fuck them all, he didn't care. What he really needed was another Stoli. What he needed was the indifference it offered.

After a stop at the liquor store, he found himself on the freeway. The university where he used to work was in the distance, its Greek columns glimmering. He spent twenty-five years pretending before he managed to work up the nerve to retire. Telling himself, Now I'll really write! No excuses, Ray. He threw himself into it, turning out two worthless novels that no one wanted to publish. Numerous short stories: all rejected. He wasn't a writer after all. A sham of a writer making motions. And finally after two years of failure he stopped. He sent nothing out. He wrote a short story or a poem occasionally and put it with the others in the drawer beneath the drawer holding the gun.

Ray had no ideas. Everything he wrote seemed vapid. He drank as much as he could hold every night and tightened his grip on his anger. Dreamed of going postal. Striding down the hall at the university and capping the director and the dean and maybe a vice-president or two. Then killing himself. Or maybe battling it out with the police. Take as many of them as he could. Before committing suicide-by-cop. He saw the headlines: *RETIRED UNIVERSITY PROFESSOR KILLS COLLEAGUES IS GUNNED DOWN*. Something like that. He fingered the gun snug behind his belt. Cars whipping by him on both sides. Six-fifteen and the freeways still crowded. All these people, where were they going? These SUVs sucking up more than their fair share of gas. Polluting the air. It would be an easy thing to shoot out a tire, set the motherfucker rolling. Beside him he pulled the Stoli from the sack and opened it. Drank a lascivious mouthful. He felt buzzed. Very.

Buddy Kerr's house was dark, only the porch light on. The garage door was closed, so he didn't know if her car was in there or not. He parked halfway down the street and watched for signs of life. Instinct told him she was in there all right. Oral sex. Sodomy. Older woman losing all her inhibitions with a younger man. Or maybe younger men plural. Two teenagers. What had possessed that bitch? Two years in prison for two blowjobs and her butt reamed. Was it worth it?

At the curb in front was a phallic Miata. Red: the color of passion. How typical. How cliché. Of course she would take up with someone like that. Her old partner, her old fuckbuddy with his sports car. Her old fuckbuddy spreading AIDs. Fuck you, fuckbuddy!

The minutes ticked by. Half an hour vanished. The sky was still bright, but the sun was setting. Ray got restless.

I don't really want to know, do I?

On the way back he pulled up behind three other cars at a stoplight. Standing on the center divider was a skinny, long-haired man with a stick in his hand. A homeless panhandler? The man walked over to the first car in line and opened the door and yelled, "Out! Get the fuck out or I'll brain you, you stupid bitch!" He brandished the stick. A woman jumped out of the car clutching her purse. The man ripped the purse from her and got behind the wheel and sped away. Crossing cars screeching to a halt. Ending sideways. A man yelling, "What the fuck!"

The woman stood in the empty space gawking. People getting out of their cars. One woman screaming into her cell phone—"Carjacking, I said!" Others surrounded the victim talking to her all at once, waving their arms. Everyone was fuming. If they could just get their hands on that bastard! More cars pulled up behind the others in line. The light turned green. Horns honking. The air filling with bluster and *carjacking! carjacking!*

Ray sat benumbed and silent. And drained. It had happened so fast! And he had not even tried to do anything. He could have jumped out of his car and shot that bastard. He could have run to the rescue. Saved the day. Freeze, motherfucker, I'll blow your fucking head off! That's what he could have said. Why hadn't he moved?

He didn't used to be so indecisive. He didn't used to be so scared.

Of everything.

Of life.

Once long ago when he was thirty-five, he had stepped between a man and a woman who were yelling at each other in a bar. The man was threatening her, his fingers reaching. And courageous Ray had jumped off his stool and told the man to back off. The man had sized him up. Calculations spinning in his eyes—can I take this guy? Ray had been in his prime, all muscle from pumping iron. Behind him the bartender held a baseball bat. Everyone waited to see what would happen. The man pointed his finger at the woman and said, I'll take care of you later! And she said, Go to hell, asshole! And that was it. The fight was over. Ray sat down and finished his beer. The woman didn't even thank him. But the bartender did. Thanked him and gave him a free pitcher of Budweiser. Yes, Ray Poe had been like a warrior that day—*heroic*.

"And here again I could have been the hero," he mumbled. And then reminded himself—"I'm too fucking old to be a hero." He burped. He rubbed his stomach round and round. He felt nauseated. He needed Maalox. Some Imodium too. He slid the gun and the Stoli under the seat. "Useless fuck," he said and burped again. Palm stroking his burning abdomen.

"Oh Ray, oh Ray," he whispered almost sobbing. "Oh Ray, why do you do the things you do? Why have you done what you've done? What's wrong with you?"

The police arrived. They had witnesses pull their cars to the curb. Ray told a cop that he hadn't seen anything. He had gotten there too late.

Back home, he put the gun away and drank Maalox straight from the bottle. Sat on the pot and let the poisons flow. Then he washed his face and neck in cold water. Went to the kitchen and poured another drink. This will stop it, he told himself. This will deaden everything.

He switched on the lights in the living room and sat on the couch staring at his reflection in the dark TV screen. His heart was still pounding ultra-fast. He wondered if every old man was a coward. Old and brittle and impotent and a coward. He wondered if testosterone would make him snap out of it. He wondered if he would do anything different if he could live the carjacking over again. He imagined himself in the thick of it. Ordering the motherfucker to freeze. But he doesn't freeze. And Ray shoots him. Ray shoots him and shoots him. There! That's for Bobbi! That's for me! That's for my mother! That's for—

What kind of car was it, anyway? What had the woman looked like? He couldn't remember anything about her except her astonished mouth. There had been an overturned sandal on the street. He could have gone over and picked it up and handed it to her. An act of kindness. A show of compassion. Poor thing. But nothing! He had done *nothing*. Moment of truth. This is who you are now, Ray.

He set his drink on the coffee table and leaned forward, elbows on knees, head in his hands. Readiness is all. Ripeness I've got, but readiness, no. No readiness in you, you old worthless fuck. He choked on the words assaulting his brain. He tried to repeat them, to yell them at himself, but a sob gushed out instead. He wept into his hands. Big baby! Big dumb baby!

"What's wrong?" she cried. "What happened?"

He looked up. He wiped his eyes. Pulled out his handkerchief and blew his nose. She was saying over and over, "Honey, what's wrong, what's wrong, are you sick? Honey, what's wrong?"

He felt his lips moving. He listened hard, but he wasn't saying anything. The afternoon and evening passed through his mind, her dead message machine, the vodka rocks, the liquor store, the university columns mocking him, the crowded freeway smothering him, the darkness of her fuckbuddy's house teasing him. The carjacker. That goddamn carjacker! He should have shot him!

"I," he said, "I thought you had left me. I couldn't find you. I called and called. I couldn't find you."

"My cell phone died, honey. I accidentally dropped it. It's dead. It's right there on the counter." She pointed to it.

There it was. Why hadn't he seen it? "I didn't see it," he said.

"Honey, you never see anything."

"It's been there all this time."

"I went to buy another after I left work." She fished in her purse. Showed him the new cell phone. "It cost me an arm and a leg," she said. "And they took forever. I hate that place. They knew I couldn't wait for a special. They knew they had me. They really stuck it to me this time. I paid a fortune for this phone. And I phoned you as soon as I could, but all I got was the answering machine. The freeway was a mess. I could have walked home faster."

He glanced at the answering machine and saw the red light blinking.

"I went out for vodka," he said. Adding, "I thought you had finally had enough of me. I wouldn't blame you. I'm old and sick and ugly and all I do is whine. I'm like my dead wife; I'm like Bobbi was. Only worse. At least she didn't wallow in self-pity. I'm disgusting. I hate myself. I'm a failure as a man and an artist. What good am I to you? Good for nothing."

"Ray, why do you do this to yourself? Why?" She shook her head. Her eyes looked painfully sad. "Listen to me, you're not old, you're not at all ugly. I love you as much as I ever have. I would never leave you. I would never hurt you. I adore you. Only death can part us and that's the truth. You know in your heart I'm one hundred percent yours, Ray. Tell me you know it, Ray. Tell me."

"I'm so depressed," he told her, feeling the tears welling again. "I can't get over her death."

"I wish you would get some help, honey. See a psychiatrist, *please*. Tell me you will. Promise me you will. A psychiatrist will give you anti-depressants, honey. You don't need to be so miserable. It's all chemistry. It's a chemical imbalance."

"Drugs will distort my mind. They turn you into a zombie. It will be someone else in here." He tapped his head. "Not me. A better me, maybe? A milder get-along Ray? The demons cast off the cliff. Or at least an anesthetized Ray Poe Prozac Person. That's what you really want. My moodiness made Bobbi crackers; it makes you crackers too. I'm driving you down the road to crazy you said."

"Ray, you hang on to your suffering like a masochist. You're after absolution. If you suffer enough you think you'll …" She shook her head. Her eyes stayed infinitely sad. "I wish you'd stop. I wish you'd believe in

241

life. I wish you'd believe in yourself again. Oh, Ray I wish, I wish you—"

"You wish I'd be the man you met all those years ago. I used to be what you might call a *real* man. Practically fearless. But conscience makes cowards of us all. You're lucky, Annette. You don't let shit like Bobbi bother you. You blow things off. My mom blew things off too, her dead husbands. Wish I was like her, instead of like my dad. That poor fucker never got over anything. Heartbreaker. My options have run out just like his did. Over the rail and bye-bye, baby."

"Ray, oh Ray." She hung her head, her dark hair falling forward hiding her eyes.

He waited for her to tell him that he wasn't finished yet, he had a lot left to give and all he needed was to keep working and everything would be all right. Tell him he's going to start sending stories out again. Tell him he's going to get back to his desk and write. Tell him he's going to work on his novels. Rewrite them until they're perfect. Polish them until they're irresistible.

He desperately needed to hear her say all that. He needed her magic now. Eagerly, like a child, he watched her mouth. And he thought of Browne again, the end of that quote about equivocal shapes: . . . *real substance beneath that invisible fabric.* It was in him somewhere. Wasn't it?

She knew what he needed. She sat beside him holding his hand. Stroking his arm. Her voice was soothing. So soothing it calmed him down. And his tears dried and his heart slowed as she assured him again and again that his luck would turn. Everything would change. Maybe starting tomorrow. Maybe that soon.

"Whatever happens we've got each other," she said. "Don't ever forget we are soul-mates, Ray, and we love each other and ultimately that's what really counts. I'd die for you, honey. I really would."

And he was thinking, Maybe tomorrow.

Maybe that soon.

Filbert

They drive off-campus, go to the drive-through at Jack In The Box, order burgers and Cokes. Norman says he's buying. "I appreciate your company," he tells Harry. While the two of them sit in Norman's car in the parking lot eating, they watch a gang of teen-agers goofing around with each other, talking, laughing. There are twelve of them, seven boys and five girls. One of the girls is leaning against a car while her boyfriend presses against her. They kiss.

"Young stuff," says Norman Ten Boom. He sighs like he is remembering old times. "She was in one of my classes last semester. Her name's Mercy. That kid doesn't know how lucky he is. When I was his age I was dumb as a mutt. I think about the sweet buds I could have picked back then, and I could just kick my ass, you know. What a mutt. It takes practice to learn the signals, don't it, Harry?"

Harry nods.

"You know how old I am?" says Norman. "I'm sixty-nine, Harry. Sixty-nine and haven't lost a step. I'm a Dutchman who is part bear, you know. Let me tell you something. I still get women, lots of them. Whatever woman I want, I get her. No, no don't smile, don't doubt me. Listen, they like my spiritual aura and my poetry and my gift of gab. That's right. I show them my books. I read them a few poems. And I talk to them like they're the most important, most beautiful things on God's green earth. I'm old, I'm fat, got this double chin and flowing white hair, but none of it matters. Nope. Because I've got this voice, Harry. I talk and they listen. I get them in bed and make them happy. I'm very potent for my age. How old are you, Harry?"

"Forty-seven."

"Forty-seven. Wish I was forty-seven. That's a good age. How many times you been married?"

"Never married, Norman."

"No shit? Man, I've been married five times. Are you gay?"

"Not gay. Just never wanted to be married."

"Playing the field, huh?"

243

"Not really. I don't even have a girlfriend these days."

"You want one?"

Harry shrugs.

"I can get you one. Get you one of those coeds. Oh, I've had my share. Coeds are easy, Harry."

Norman's eyes narrow as a woman in a loose dress walks by carrying a bag with the restaurant's logo on it. She gets in a car and sits there with a man sharing french fries and drinks.

"What you think she looks like under all that shimmy-shake, Harry? Anything new?"

"Be new to me," says Harry.

"These girls letting it all hang out don't know a thing about a man's mind. They don't leave anything for meditation! Damn stupid, weeping shame. You would think women would have better instincts, they're supposed to be so goddamn mother-earthy. All that poetic horseshit they want us to believe about them, what a load of wishful thinking. Men are the ones with earth in their veins. I know these things, Harry. Men are the ones close to nature." Norman points a stern finger at the cosmos. "Men just won't get tamed, know what I mean? Mud and blood and thunder. Boners thick as drive shafts. Women don't get it. All they know are hair-do's and manicures. Hey, yum-yum, gimmee a nibble, look at that little twat with her shorts up the crack of her ass. Cute little previews, huh?"

"A couple of honey dews," says Harry.

"You want her?" says Norman. "You want her, I'll make it so."

"Go on."

"I'm not lying. Listen, I know these things. The bear in me casts a spell that women can't resist. Say the word and she's yours. Hot pussy in the back seat. Hot twat. Yum, tastes like tapioca."

"Norman. I'm way too old for her."

"Age doesn't mean shit to young women. I'll have her over here in two minutes." Norman opens the door and starts to get out. Harry panics.

"Hell no, man, hell no! Stop that! What's the matter with you? Are you crazy?" He grabs Norman's arm. "You don't proposition someone like her. That's jail bait. I bet she isn't sixteen even. Come on, let's get back to campus before you get me in trouble. I've got office hours pretty soon."

"It's what all my colleagues think. They think I'm crazy. Crazy like a fox. You're new, Harry. You stick with me and I'll teach you what Minnesota living means. Don't squirm. Don't blush. Harry, you're blushing."

"Can we go, Norman? I'd like to get back."

Norman looks at his watch. "My next class doesn't start for another hour. Kick back, relax. Enjoy your lunch, Harry. You're my guest. I appreciate you taking me up on my offer. I'm sick of that cafeteria food, aren't you?"

"I have to get back, honest."

"Eat. Eat."

"I guess I'm not hungry."

Norman shakes his head with disappointment. "You know what, Harry? You don't know how to live. That's what real trouble is, not knowing how to live. You can have no fun in life if you don't take chances." He points at the girl with the pair of previews. "Who cares if she's sixteen or six or sixty? What I'm saying is, don't pass anything up. What're you saving for? When the juices dry up, they're gone forever. Spring turns to winter, you get me? Real life is at the edges, Harry. Make something happen, son. Look here, I'll show you what I mean."

Again Norman starts to get out, and again Harry grabs him. "I mean it," he says. "I don't want her. That's not my style. I'm no Casanova. I'm not good with girls. Girls scare me."

"I'm not doing that," says Norman. "Just watch and learn. Let me show you how to stir things up. Watch me create a little chaos and get everyone excited. Everyone needs a little excitement in his life."

"I'm not into chaos either," says Harry. "I crave calmness, a calm life, Norman."

"I'll be back in ten minutes. Maybe less."

Norman Ten Boom strolls down to the sidewalk and stops at a mail drop. He opens the slot. He looks in. Then he looks around to see if anyone is watching. The kids in the parking lot are preoccupied with each other. No one is noticing Norman.

Opening the slot again, he shouts, "Come out of there, you

weasel! Oh, listen to him bawl, now it's too late. Papa was right, wasn't he, weasel? But no, we don't listen to Papa!"

A bald man with a prissy mustache passes by with a Chihuahua on a leash. He stops a few feet from Norman and watches him. The dog makes vicious, squeaky noises. Norman indicates the mail drop.

"Sniffs him in there," he say. "Sniffs my baby boy."

"What's that you say?"

"Set him on top." Norman pats the mail drop. "And I turn my back to see if the bus is coming, and down he goes. Kids are like weasels, they're like two-foot snakes, wiggle their way into anything. This one's done it before. He thinks he's funny. Don't think you're funny, little Norm!"

"Wow, you better tell somebody," says the man. He looks around as if maybe there's a hero standing by, ready to come to the rescue.

While the man has his back turned, Norman grabs the pop-eyed Chihuahua, unhooks his leash, and drops him into the mailbox. He yells down the slot, "Pet the doggy, Norm! Pet the nice doggy now."

The man gawks at Norman. "What the!" he says. "My God, what have you done, fella?" He touches the mailbox, his eyes blinking like he's sending Morse code. He backs off and looks around as if he's not sure of what is going on here, like maybe it's Candid Camera, or maybe Norman is one of those sidewalk magicians and it's all an illusion, the dog is up his sleeve or something.

"Everything is fine," Norman tells him. "Everything's cool."

The man's mouth gapes wide as a fist. His eyes are saying, wait a minute, this can't happen to a man just out walking his dog, what's the trick here? He opens the mail slot and calls softly, "Filbert? Filbert?" Filbert squeaks a few times, then comes unglued, barks like he is going insane, goes—*yi-yi-yi!*

"Listen to him!" says the man.

"A boy and his dog," says Norman. "A boy and his dog."

"Good God, this is terrible!" says the man.

The teen-agers have stopped molesting each other. They are catching on to something happening. They move closer to listen. The dog's bark has turned into a faint squeal, a wee howl, ghostly and mournful, like the soul of a puppy passing by: *oowoowoowoo*. Norman drapes his bulky arm

246

over the mail drop and runs a hand up and down its side. "It'll be fine," he says. "We'll get you out of there. Don't cry, little one." His eyes roll upward. He says, "I told him to behave, didn't I, Lord? Oh, the damn *dwarf*, don't make him suffer, Lord! He doesn't mean harm."

"Dwarf?" says one of the boys, cocking his head curiously.

"What's going on?" says one of the girls.

"Someone chucked a baby in the box," says the boy next to her.

"A baby! Oh, my god!" says the girl.

"Filbert," wails the bald man.

"Filbert," she repeats.

Voices whirl in the air. The word goes round. "Baby in the box. Baby Filbert."

Eager-eyed boys and girls descend on the mail drop. Norman has the slot open. "Say what? Say what?" he says. "He's crying. I can hear the little wee-ness crying."

The thin, ghostly wail of the dog bleeds upward: *wooo-ow-wooo*.

"Ohhh," the girls whine.

"Better do something," says another boy, his voice all business.

"Baby's dying?" says someone else. "Is that what I hear?"

Filbert's owner takes over the slot, crams his head halfway down it and croons, "Daddy's here, precious, Daddy's here."

"Oh, won't somebody help the pitiful thing?" says Norman. He takes out a hanky and blows his nose, wipes his eyes. He pulls his hair. He beats on the mail drop with his fist, and the bald man jumps back.

"You trying to break my ears?" he yells. His eyes say he's had it up to here with Norman.

"My heart can't take it no more," says Norman. "I'm cracking up. It's the stress. My wife left me for a piano player. Dumped the kid and run off. I'm cracking up! Can't stand no more!"

"What's he say?"

The word goes around as a larger and larger crowd gathers. "Dumped it!" "Brand new infant!" "Crack baby!" "The mother run off!" "Umbilical cord wrapped around its neck!"

Norman beats more against the steel sides of the drop. "Why me? Why me?" he cries.

"Careful," says one of the girls. "Don't scare him."

"You're right," says Norman.

"Daddy's here, Filbert. Daddy's here," croons the man.

It goes on for some minutes, everybody trying to decide what to do. Some boys want to tear the drop off its foundation and turn it over. Others say it's too dangerous, they might kill the baby. More and more people come by, asking what's going on. Cars slow down, stop; there is a traffic jam. The crowd grows and grows. Harry hears one man in the back tell the person next to him that there is a chopped-up infant in the mailbox and the killer is its mother. She jumped on the bus and got away.

"You know, the thing of it is," says the other man. "I'm not shocked. Nothing surprises me anymore, that's the thing."

"I hear you," says the first man.

The manager of the Jack in the Box comes out. He hears that the teenagers stuffed a dwarf down the mail drop. He runs inside and phones the police. In the midst of it all, Norman slips away. He and Harry watch the people gather deeper and deeper. The bald man is still talking down the slot. A girl is yelling for everyone to shut up, she is trying to hear the baby. The manager comes back with all his employees following him. They're all talking at once. They're mad as hell. They want to kick the shit out of those teenagers. The teenagers don't know what's going on. Everybody is shouting at them. They shout back, they make rude gestures. Threats are made. Fists fly. Bloody noses sprout like red carnations. Cries and shrieks, bellowing and cussing corkscrew through the air. In the distance, the sounds of sirens can be heard.

Climbing back into the car, Norman starts the engine and says to Harry, "Thanks for your patience. We'll have to do this again sometime."

"Like hell," mutters Harry.

They drive back onto 14th Ave SE. The sirens get closer, and soon a fire truck goes by blasting on its horn, red lights flashing. An ambulance screams, followed by a police car swooshing. It's a sight. Everywhere is wailing, clanging, glistening, glittering, scintillatingly shimmering bubbles of effervescence fizzing against the backdrop spectacle of downtown Minneapolis hellbent to rescue the little wee-ness nooked in a mailbox.

"These are good people," says Norman. "Fine Americans."

DUFF BRENNA is the author of nine books, including *The Book of Mamie*, which won the AWP Award for Best Novel; *The Holy Book of the Beard*, named "an underground classic" by *The New York Times*; *Too Cool*, a *New York Times* Noteworthy Book; *The Altar of the Body*, given the Editors Prize Favorite Book of the Year Award, South Florida *Sun-Sentinel*, and also received a San Diego Writers Association Award for Best Novel 2002. He is the recipient of a National Endowment for the Arts award, *Milwaukee Magazine*'s Best Short Story of the Year Award, and a Pushcart Prize Honorable Mention. His work has been translated into six languages. His memoir, *Murdering the Mom*, is forthcoming from Wordcraft of Oregon, June 2012.

CPSIA information can be obtained at www.ICGtesting.com
Printed in the USA
LVOW130306100512

281142LV00003B/99/P